"One thing

have I desired

of the Lord,

that I will seek after;

that I may dwell

in the house of the Lord

all the days of my life,

to behold the beauty

of the Lord,

and to enquire

in his temple."

Psalm 27: 4

The Story of God's Plan of Salvation

In The Physics of Our World

Helen Glowacki

Novels by Helen Glowacki

When God Broke Grandma's Heart
When God Took Grandma Home
When Grandma Chased the Spirits
The Granddaughter and the Monkey Swing
The Story of God's Plan of Salvation
Abiding Faith, Hidden Treasure
And Then They Asked God
Caleb's Testimony
Caleb's Zeungis (German Translation)

Why God Why Series by Helen Glowacki

To What Purpose?
Why God Why?
Why Trust Scripture?
Life after Death And The Coming Tribulation
What Does God Want Me To Do RIGHT NOW?
Do Our Little Sins *Really* Count?
What Do Angels Do?

Other non-fiction Books by Helen Glowacki

Politically Incorrect: When Enough is Enough
Overcoming Depression: How to be Happy
What No One Is Telling You about Addictions

****

Available through Amazon.com and the
Authors Website: www.helenglowacki.com

Face book: http://www.facebook.com/pages/The-Grandmother-
Series/155300907853909?ref=ts and
http://www.facebook.com/pages/Helenglowacki/

The Story of God's Plan of Salvation

In The Physics of Our World

Helen Glowacki

Copyright © August 2012 by Helen Glowacki
Library of Congress Control Number: 2009901900
ISBN: Softcover: ISBN 978-0-9847-2114-6
          EBook: ISBN 978-1-4535-9462-9
          Tabletop Edition: ISBN 978-0-9893-8074-4
          Tabletop Edition: *German language:* ISBN 978-0-9893-8073-7

The novels by Helen Glowacki are works of fiction. References to real people, events, organizations, or locales are intended only to provide a sense of authenticity and are used fictionally. All other characters and all incidents and dialogue are drawn from the author's imagination and are not to be construed as real. Any resemblance to actual persons, living or dead is entirely coincidental.

The non-fiction books by Helen Glowacki represent the opinion, research, religious beliefs and scriptural interpretations of the author and not meant to be used in lieu of the advice of ministerial, theological, medical or psychological experts.

This book was printed in the United States of America. The King James Version (KJV) of the Bible, which is public domain in the United States of America, has been used for all scriptural references throughout this book. The application of which is based upon the opinion, research and religious belief of the author.

German translation by Katharina Leipp, Muhlacher, Germany. Cover assembly and artwork by Darren Robinson, dr Design & Associates, West Palm Beach, Florida, USA.

For more information or to purchase additional copies of this book visit www.Amazon.com or visit the author's website @   www.helenglowacki.com or email helen@helenglowacki.com.

MISSION STATEMENT

To Serve

God

With All Our Strength

And

All Our Heart

Helen Glowacki

NOTE TO THE READER

The King James Version (KJV) of the Bible, which is public domain in the United States, is used throughout all the books written by this author. For further study, the author recommends the New King James Version (NKJV) of the Bible as easier reading and less usage of the old world language while remaining true to the original text.

This book contains an index of the scripture used to formulate the content of this story. They are taken from the King James version of the Bible and can be found on page 271 to assist in further study.

The non-fiction books by Helen Glowacki represent the opinion, research, religious beliefs and scriptural interpretations of the author and are not meant to be used in lieu of the advice of ministerial, theological, medical or psychological experts.

The novels by Helen Glowacki are works of fiction. While some events in these novels reflect the expertise and support of those in particular vocations, references to real people, events, organizations, or locales are intended only to provide a sense of authenticity, and are used fictitiously. Characters, incidents and dialogue are drawn from the author's imagination and are not to be construed as real. Any resemblance to actual persons, living or dead is entirely coincidental.

FORWARD

By Dr. Walter Forman

Overhearing a conversation about the Grandma Series of novels written by Helen Glowacki, I purchased one for myself and then another and another. I was impressed by the wealth of information in these books and how Helen wove her tales to the perfect word of God. When I personally met Helen, through the person who introduced me to her books, I told her how much I enjoyed her books and spoke about the value of our various ministries in drawing adults and children to the word of God. Mine was the *Good News Fishing Ministry* which helps children in need by providing them with a happy experience close to nature and introduces and reinforces the gift of the saving grace of Jesus Christ. It was during this discussion that Helen told me about this new novel which was applicable to children of all ages and which explained the process by which God develops mankind into those with whom He will share His kingdom. After reading it I realized what a special opportunity it was to find books like Helen's which provides a great story, teaches the wonder of God's goodness and patience and His love for us through the plan He created to help us be all He wants us to be. The story also shows us that each of us are separated from God by sin but that He loves us so much that He sent His Son Jesus Christ to earth to die for our sins thus allowing us a future with Him. I hope that if you have not yet known of God's plan of salvation, after reading this book you will have gained the understanding to do so. All of Helen's novels are wonderful to read; they are a balm for the soul and an education for the seeker. Words cannot express how much good I believe books such as these will do for so many and for that reason I pray that Helen's books will all become best sellers.

ACKNOWLEDGEMENTS

Special thanks to Katharina Leipp of Muhlaker, Germany for translating this book *God's Plan of Salvation* and *Caleb's Testimony,* as well as many of my articles into the German language. She has been a wonderful friend, a terrific editor and an incredible support! Thank you! Thanks to District Evangelist Revishaq Bashir who has so lovingly shared my books with the Sunday school teachers in Pakistan and encouraged me to continue to send my books to the congregations in that country. Thanks to my husband Wally who provides me with so much love and support and makes my computer behave. Thanks to my children and grandchildren for the constancy of their encouragement, and to my dear friend, the Reverend Herold Ambroise for his fervent prayers on my behalf. And always a special thank you to Richard Levinson for providing me with the first opportunity through which I could develop my writing skills. My thanks also to my brothers and sisters and ministers in faith who give so freely of their love and prayers and support, and to my Face book friends who also pray for me and support my ministry. My thanks to Darren Robinson for his meticulous assembly of the cover and the interior artwork, and to Daniel Patrick Landolfi for his cheerful inspiration, his incredible faith....and works....for maintaining and improving my website, and most of all for his enduring friendship. I am grateful for the support of those who have helped promote my books in Germany, South Africa, Pakistan, Zambia, Australia, the United Kingdom and many other countries.

But most of all, my heartfelt, humble thanks to our Heavenly Father for His inspiration, guiding hand, protection, and never-ending love. May this work bring joy to His heart and help find that last soul!

MESSAGE FROM THE AUTHOR

This book, *The Story of God's Plan of Salvation,* is the fifth book in the Grandma series. While it is a wonderful story for children, a whimsical fairy tale of sorts, it beautifully describes for adults what our Heavenly Father wants us to learn. It tells the story of how and why God created such a loving and all encompassing plan for each of us and placed it into His creation to develop the Bride of Christ.

God's plan of salvation is part of what we know as "the physics of the world", those things which occur naturally in our universe. An example of physics is when we throw a ball into the air and rather than stay where we throw it, it comes back down. Other examples include the disappearance of light when the sun sets at night, and the elements found in rain which nurture and feed the soil in which our plants grow.

It is important that we also understand that physics is used to create the spiritual laws of the universe which provides us with everything we need to become a child of God. Only God can change what physics will do both naturally and spiritually and only God can change our heart as we learn of Him and heed His words.

Thus for this book I created a special sentence to describe the phenomena of physics; a sentence which is repeated often throughout this book in the hope that all who read it will begin to recognize the magnificence of what God did for us even before we were born. The sentence I have chosen to use throughout this book is: *This was just the natural law of the universe, the physics of things which God had built into His magnificent and loving plan of salvation for all the inhabitants.*

It is through God's incredible acts of love; the beauty and power we see in nature, His instructive words in scripture, and those He gives us as an example of what we are to strive for, that we too can learn God's plan for us, learn about His desire for our eternal future, and appreciate the sacrifices He has made for us. Through these we learn of the profound miracle that we see that creates love in our hearts and helps us change from our Adam-like nature to become more like Christ. It is through God's Plan of Salvation that we are given the opportunity to develop a love so powerful that it can defeat the enemy called Satan who seeks our destruction.

God wants us to desire to overcome the selfish nature which Satan placed into Adam and Adam passed on to us. God wants to touch our hearts with the purest love and make us suitable for the kingdom of Heaven. But God has allotted us only a certain amount of time to learn these lessons, make these changes, and decide with our free will if we are willing to do what He asks. He wants us to understand that every soul will continue to live *even after death* and will be assigned to one of three places: The City of God, The Kingdom of God, or The Lake of Fire where Satan will be bound for all eternity. Those are our only choices. Therefore, God has provided us with a plan which will demonstrate that each of us must decide his own future.

Learning and changing is not always easy to do. Sometimes it takes a great deal of work and practice. The sinful nature, which all of us battle, makes our learning process slow, and limits our understanding of heavenly matters. It is the sinful Adam-like nature which locks us into a personal arrogance and a spiritual complacency which tells us that we do not need God and certainly do not need to follow any rules He laid down for mankind to follow to gain a place in Heaven. But God understands our limitations and, throughout scripture, describes the future He offers us and provides ways for us to better understand what is at stake.

In fact, God's words are just as alive and relevant today as they were thousands of years ago. They are to help us learn what God seeks to accomplish and why Satan seeks to block that accomplishment. It tells us that there are rules we must follow if we want to be a part of heaven, and that it is through God's plan that He works to provide us with what we need to reach this goal. Though Satan has incredible power, God has placed limits on what Satan can do, always give us a way to escape Satan's wiles, and has created a future for us of such perfection that we cannot even begin to imagine its magnificence.

The parables of the Holy Bible use the circumstances of everyday life as it was during the time when the Bible was written and can be applied to our present life. Thus when God tells us that our future will have streets paved in gold, we will wear crowns of valuable jewels, there will be food growing on trees and harvested monthly, evil will be bound forever, that we will be married to Christ and live in His mansion, we can gain an understanding of the value of what God is offering us. From these words we begin the hope...and the work.... of being found worthy to participate in this future. Whatever our personal struggle; illness, poverty, tragedy, hunger, or loneliness, these descriptions of our potential future are appealing and help us see that heaven is worth fighting for. God's love for us is so great that He endures our hardened hearts, our willfulness, our arrogance, and our selfishness as long as we try to do our best.

As we experience times of turmoil, it may be difficult to understand why evil appears to prosper; but that prosperity is for a limited time. For us, as we live on earth, locked into the battle our training requires, we learn to look toward the rewards of an eternal future with God which is well worth what we go through. God's plan is to separate good and evil for all eternity. Thus, the purpose of God's plan is to help guide us toward learning His words and making decisions which allow Him to help us separate ourselves from evil. The words He provides for us through the Holy Bible offers us the information we need to change ourselves, and thus change our circumstances. When we complete this process and have chosen God's way over evil, our future will be free of all tears and sorrow.

God also teaches us to comfort one another. *"Bear ye one another's burdens, and so fulfil the law of Christ"* (Galatians 6:2) and explains that we have the opportunity to become a treasure to others by being the role model God wants us to be. Being a blessing to others brings a blessing to our own lives. As we move through our stages of development, God wants us to share our hard-earned wisdom with others and become ambassadors of Christ by loving, forgiving, teaching, supporting, helping those around us, and bringing testimony to everyone we can. When we have developed this heart's attitude, God can change circumstances, change relationships, create love in its purest form, and bring us understanding, even though He is bound by the rules of righteousness under which He has chosen to labor.

This story appears at first to be whimsical, similar perhaps to a fairy tale. But as it unfolds, the plans laid down long ago by the Father and His Son and the Holy Spirit to create the Bride of Christ come to light. It is a story which explains why tragedy strikes, what its purpose is, and what we are to do in these circumstances. It shows us what our ultimate goal is and what an incredible and magnificent feat of engineering God placed into His Plan of Salvation. It is a story which is told from the perspective of the angels who reside in the Heavens but watch those on Earth. They know God's plan and see our struggle, errors, vanity, and shortsightedness.

From the beautiful heavens in which they live, the angels see the coldness and bleakness of a planet without love, and see the evil which seeks to harm the inhabitants of that planet. They know why it takes us so long to learn and to change, but they also recognize our victories and cheer them. This story is for the very young and those still learning for it is a wonderful story filled with easy to understand lessons for both children and adults which will help sustain us in our personal struggles. It is also a story for the old and infirm to comfort them in their very different struggles, helping us know that God understands what we feel and what we battle, and is by our side in all circumstances. It gives us whatever measure of strength we need to carry our cross. It demonstrates how much we mean to God, why evil wants to harm us and how we can fight back.

It is a story to be shared with others so one can offer testimony by providing the reader with a story to tell, recommend, read to others, or gift to others to help spread the Gospel of God's loving plan for all of us. Even very young children accept the lessons in the story without need of explanation, and over time, the words they hear increase their understanding and they begin to recognize their role in God's plan. With emphasis placed on the protection God provides for those who love Him, we learn of evil without fearing it, and learn how to thwart its influence in our lives. This helps us understand why people often behave badly and inhibits the personal blame many experience for the bad things which sometimes engulf us. Understanding the work of evil gives us the wisdom to trust that God is with us, and that our prayers are powerful and can cause evil to flee.

Many hunger to understand God's words, and God gladly reveals to the seeking heart the mysteries of the Bible. *"Then opened he their understanding, that they might understand the scriptures"* (Luke 24:45). Many feel a sense of relief to know that God does understand the difficulty of personal growth and the emotional pain attached to our failures. Sometimes this simple truth is what will touch a heart and draw someone to God. Knowing that others have expressed what they themselves have felt and suffered yet triumphed over, helps immensely to bring peace to a troubled heart and release any long term guilt.

The Grandma series of novels of which this book is a part, have evolved into a saga about a grandmother whose trials and tribulations brought her heartache but which God turned into a blessing by teaching her of the wonderful plan He had for her life. It brought her a beautiful and enduring trust in God and prepared her for the legacy she would leave her family. As she learned the precepts found in God's words and in His Plan of Salvation and began to put them into effect in her life, she was inspired to formulate the manuscripts and journals which her children and grandchildren would one day read. They became my stories.

Through these, Grandma teaches her family that God wants them to have the best of everything, even in the vigorous training program which this earth was formed to provide. The Grandma of my stories desires that her family learn from her mistakes and learn that God will forgive those mistakes; that it is okay to be swayed by a moment of despair as long as we turn to God and ask for His help in getting back up to fight again another day. All of us share similar struggles and sometimes need to be reminded that help and solace is available. In fact, God tells us, *"But ye are a chosen generation, a royal priesthood, an holy nation, a peculiar people"* (1 Peter 2:9) and therefore miracles still happen today. All children of God suffer under the work of Satan and are not alone in their worries, fears, insecurities, or personal struggle. It is Satan who wants us to feel guilty, to be discouraged; to be reminded of the limitations of body and mind. But reading God's words assures us that despite what our situation might appear to be, God can fix all things and walks with us. His words assure us that He looks on the willingness of the heart, not the weakness of the body.

All the children of God come under the enemy's attacks, but through such attacks, we are "tried in the fire" and evolving through God's patient, loving training process. God's magnificent Plan of Salvation brings us into the fullness of God's glory as He seeks to create the Bride of Christ, and the kings, priests, lambs, and sheep for His new kingdom. Thus, the land in which we live is a training ground, a practice place which is ruled by an enemy who does not want God's Plan of Salvation to succeed.

This story is about the purpose of life and also about the birth and development of love. It is about how pure and selfless love is actually the passport to heaven where evil cannot exist. It explains why life, as we know it, is not fair and why we cannot avoid pain and heartache. It tells us that God promises that if we follow His word, we can leave those experiences for something far better. He promises that in heaven, we will be free of Satan's fiery darts. *"And God shall wipe away all tears from their eyes; and there shall be no more death, neither sorrow, nor crying, neither shall there be any more pain; for the former things are passed away"* (Revelation 21:4).

As we move toward a better understanding of God's Plan of Salvation, we become a blessing as we share our knowledge with others. This is what God wants of His children......that while we are here on earth we do our best to convey what God has taught us. Grandma learned that if she listened to God's word and followed as best she could, He would direct her ways. Thus, she could avoid some of the disappointments of life because she understood how evil worked and what God taught about dealing with evil. Grandma learned to make better decisions and to develop a heart with the capacity to love, understand, and provide the empathy which would allow her to accept the faults she would inevitably encounter in others... and to forgive those faults even if she had to flee their evil. Through this development, she found happiness, not in the form she had originally imagined, but a happiness which filled her soul. She learned that she did not need what she'd imagined she did. Through this understanding and her striving, her heart found peace.

The words of scripture open to us in this book as a flower opens its petals to the sunlight. *"The eyes of your understanding being enlightened..."* (Ephesians 1: 18) Sadly, many who read the Bible see only a small part of God's plan. They do not accept God's words literally nor do they believe that God's words are all encompassing, and for all times, nor that God clearly asks certain things of them. But if we pray for this understanding, God will reward us with an unshakable faith and a loving heart. God's miracles are not only huge earthshaking experiences of faith and but are also smaller everyday occurrences which bring us joy, strengthen us, and change our lives by increasing our understanding and allowing God to enter our hearts.

I hope that you enjoy this novel. I wish for you God's richest blessings and pray that God will give you the desire to seek His word, the wisdom to understand it, the strength to follow it, and the willingness to share it. For it is only a short time that we labor here, and it is for all eternity that we will sit at the feet of God. *"To him that overcometh will I grant to sit with me in my throne"* (Revelation 3:21)

Helen Glowacki

Table of Contents

Prologue
Sarah Remembers

Sarah understood the extraordinary magic of being loved and of loving others. She felt that love was similar to standing on a mountaintop overlooking a vista of hills and forests or a huge valley which stood guard over a winding river, or even being at a beach or on a cliff overlooking the sea. She could feel it when sitting under a sky filled with twinkling stars and thinking about the wonder of the universe or when walking in the shade of old oak trees listening to the happy chatter of birds. To Sarah, love was what she felt when she saw a rainbow, or a field of wildflowers, or when she heard the music of the wind whispering through branches and around buildings. Love was a gift for the heart; soothing and gentling. It was the teacher of the soul because it was humbling, powerful, demanding, and often a mixture of joy and of pain. She knew that pain provided the opportunity for growth and allowed the lessons of life to change the selfish heart of man into the giving heart God sought in His children. Only love could produce the miracle of change. She was grateful for the instruction she had received as a child, grateful for what she had been taught about the love of God, and grateful for her grandmother who helped her understand God's words, kept her involved in church, and insisted that she complete her education. Sarah knew that this was a great blessing. And she felt that today was a very special day for her.

It was the second day after she and Matt had returned from their honeymoon and the first time that Sarah would be alone in their home. She wanted to take a minute to think about all that had gone into their wedding plans and what their future held for them. She and Matt would begin their life together and would be creating their own memories, their own life story. Before the wedding, they had moved Grandma's wonderful antiques and treasured furnishings in their home and looked forward to enjoying their beauty and the memories they held. Sarah wanted to walk through each room, admire everything which had once belonged to Grandma and send thoughts to Grandma to let her know how happy she was, and what a lovely home she and Matt created from the possessions she had left them. But most of all, Sarah wanted to assure her that she and Matt would carry on her legacy of love and faith. Grandma's clocks, desks, armoires, lamps, exquisite porcelains, and oriental carpets, all brought back Sarah's memories of

Grandma; and her heart tingled in anticipation of this first day when she could think about, feel, and remember all her blessings. She was so thankful for her family; Caleb and Ann, Josh and Debbie, who were her brothers and their wives; and Matt's sister and husband, Barbara and Jim. They were their best friends and had been a part of their wedding. They all lived only a short drive from this house, the older home they had purchased and renovated before their wedding. Knowing that Matt would not arrive home for another few hours, Sarah was alone with her thoughts and memories, with Grandma's beautiful furnishings....and with the manuscript they'd found in Grandma's old desk. Just last night she and Matt had discovered one of Grandma's many manuscripts in the antique desk they brought to the house from the storage unit a week before the wedding. They had not noticed the manuscript when they discarded some of Grandma's papers before moving the desk into storage after Grandma died. But last night, as Matt began to transfer some files into the desk, he saw the manuscript stuck in the back of a drawer, pulled it out and placed it on top of the desk. A quick perusal of the manuscript brought a vague remembrance to Sarah that Grandma had read her the story which was written in its pages. Her heart pounded with anticipation, and her mind raced with a million memories if indeed, it was what she thought it was. Now, alone in the house and knowing that Matt wouldn't arrive home until late, she hoped that she would have time to read the story. *Perhaps I can curl up on one of the wing chairs with the manuscript and read until Matt gets home.* Memories of Grandma's big old Victorian house with clocks chiming and ticking, cedar-smelling armoires, and oil-scented desks for hiding under, flooded into Sarah's mind and with tears slipping down her cheeks, she wished that Grandma was with them; wished she could see the house, could discuss the pros and cons of where to put each precious piece of furniture. For a moment, sadness swept into her heart, and she sobbed aloud, thinking how much she missed Grandma. But Sarah accepted that some things couldn't be changed and believed with all her heart that they would all be reunited again one day when God's Plan of Salvation was completed.

As she pulled into the driveway and then into the garage of their new home, Sarah decided not to enter the house from the garage but instead, to enter through the front door by walking outside and around the house. She wanted to savor the experience of their home both from the outside and the inside and compose her thoughts and feelings before she walked in the door. She wanted to enter the house just as she had so often entered Grandma's house—by the front door, *listening for the silence.* Now, still standing outside and looking toward the magnificent old trees she realized how much she loved the serene setting of the house, the rustling of the leaves, the chirping of the birds, and the vantage point she had from the front porch. From there she could view the lovely tree-lined street with the spacious old houses and their distinct old-world styling. She loved the architectural features of all the houses along the street, each so different, yet each sharing the beauty of history. She loved the hot, humid early September evening, and sensing the promise of the dryer, cooler air of fall. Her gaze moved across the street to Mary and Kevin's house and she smiled at the lovely colors of the impatiens in full bloom, planted all along their walkway. She had so much joy in the friendship she and Matt shared with them; they were both so pleased to have met Mary and Kevin and their newly extended family of Rebecca and Elizabeth. It would be great fun to be neighbors. Matt would be helping Kevin renovate his carriage house this fall for Rebecca and Elizabeth. They would all help; even Ann and Caleb, Barbara and Jim, Josh and Debbie,.....even Jayden had asked to help. She and Matt both looked forward to the many nice fellowships the whole group would share. They'd be having their lively conversations again. They loved these happy times together. Sarah smiled as she watched a butterfly fly pass in search of a flower, and mentally apologized to the butterfly, explaining that she and Matt wouldn't be planting flowers until spring. Sarah loved flowers and looked forward to the garden which she and Matt would create. Her head swam with thoughts of birds and butterflies, a gazebo upon which climbing vines of flowers would grow, a little fountain, maybe even a tiny little pond. It would be so much fun to work together to create their little Bethany, and the best part was that they could share their creations with all the others.

Sarah turned to the front door and put her key into the lock. She was excited. In just a few seconds, she would enter the hallway; and she would stand there, *and she would listen.* She would listen for the quiet. Grandma had always done that. Grandma would step through her door, close it softly, and listen for the quiet; then she would listen for the ticking of her clocks. And if she'd timed it right, she could wait and listen for the chimes. Every clock had been set about thirty seconds apart; so once the chiming of one clock began, the others would follow, one at a time, for quite a while. That was because Grandma had a chiming clock in every room in the house, sometimes two in a room. Now Sarah had these clocks, and Matt had lovingly and meticulously set them thirty seconds apart so she could enjoy them as Grandma had. The key turned effortlessly. Sarah pulled the latch down, pushed open the door and stepped through the opening. She closed the door quietly behind her. Then she stood still, listening. First she listened for the quiet. When her ears picked up the beauty of the quiet, she thanked God for this home, for Matt, for Grandma, for all she had learned. Then she took a deep breath and listened for the ticking of the clocks. When she could hear the ticking, tears of joy came to her eyes; and she remembered so many special times in her life, so many unique things which Grandma had taught her. She remembered Grandma swooping her into her arms when she was just a little girl, and laying her finger against her lips, saying, *"Shhhh."* Sarah would imitate Grandma and also say, *"Shhhhh,"* with her own little finger against her tiny lips. They would listen, heads together, ears straining to hear the silence, eyes wide open with anticipation of what was to come. Then.... after a little while.... Grandma would repeat the ticking sound she heard, saying, *"Tick-tock, tick-tock"* or *"tick-tick, tick-tick"* or *"tick-tock-tock, tick-tock-tock,"* because each clock had a different sound.

And so Sarah learned to listen and soon she was able to identify the different kinds of ticking, later even naming which clock made which sound. When the chiming began, she and Grandma would run from room to room to the clock which would chime next. Grandma always knew the order of the clocks' chiming, and eventually, Sarah learned too. Sometimes Grandma would play a joke on Sarah and switch the clocks between two rooms, and Sarah would run into the wrong room and then have to listen again to find the room where the clock was chiming. They would laugh together at their great game. Sarah wished Grandma were here, wished she could see her new home, and wished Grandma could listen to the clocks with her, even if just for five minutes. Then maybe Sarah would be satisfied and not have this hunger and longing in her heart. But this was not possible, so Sarah reminded herself that one day, they would be together again. It would be a very special day, and Grandma would tell her that she was proud of her. Suddenly, Sarah realized that the chiming of her clocks had begun. She had stood for so long, listening to the quiet and the ticking of the clocks, thinking, and at the same time remembering, that she forgot about the chimes! Miraculously, just when she needed a distraction, the clocks began to chime, so she smiled and stood quietly until the chiming stopped. Somehow the chiming had been a message to her that all was well, that God was in control, that life was where it was supposed to be. She felt peace. When the chiming ended, Sarah moved from the entry hall, through the parlour, and into the study. She laid her purse on the console table and placed her briefcase on the floor next to the desk. Then she moved the manuscript which lay on top of the desk to the table next to the wing chair where she planned to sit to read the manuscript after her tour of the house. Then she changed from her business clothing into something more comfortable.

A few minutes later Sarah walked into the living room and stood to admire the highly polished mahogany and cherry woods of Grandma's tables, secretary desk, and chair frames. She loved their classic lines and elegance and remembered shopping for some of these items with Grandma when she was just a little girl. Then she walked to the dining room, admiring the huge hutch and the gold-rimmed dishes, so expensive now yet something that her great-great-grandmother had received free of charge each time she went to see a movie. Grandma had told her how her grandmother would tell her what to ask for as they entered the movie theater: a butter dish, a cup, or a dessert plate. So Grandma too had cherished these same dishes because of the memories they had for her. As Sarah moved from room to room, she accomplished what she'd wanted to do—remember Grandma, thank her, appreciate all she'd been to her. She'd wanted somehow to start her life in this house by letting Grandma know how she cherished the memories, the example she'd been, and the instruction she'd provided to Sarah about God. She was also grateful that Grandma had instilled into her heart the ability to move on and enjoy her current happiness without bitterness, blame, or a sense of loss. She wanted to thank God for giving her such a wonderful role model in Grandma. And now she'd done this and felt that she was once again ready to move on. After making herself a quick snack, Sarah carried a cup of tea into the study, curled into the wing chair, and began to read Grandma's manuscript.

After reading just a few paragraphs, Sarah realized that she had been correct in her first impression—Grandma had read this story to her many years ago and to Caleb and Josh too. It was their favorite bedtime story, and they clamored for Grandma to read it whenever she was visiting. They never tired of the story and asked question after question while Grandma patiently answered them and explained every detail to them. Sarah realized that this was the story which had helped her understand God's plan for them. It had been a wonderful way to learn of God! And it had helped them when things in life had seemed so unfair. Sarah felt a sudden thrill course through her body as she realized that now she would have the story in hand to read to her own children. She couldn't wait to share this story with Matt. *In fact*, she thought, *I will make copies and have them bound and give them to each family. I will give one to Mary and Kevin, to Ann and Caleb, to Josh and Debbie, to Barbara and Jim, to Elizabeth and Rebecca, and even to John and Jayden!* Then Sarah began to read in earnest, half remembering the words, the story familiar yet new, and was struck by the wonder of Grandma's unexpected gift to them. She once again admired Grandma's beautiful handwriting, the script she'd learned as a child. Within minutes, Sarah was engrossed in wonderful memories of the questions she and her brothers had asked and the explanations Grandma had given, of the awe they all felt as the inflections in Grandma's voice pulled them into the drama of her story. And so Sarah read the manuscript from cover to cover and once again marveled at the incredible magnificence and perfection of God's great engineering feat, the physics of the world he'd created for them and most of all, His incredibly loving plan of salvation.

****

Chapter One

<u>The Birth of Prayer</u>

The Poems of Chapter One:

Rejoicing in hope,
patient in tribulation,
continuing instant in prayer.

—Romans 12: 12

Once upon a time, in a land of marshmallow clouds drifting in skies of the most beautiful blue, where music played and everyone sang, there lived a multitude of angels who carefully watched the planet below them....and waited for God's plan of salvation to unfold for the inhabitants who lived on that planet. All across the land of the angels far up above, flowers grew everywhere one could look, and were always blooming, full and perfect... filling the soft, warm breeze with the wonderful fragrance of their perfume. The flowers basked under a light so bright that it caused everything to shine vibrantly and clothed this lush and lovely land with its ability to enhance the beauty of everything it touched. The clouds were the whitest white imaginable and the grass the greenest green. Even the trees were exquisite in their perfect symmetry and beautifully shaped leaves in graduated colors of gold, green, and rust. An all-encompassing aura of love permeated every living thing in the land of the angels and filled the soul with warmth. A great sense of peace and comfort could be felt by everyone who lived in this beautiful land. This was because pure love flowed everywhere in the heavens, and ruled in every heart. The angels hoped that someday everyone God had created could live in this verdant place of peace high in the heavens, far above the spinning planet below which they could easily see was slowly, insidiously dying. In fact, the cold, bleak planet below the land of the angels seemed as if it harbored a terrible sickness which was gnawing its way through everything good. Yet none of the inhabitants of the dying planet recognized that the initial perfection of their creation was becoming anything less than what it originally was. They did not see that its life was limited; they thought that everything would always go on as it had in the past and sadly, many became complacent, and thought of nothing other than themselves. But the angels could see the sickness. They saw it growing.... eating at the planet from the inside, determined to destroy its goodness and its beauty. The sickness was evil, and it fed and thrived on anger and hate. This is why the planet was doomed. The angels even knew why planet would die, why the planet had been created, when it was created, and what its replacement would be. But this was heaven's secret and the angels were not allowed to reveal what they knew. They could not share their knowledge with the inhabitants of the planet far below them. They could never breathe a word about the planet's future unless God told them that they could. They could only watch and wait for the completion of God's magnificent plan.

Despite the concern the angels felt as they watched the evil sickness devour the planet below them, they weren't distressed by what they saw or what they knew, or about the planet's inevitable death or about the future of its inhabitants. This was because they knew the great secret which was placed into God's special plan for those inhabitants. They understood the incredible plan God had engineered, and what the outcome would be. They understood that the inhabitants who lived far below them were in the midst of a great battle, in the midst of a struggle between good and evil and therefore in the midst of the development of pure love in the heart of man. Love was the only weapon which could overcome the sickness and the evil which wanted to destroy God's creation. They knew that someday, the inhabitants would have to choose between what good offered them and what evil had to offer. They knew that the inhabitants didn't yet know that one brought them truth and the other only lies but that as they began to learn what good brought and what evil brought into their lives, many would try harder to withstand the evil. The angels knew that those who did respond to goodness and made the decision to fight against the evil would please God very much.

The angels also knew that in Heaven there was a great book filled with the names of those who would search for good, those who wanted goodness in their lives and wanted no part of evil. This book lay open upon a beautiful table made of marble and gold and was very important because it contained the names of those who God saw as righteous. In Heaven, the word "Lamb" referred to God's Son who was also known as the Lord Jesus, and also known as Christ for whom God was gathering souls who would come to dwell with them one day. Therefore the great book was called the Lamb's book of life because it would contain all the names of those who would choose to follow Christ and reign with Him in heaven when God's great plan was completed. Those people would be called the Bride of Christ. To have their names entered into the Lamb's book of life the inhabitants of the cold bleak planet under the heavens would have to learn to love and through that love choose good over evil of their own free will. If the inhabitants chose to seek this goodness and love, they would escape the destruction which would someday come to their planet.

There was another great and wonderful Book which God created for the inhabitants of this planet. It was called the Holy Bible and was given to the inhabitants so they would know exactly what God wanted them to learn. It was filled with great and perfect wisdom, and could teach the inhabitants how to overcome evil by learning how to love. In the pages of this Holy Bible were the wonderful words of instruction which God provided for the inhabitants to help them learn of Him, of the love He had for them and what He wanted to give them. This Holy Bible contained everything which the inhabitants needed to know about the struggle between good and evil and how evil came into existence and what would happen to evil and evil things when God's plan was completed.

Therefore it was important for the inhabitants to learn to use the gift of wisdom found in the pages of this wonderful book, The Holy Bible. It would teach them how to overcome evil and how to be sure that their names would be written in the Lamb's book of life. The Holy Bible gave them examples of how God placed His plan of salvation into the physics of the world and what God required from those who wanted to be a part of His kingdom when He created the new heaven and earth. Therefore God divided the Holy Bible into sections where the people could study the beginning of God's plan, the way Satan brought harm to Adam and Eve who were the first people God created. They would learn how Christ sacrificed Himself to help His people, and teach them how to fight against evil. They were also given a warning about what would happen to those who became evil. The Holy Bible was a large book which had many smaller books inside its covers which describe those things which the people would need to learn so they could understand what lived in God's heart. The very last of the smaller books of the Holy Bible was called the book of Revelation and in Chapter 21, verse 27, God described the heaven which He hoped the inhabitants could someday enter and the requirements to enter that heaven, saying, "And there shall in no wise enter into it anything that defileth, neither whatsoever worketh abomination, or maketh a lie, but they which are written in the Lamb's book of life." Those whose names would be entered in the Lamb's book of life were those who would be willing to learn from the Holy Bible, those whose hearts desired to learn of and practice love toward their fellow man, those who weren't lazy or complacent but sought to overcome evil, those who would not choose evil. As time went on, many of the inhabitants began to see the difference between good and evil and became thankful for what God was offering them. When God saw that the inhabitants were not only thankful for what He had provided for them but also demonstrated their thankfulness, it brought great joy to His heart. For these were the inhabitants who were becoming "different"; they were becoming the "peculiar" people God spoke of in another book in the Bible which was called "Peter". In 1 Peter 2:9 God told them: "But ye are a chosen generation, a royal priesthood, an holy nation, a peculiar people."

The inhabitants didn't yet understand the part of their nature which was godly, but they did understand that they felt a void in their heart, and wished they could fill that void. It made them hunger for something which they did not yet understand. They only knew that the void brought them discomfort and sometimes a sense of despair.

They didn't yet realize that this void was a lack of love; the pure self-sacrificing kind of love which living by God's words could provide for them. Filling their heart with love would bring them great satisfaction and joy. But they didn't know this yet. The angels who watched the inhabitants on the planet below and waited in patience for them to learn were, in reality, watching God's great and magnificent plan unfold. The plan was called God's plan of salvation and had been created by God, the Father, by Christ, the Son of God, and by the Holy Spirit which God sent to dwell in the heart of man to comfort them and to teach them to overcome evil and choose for themselves whether they would live under hate or under love.

When the plan of salvation was completed and the Father, the Son, and the Holy Spirit deemed it perfect, God placed it into the natural laws of the universe....the physics of His creation....to help the inhabitants of the planet far below the heavens learn everything they would need to become a part of God's new kingdom. Therefore the plan of salvation became an integral part of everything in the universe and was unchangeable. The plan was righteous and gave everyone the same opportunity for success. The plan would provide every inhabitant with the knowledge of how they could choose....of their own free will.....to live with God and all the good He represented. Thus the great plan of salvation for all mankind was built into the natural law of the universe, the physics of the things which God placed into His magnificent Creation.

One element of the physics of the world allowed the conversations of the inhabitants to reach the heavens. These conversations would be used to gauge the development of love in the inhabitants, but it would take time for the inhabitants to understand the importance of their conversations and how these would measure their understanding of what God was offering them. In fact, at first, the inhabitants did not even know that the natural law of the universe, the physics of things which had been built into God's plan of salvation, caused their conversations to be carried to a certain point high above the planet where the swirling currents of the breeze picked them up and brought them to the heavens where they were entered into the great heavenly computer and saved. The currents grasped and transported the conversations up to the land of the angels. The inhabitants did not know of, nor understand, this phenomena because they were not yet aware of the great and magnificent plan or the physics of the world which God had developed for them.

Nevertheless, through the natural law of the universe, the physics of things, the conversations of the inhabitants were moved into the different atmosphere surrounding the beautiful and verdant land of the angels. When these arrived at the heavens where the angels lived, they were recorded and categorized. Most of these were then locked into a great computer where they would remain until God's Plan of Salvation was completed. However, before its completion, a day of judgment would occur when every inhabitant who had ever lived or ever died would have made their choice between good and evil. The archived conversations would be used on this day to separate those who chose good from those who chose evil; it would separate what the Holy Bible called the "goats" from the "lambs".

The Holy Bible had taught the inhabitants that the goats would be those who had not chosen to fill their hearts with love and who had chosen evil rather than good. They were those whose names had never been written in the Lamb's book of life and they would never be able to enter heaven. Their conversations which had also been recorded and categorized, would demonstrate the choices they had made throughout their life. This was just the natural law of the universe, the physics of things which God built into His magnificent and loving plan of salvation for all the inhabitants. Some of the conversations however, would be recognized as very special conversations. They were the conversations which were directed to God rather than to other inhabitants. The angels called them prayers. These prayers blossomed from the thankful hearts of the inhabitants who found great peace when they spoke directly to God because these prayers expressed their love for Him. These special conversations were also recorded and categorized, but they were separated from all the other conversations and went directly to the glittering palace which sat high on the majestic mountain at the highest point in the heavens.

The palace was surrounded by a light so beautiful that its multitude of crystal prisms reflected what appeared to be a million rainbows, bouncing a sparkling tapestry of color across the huge edifice. Because the conversations which were called prayers were considered so special, they were handled with great love. Counterfeit prayers, full of repetition or spoken for show, were easily recognized for their lack of sincerity and were not accepted. Only genuine prayers would pass on to the glittering palace. Prayers were judged genuine if, and only if, they contained a certain element which identified them as coming from a pure heart. Only the prayers coming from a seeking heart which held no guile could pass to the palace. Counterfeit prayers would be caught and recorded and categorized like the other conversations, but they did not go to the palace. Only pure prayers with no falsity went to the palace. In fact, the Holy Bible taught not only the value of prayer, but what a prayer should contain. If someone prayed just to impress someone rather than to seek an intimate conversation with God, it was not accepted into the Palace.

In the book of Luke which is found in the Holy Bible, God warned the people not to pray the way a Pharisee prayed, explaining that the Pharisees exalted themselves and spoke for show and were not sincere. In the Book of Luke, Chapter 18, verses 11 and 14, God warned the people that prayers which did not contain love or true thankfulness, were not from a humble heart and would not be accepted. Prayers which did pass to the great palace made the angels happy. They knew these prayers were cherished. They knew that the inhabitants who sent these prayers to God were loved very much by those in the palace. Most often, these prayers came from those whose names would be written in the Lamb's book of life which lay open on the table made of marble and gold and were of utmost importance to those who engineered the natural law of the universe, the physics of things. These prayers always received a response. An immediate response. For God had said of these prayers in the Holy Bible: "And the publican . . . saying, God be merciful to me a sinner. I tell you, this man went down to his house justified . . . he that humbleth himself shall be exalted" (Luke 18:13,14).

The learning process came more easily to those inhabitants who had an open heart and a loving nature. But this process still took time because God wanted everyone to know how to make a positive and well-informed decision. Thus, God planned for every inhabitant to have the opportunity, and plenty of time, to learn. God knew that it would take some of the inhabitants longer than others to learn, but eventually, everyone would be given the same opportunity and enough time.   The angels smiled when they remembered that before the inhabitants first began to recognize that they were loved and cared for, they thought that the good things which came their way were just by coincidence. They hadn't yet understand that God was working in their lives to show them who He was and, through His love, draw them to Him. But as they experienced what they thought were coincidences, they began to recognize the care they received from God and thus their prayers began to change.

Coincidence

I knelt in reverence to send a prayer
to my Heavenly Father above,
but the answer seemed a coincidence,
not a sign of the Father's love.

Yes, while I asked on bended knee,
in prayer, with folded hands,
I doubted that I had been heard
and mattered in God's plans.

At first, it seemed coincidence,
this answer to my plea,
this is truly how I saw it,
for what else could it be?

And so it went the first time,
the second, and the third,
until one day I realized

my prayers were being heard.

And thus I came to listen
to God's plan for my life,
and learned the awesome power
that prayer has over strife.

****

When God heard these prayers, His heart was touched and He was happy that His great and magnificent plan was beginning to take effect. The natural law of the universe, the physics of things which He had created to protect and teach the inhabitants was progressing. His plan was bringing about the development of His peculiar people; those who would understand the nature of evil but, through the learning process instilled into God's plan, would seek pure love instead. There was singing and rejoicing as these new prayers were heard in the heavens. The first of God's peculiar people had begun to understand!

Sadly, however, though God always provided a response to these special prayers, some of the inhabitants who sent the prayers did not always understand what the response meant. Often, they had their own ideas about what answer they should receive from their prayers, and therefore they did not accept or even recognize the response God gave them. The angels, however, always understood the response the inhabitants had been given because they knew the plan and realized....through the natural law of the universe, the physics of things.....how the response would benefit the inhabitant. It saddened the angels when they saw an inhabitant who had lost hope and patience when they received a response they did not expect nor understand. So the angels sometimes whispered comforting words into the ears of the inhabitants, words which God had asked them to say. They saw the tears of confusion in some of these inhabitants and were moved as they recognized that a pure and seeking heart looked for a response but could not seem to understand it.

The angels wished they could explain to the inhabitants that in time, their worries would be abolished; and that in the meanwhile, despite what they thought, they were being cared for. They just had to trust God and be patient. The angels often wished that they did not have to keep their secret. But they did. That was the natural law of the universe, the physics of things, the method by which God had developed and engineered the great and magnificent plan of salvation for His people. The people would have to learn trust and patience, for someday they would have to choose whom they would trust for all eternity. The angels saw how the prayers of the inhabitants changed as they grew in faith; the prayers began to include the words: "Thy will be done" and "I trust in Thee." This brought joy to the hearts of the angels and to the heart of God. These special inhabitants of the dying planet were indeed learning. The tears of confusion had done their work. For while some of the inhabitants chose to walk away from God, others stayed with God and waited upon His good favor. The inhabitants who stayed had chosen wisely.

In fact, the training which the inhabitants were now enduring would come to an end once they had accumulated the knowledge of good and evil and were able to make their choice. Some inhabitants would move quickly along this path, others slowly, but God gave every inhabitant an opportunity to achieve the goal. Prayer from a pure and seeking heart would lead to trusting God and this trust would lead to the development of a noble heart which could be made worthy to become a part of God's family. Prayer was the very first step toward this goal. In the Holy Bible, in the book of Psalms Chapter 102, verse 1 were written the words: "Hear my prayer, O Lord, and let my cry come unto thee." and if the people prayed with their heart, wanting to converse with God, their prayers would go directly to the glittering palace. Thus the inhabitants demonstrated their growth and development and a greater understanding in their newly accepting, trusting, gentled hearts. Progress had been made and God's plan was moving along as intended, with the proof of this evident in the prayers the inhabitants were now sending to God.

Dear Heavenly Father

When I'm on my knees and praying,
oftimes with heartfelt pain,
and beseeching You to help me,
You show my faith much gain.

I know, my Lord, Your wisdom,
and the reason You'd deny
is to help my soul to grow,
when on Your word I will rely.

So I try to be more patient
and reject what's just my will
and let all my Lord's decisions
be those I would fulfill.

And yet, my gracious Father,
so more often do You grant
such miracles to come my way,
Thus the seeds of faith You plant.

I'm so often quite astounded
at how good You are to me
and feel intense unworthiness
of the blessings that I see.

For you've answered all my prayers, my Lord,
and shown me of Your love,
thus I hunger to be close to You
and to Lord Jesus up above.

Oh Father, I am unworthy,
yet You've chosen me to hear
that very special Word of God
that's precious and so dear.

For my eyes have now been opened,
and my heart is one with You
because You've deigned to choose me
and my life to thus renew.

You've done so much for me, my Lord,
what can I do in return?
I can love You most of all

and try very hard to spurn

the promptings of the evil one,
the one I so despise,
and keep my sight on Heaven,
not on the serpent's deep, dark lies.

I can tell others of my happiness,
of being Your own child,
of how close You are to those You love,
and of the treasures You have piled

for each of Your own children
in the Heavens up above
that You offer each and every one
who will give You all their love.

I love You with my heart and soul
and glorify Your name,
and I'm awed by Your goodness
and the fact that Jesus came.

My sins are mercifully washed away,
and I can start my life anew
as I hunger for the time to come
when I can bid this earth adieu.
Amen
******

Sometimes, however, because evil was not yet bound, many of the inhabitants of the cold, bleak planet strayed from the pure love and understanding God wanted for them. During these times the angels were saddened, but they had hope that these circumstances would change. The inhabitants had learned that the land of Canaan, which was described in the Holy Bible, represented righteousness and goodness and was a place where love could dwell. They also learned that the land of Egypt represented unrighteousness and evil and was a place which would eventually harm their souls if they chose this place to live. So when one of the inhabitants succumbed to the temptations of evil, it was as if he had moved to Egypt. And when he returned to righteousness through repentance, it was as if he returned to the land of Canaan where he belonged, where God wanted him to be.

Whenever the inhabitants gave in to the whispers and temptations of evil and slipped back into the land of Egypt, when they sampled the wares which evil freely offered them and used to entrap them, the angels had a heavy heart. The Father and the Son and the Holy Spirit had engineered the magnificent plan of salvation so the birth of pure love in the hearts of mankind could evolve and sometimes sadness was the best learning process to help mankind recognize what his choices were and help him understand the difference between good and evil. It was the way that they would learn that they had free will and would be called upon to make a choice when the days ended and the plan of salvation was completed. For there was a time and a season for everything as God had explained in the Holy Bible. In the book called Ecclesiastes, Chapter 3, verse 1, God said, "To everything there is a season, and a time to every purpose under the heaven." Then in Galatians 6:9, God explained the miracle of His plan, saying, "And let us not be weary in well doing: for in due season we shall reap, if we faint not."

Therefore, many of those who had strayed from God's direction because of evil, came back, again seeking His love and His forgiveness, hoping to learn His words and walk in righteousness. These inhabitants had learned that living a life away from God and living in the midst of evil was not what they wanted for their lives. When any inhabitant of the cold, bleak planet came to repentance and again sought God, the heavens rejoiced; the angels sang, God smiled and the plan moved ahead. It was the learning process which would allow man to recognize that they must make a choice; that no one else could make that choice for them....it had to come from within. And from these lessons yet another kind of prayer was born in the heart of man and began to reach the heavens. These were prayers which demonstrated what the inhabitants learned when they left the presence of God and what they felt in their hearts when they came back. It demonstrated that the inhabitants now understood that God never left them even though they had left Him. The angels could see that now the people understood the difference between living, metaphorically, in Canaan or in Egypt.

On the Brink of Canaan

I had been in Egypt and sampled many wares,
searching for I knew not what and carrying all my cares

Then God doth led me elsewhere; to the wilderness He led
where my soul began to hunger, where my poor heart bled.

And so I wandered lonely, confused, half in, half out,
until I saw the cross of Christ thus conquering all my doubt.

Now I pray to enter Canaan, dispossess the evil one,
and let God's Holy Spirit ordain me as a son.

But Satan will not let me gain ground too easily;
he seeks to stop my progress to a life of victory.

And I must ne'er forget that I stand as God's own child
and face this awesome battle with trepidation yet so mild.

Though my goal be aimed at Canaan, and my heart and soul so set,
the evil one takes hold of me and lets pain my flesh beset.

To fight the pain and carry on is a slow and tortuous task,
yet all my strength is from the Lord when on my knees I ask.

Yes, I am gaining Canaan, inch by inch of ground,
and it's me the Lord's whole legions do support and do surround.

For as I enter Canaan and gain each foot of ground,
it's me the Lord's whole legions do protect and do surround.

****

Finally, the lessons of prayer and the heartache of evil seemed
to be understood by the inhabitants of the cold, bleak planet beneath
the land of the angels. Mistakes were still made, but many stayed

faithful to God and valued what they were given. The great and magnificent plan of salvation was in effect; and the natural law of the universe, the physics of things, was a miracle to watch as it unfolded and the ability to love evolved. But then came a day when the inhabitants were tested in their understanding of prayer, and they were faced with what they thought was silence from God. They were made to wait for the answer to their prayers so their patience and their faith could be tested. This was to teach the inhabitants to cling stedfastly to the gift of prayer and continue in their trust of their Heavenly Father when evil launched its attack against them. This too was part of God's plan of salvation, His desire to help His children. Sometimes, when the inhabitants had to wait for the answers they requested when they prayed, they asked questions about their lack of understanding, about the timing of the answers to their prayers, and about the feelings and concerns which burdened them. And God was glad that His people were now learning to converse with Him openly. He was happy to see them trust Him and wait patiently for His help. He was so touched by this that He granted other blessings to His people so they would recognize that He was still with them even if He did not provide immediate answers to the current concerns they voiced in their prayers.

And so the inhabitants came to recognize God's gifts and developed even more love for and trust in their Heavenly Father. Their prayers still went through the test of sincerity, and when they passed this test and went to the palace, God listened and understood. Those who chose to wait for God's answers and trust Him to answer in His time grew in faith. God's heart was moved as the inhabitants told Him that they accepted His will for them no matter what that would be. And God smiled, and the heavens sang again with joy, and God rewarded them for their patience and for their unwavering trust. This had been the lesson of prayer which God gave His children. Now the magnificence of God's plan of salvation could move into the next phase of completion, which was to create within the heart of man a hope for his future, a hope which was so strong, so great that it would be unshakable, even when evil came to whisper doubt. Thus, as new prayers rose to heaven and the inhabitants demonstrated the role which prayer now played in their life, they were ready for more. This first step in God's magnificent plan of salvation now lived in their hearts. The new prayers proved their progress and caused the angels to sing a new song and the heart of God to rejoice.

I Will Await You

So often I've heard from the Altar
that I'm special and precious to God,
and when times are painful and trying,
I'm being shaped by His love, not His rod.

When I read in the wonderful Bible,
that our prayers are heard each day,
I hope and I wait while I'm trusting
that my help will be on the way.

But when day after day it's not coming,
and I try even harder to please,
sometimes I feel very discouraged
and wish for a way to find ease.

Yet I know that God has not forgotten,
I know there's a reason to wait,
I know that there's something still needed,
and that God is never too late.

So I pray even harder than ever
that I learn and grow and forgive;
I immerse myself in God's teaching
so the Lord's is the way that I live.

I want to bring joy to Your heart, Lord,
by the attitudes and hopes that I hold,
and I want to be part of the Bride, Lord,
if saying so isn't too bold.

Please, God, forgive my impatience;
please know I thank You so much.
Please know I realize that your words
and decisions are what I must clutch.

Thank you for keeping me close, Lord,
to the faith, to the hope, and in trust;
Please forgive my great sorrow
despite knowing your decisions are just.

So help me, my wonderful Father,
please help me to please You in all;
help me to do what You want, Lord,

and to accept what You've sent and not fall.

****

These prayers pleased God and worked a sort of magic on the inhabitants' conversations. The conversations of the inhabitants were no longer demanding or accusing; they were more loving and appreciative. And God could see that His great plan of salvation—the plan which He had placed into the natural law of the universe, the physics of things—had successfully completed its first phase. The development of man now had the foundation of prayer to sustain it; the great phenomena of perfect prayer to bring growth and comfort to the souls of the people continued to unfold. There were other phases of God's plan of Salvation yet to come. And thus began the process of God choosing a bride for His beloved Son, the Lord Jesus. The Bride would help the Lord Jesus during the thousand-year kingdom of peace when evil would be bound for a time. Only the Father knew the day and the time when He would send His Son back to the inhabitants' planet to get His Bride; those who had proven themselves by choosing to live by God's statutes. Even God's Son, the Lord Jesus, did not know when God would tell Him to fetch His Bride. God explained this to His people in the Holy Bible in the book of Matthew Chapter 25, verse 13: "Watch therefore, for ye know neither the day nor the hour wherein the Son of man cometh." In Matthew 25:21, God explained the reward for faithfulness: "Well done, thou good and faithful servant; thou hast been faithful over a few things, I will make thee ruler over many things: enter thou into the joy of thy Lord." The inhabitants knew from the Holy Bible that there would be a time of great destruction on their planet when God sent His Son to take them to heaven. Thus many heeded God's words, believed them, and tried to follow His statutes. But few of the inhabitants fully understood that God had put a magnificent plan into place which would help them ready themselves for that day. Nor did they realize that evil watched them and worked to stop their progress. But now, with prayer established in their hearts, the inhabitants of the cold, bleak planet below were ready for the next step. They would be comforted by the power of prayer as they entered their next learning process, the next phase of God's plan of salvation, the natural law of the universe, the physics of things that God put into place just for them.

This next phase of God's plan was to be the development of hope.

"Pray without ceasing."

1 Thessalonians 5:17

"O Lord, Give me Understanding
according to thy word."

Psalm 119:169

Chapter Two
The Development of Hope

The Poems of Chapter Two

Rejoicing in hope; patient in tribulation.

—Romans 12:12

But if we hope for that we see not, then do we with patience wait for it.

—Romans 8:25

The angels rejoiced as the inhabitants of the cold and struggling world beneath them finally seemed to master the art of prayer. They saw that the inhabitants began to understand the Father's love in the answers to their prayers. From this, the angels knew that eventually, the desire for righteousness would also come to live in the hearts of the inhabitants. They saw that the inhabitants recognized the righteousness and love in God's heart and that it became their example to guide them in their own choices and thus sustain them. Yet this was just the beginning. Although the angels could see a change in the inhabitants of the dying, bleak world beneath them, there was still much work to be done and still an enemy who wanted to stop their progress. The angels also noticed that circles of silver began to appear over the heads of those who had learned to pray correctly.

The inhabitants could not see these circles of silver themselves, but the angels could see how beautiful they were and how each circle of silver reflected the aura of love emanating from the heart of the one who wore it. The halos were somewhat pale, almost white in color, not the bright refined color of gold which many angels wore, but they were a sign that the natural law of the universe, the physics of things, had been working and had produced a purity of heart in the prayers of those inhabitants. After all, this too was a part of the great and magnificent plan God had created. As these special people (the ones with the silver circle hovering above their heads) began to know love through prayer, they also began to hunger for something more. They weren't yet sure what it was that they longed for, but they knew it was a driving force in their hearts, a desire to fill yet another void they could now recognize still lived in them. All they knew was that they felt wonderful when they prayed with a sincere heart. They wanted this feeling to stay with them and knew they needed something more to make that happen, yet they weren't quite sure what that was. But this too was just the natural law of the universe, the physics of things, the way God had engineered His plan.

As they prayed and asked for guidance, these inhabitants were inspired to set higher standards of behavior for their lives. They realized that their hearts rejoiced when others around them behaved in a loving way toward them and when others prayed for them and that they too needed to do this for others. They began to understand that they became sad when they were with those who did not love, would not pray, nor try to follow God's words. So they began surrounding themselves with those who did try to love and to pray and to follow God's words. This inspired them to do better themselves and to share this joy. They saw that when they did this, the void in their hearts seemed to lessen. This encouraged them to believe that if they could succeed in their quest to surround themselves with what was good, they could fill some of the emptiness in their hearts even though they continued to hunger for what they could not name. Then God told the angels that they could whisper to them to help them understand that they needed to start with hope; the hope to always walk with God, always come under His love, always do what was needed to please Him....but they didn't yet fully understand all the wonderful things that hope could mean to them. However, the angels knew the secret to filling the void which the inhabitants felt. It began by developing such a strong hope that it would become faith which would lead to trust, and that trust would then lead them to the purest love and love filled every void!

The angels knew that having faith in their hope and trust made love blossom. But the angels were not allowed to tell the inhabitants everything for there was much that they had to learn themselves. The angels saw the struggles and the failures of the inhabitants and knew why the failures came. But they couldn't share every answer about how to avoid failure, for failure, they knew, was the very best teacher. So the inhabitants with the little silver crowns continued to search, continued to feel emptiness, continued to seek a way to fill the void in their hearts, and to struggle toward understanding what they were supposed to do. Thus, the angels did what they could and were happy when the inhabitants recognized that they felt great joy and peace when they were with others who sought God, sought to learn. Thus friendships were born which brought them a sense of safety.

The angels knew why the inhabitants were attracted to those with goodness in their hearts, those who prayed and also wore the little crowns of pale thin silver. The angels knew that the inhabitants felt this way because there was no evil amongst that group. As their friendships blossomed, the inhabitants began to pray for their friends as well as their families. When they gathered together, they prayed together. They began to help one another pray and to hold on and trust in God when difficulties arose. They developed a strong hope that the bad times would eventually change and this kept them going. When the other inhabitants joined them in prayer, encouraged them, and inspired them to remain strong, they didn't become discouraged as quickly, and the void in their heart seemed to diminish a bit. Those who recognized this phenomena shared their experience with others. They were amazed to see that the void in their hearts, the sensation of coldness and emptiness, would disappear when they helped one another. This brought them joy. And soon they realized how precious their hope was. It was a sort of assurance that God would help them through all circumstances; it began to live deep within their heart and became very special to the inhabitants because it affected how they felt; it was the beginning of faith. Understanding the importance of hope was a miracle from God and as they acknowledged God's hand in this precious gift, they brought thanks to Him in prayer.

But of course, this too was a part of the great plan, the natural law of the universe, the physics of things, which God had created for the development of His children. Very soon, as the inhabitants began to realize the combined value of prayer, hope, and trust in God, they began to pray a new prayer. Their conversations reflected their desire to retain the brightness of hope in their hearts forever, for hope gave them patience and gave them peace. Their desire and their effort pleased God, and the harps of heaven played their beautiful songs, and the angels rejoiced once again. The heavens rang with joy, and in the palace, God smiled!

Keeping Hope Alive

Let me keep my hope alive, for it's always deep within;
and let not sadness hold me, though that's a battle hard to win.

Help me set my spiritual goals and follow fairly well
so, Lord, Your Golden Rule can stay in me to dwell.

Once Your Spirit fills me and my hope is always there,
I know I'll walk with You, my Lord, and be happy in Your care!

We are all from God yet different in our separate ways.
We search for love together, and should to one another say,

"I have needs and cares, but I know that you do too,
so let us try to understand and to one another always be true."

Let's try to help each other when we feel discouraged
and work hard when we're together to always be encouraged.

And even when we're downhearted, give each one a smile;
love one another to make life all worthwhile.

Let us keep our hope alive for that precious wonderful day
when Christ will come again for us; it might even be today!

****

As the inhabitants who were searching for fulfillment experienced
the blessing of warmth in their hearts from their prayers, hope, and

fellowship with God and one another, they began to understand so much more about God's love and make that understanding known through their conversations with Him. The angels cheered to see that many of the inhabitants of the cold, bleak planet finally felt the joy of this great achievement. As these inhabitants began to understand, they also began to teach others so they could share their joy and instill hope in other hearts as well. This was, after all, one of the parts which God wove into the natural law of the universe, the physics of things long, long ago to help those who would one day want to be helped. The angels sometimes wished that they could explain more; could hurry the slow and painful process of learning for the inhabitants of the cold, bleak planet below them. The angels could whisper the hints which God gave them permission to share, but the angels could not explain. They were sworn to secrecy; and they too were bound by the natural law of the universe, the physics of things, the free will which God wanted the inhabitants to use. Therefore, the inhabitants had to discover the answers on their own and make these choices on their own. Their hearts had to reach the point where they would desire the warmth of love, seek ways to obtain it, live in the hope of attaining it, and finally make a decision to be loyal to the goodness which could help them hold onto this wonderful quality. In time, many of the inhabitants of the cold, bleak planet beneath the warm, bright land of the angels did experience the warmth of prayer, the warmth of keeping their hope so strong that in times of distress, they could maintain their trust in their Heavenly Father. They learned that helping and teaching others allowed that warmth to grow and spread through their hearts and stay awhile. They understood that to help one another maintain hope was very important because of the outside forces of evil which tried to take hope away...thus it was easily lost.

Over time they began to trust one another with their concerns and ask one another to intercede for them in prayer. This was the beginning of truly loving one another and as they found the courage to reach out to one another by helping and teaching and sharing and trusting, they formed the wonderful bond called friendship. These precious friendships helped them and sustained them in times of trouble. But because the evil hated to see their progress, another lesson had to be learned. They were to learn that trust could be easily destroyed and when trust was destroyed, friendship could be destroyed as well. Then, without the prayers and encouragement of one another, they could lose their hope. Therefore evil tried to destroy all friendships.....for if evil could damage the inhabitants trust in one another, it could destroy the friendship. The inhabitants were to learn that trust was a precious commodity which needed to be carefully protected. Trust was something that evil would target and destroy whenever it could. Evil hated trust and thrived and grew on distrust. This was difficult to understand because evil hid within the inhabitants' own human nature where it could be awakened at anytime and work to break trust. In fact, evil fed on broken trust and the pain and fear and loss of hope this brought.

When this happened, disagreement and bitterness reigned and evil was satisfied because it had not only launched another attack, but succeeded as well. As evil wormed its way once again into the hearts of the inhabitants, it caused them to hurt one another by breaking the bond of trust and friendship with one another. Distrust and separation between the people grew. Then the cold and empty void grew in their hearts, first chilling, then destroying any warmth that tried to linger. Many fell away from prayer because they were angry. Many looked to return hurt to those who hurt them. Many suffered. For years, the inhabitants struggled in their loss until their hearts were cold once again and their state was one of unrest and unhappiness. They had no hope for a better life. But as they felt the discontent and lack of joy and began to wonder why this had invaded their hearts, they began to remember when they had been happy. They began to remember the warmth and the joy which love and hope had brought them. They spoke of how much they longed for the comfort that they once had. As they talked with one another, slowly they began to understand that what they once felt had come from the peace they had attained between one another and from the love this fostered and supported. They came to realize that love and trust had brought this peace and that it was very important to their well-being.

They began to understand how they had lost their peace and wondered if there was a way to get this back and then protect themselves from losing it again. Their hope began to resurface and this was good. The idea of protecting what was good in their lives was a new idea to the inhabitants, and the angels were glad that their whispers had worked. They were glad that the inhabitants had listened and remembered the days when joy had filled their hearts. The angels were glad that the inhabitants were thinking about how to regain what they had lost and how they could retain the warmth once they got it back again. The great and magnificent plan to help the inhabitants of the cold, bleak planet beneath the verdant land of the angels was still working, still making progress. The longing in the hearts of the inhabitants to go back to the times when they had been happy began to produce the desired effect. Of course, this was all a part of the incredible, all-encompassing plan which God had developed for His children, those whom He loved so much. God wanted them to desire to love. Then they would know how to gain what only pure love could provide.... for without love they could not become all that God wanted.

But the inhabitants first had to understand what the building blocks were to achieve pure love. Again the angels whispered into the ears of the inhabitants to help them remember and help them see that hope was the foundation for everything. Hope fostered trust, and trust fostered faith and faith fostered love, and love produced the giving heart. Love filled every void and could heal all things. Love could overcome evil and if the inhabitants would choose the building blocks of hope and trust.... and learn how to truly love, of their own free will......they would have all God wanted for them. For God would never **make** them love.....love was a choice. The inhabitants now knew what it was like to be without these gifts, and could make a comparison between having them and not having them and were now able to choose for themselves what they wanted. If they chose love, however, they would have to work to protect it and not allow evil to destroy it.

This was a part of learning the difference between good and evil. The angels knew that mankind's struggle between good and evil had been born when Adam and Eve, who were the first beings God created, disobeyed God and ate of the tree of the knowledge of good and evil. This caused a terrible battle for the heart and soul of mankind because the force of evil now had a right to work to gain the soul of all people. God had warned them not to eat of this tree, but they had been tempted, and they had succumbed. They had eaten of the tree, and thus they were destined to engage in this terrible struggle. God explained in the Holy Bible, in Genesis 3:4, how the evil entered a serpent and tempted man to eat of this tree by telling him, "For God doth know that in the day ye eat thereof, then your eyes shall be opened, and ye shall be as gods, knowing good and evil." Yet despite their disobedience and their destiny to learn of evil, their loving God provided a way by which all of mankind could overcome evil if they chose to do so. But the inhabitants didn't understand the full consequences of that disobedience yet. Only the angels did.

So now, in the midst of their learning process, the inhabitants began to converse with one another to see if they could find a solution to their concerns; a way to protect the gains they could make if they could indeed find a way to win back the trust and love they had so foolishly lost. Although finding ways to protect these gifts seemed almost impossible; they struggled for a long time to make it happen. Finally, they realized that they needed to ask God to help them. They asked, and God did help them and slowly they understood that God would not intervene unless the inhabitants asked Him to do so of their own free will. They had to make that decision themselves and then God could gladly step in. Because man had eaten of the tree of the knowledge of good and evil, they had to finish what had been started. Mankind had entered into a battle where two forces, one for good and one for evil, would try to win their hearts, their loyalties, for all eternity. The final choice had to be their own. The disobedience of man had given evil the right to work in the hearts of the people and Satan.... who was the father of all evil and who had once been an angel in heaven.... now worked to stop God's plan to save mankind. The goodness and righteousness of God, did not allow Him to forcefully take from Satan what Satan had won when man fell to the temptation Satan set before them by disobeying God. Mankind now had to gain full knowledge of both good and evil and then choose which he would follow.

Because of man's disobedience, God's righteousness required Him to give equal time and equal rights to Satan who wanted to place evil in the hearts of men. But God's plan of salvation would allow man to escape Satan and his evil ways and give them the opportunity to choose to live for all eternity with God after evil was bound forever. Mankind would have to learn about both good and evil and choose between them.....and while the way would be difficult, this too was a part of the great plan, the natural law of the universe, the physics of things, which God had created for the development of His children.

One day, one of the inhabitants began to recite a poem to a group of other inhabitants. She explained that she believed she had received an inspiration to write this poem and that it explained what they could do to protect trust. The inhabitants were very excited by this prospect and wanted to hear her poem. Hope was once again in their hearts. Before this inhabitant read her poem to them, she asked them to listen for one specific word in the poem and how this word seemed to provide the answer to what they needed to do. She told them how strongly she felt that this was a key to helping them in their quest. She explained that in her poem she had used the word **respect** and admitted that she had been surprised by her use of this word, not usually thinking about what an important word it was. Yet when she had reread the finished poem, she realized that respect was the key the inhabitants needed to protect trust and foster love.

The angels smiled, for God Himself had told them to whisper this word to her as she wrote her poem. She began to read her poem aloud to the other inhabitants, and as they listened to her poem, their hearts were moved by its content. They thought about her words and asked her to read the poem to them again and again. The more they contemplated her words, the clearer it became that if they employed this word in their lives, applying it as they interacted with one another, it would help them. Suddenly, they could see that respecting one another was one of the secrets to protecting trust. Hope grew stronger. God had answered their prayers. He had commissioned the angels to whisper this word into the heart of the inhabitant who wrote the poem. Her heart had been receptive to the whispers of the angels because she had prayed with a pure heart, asking God to help the inhabitants find their way back to Him. This was key, for the whispers would not have worked on an impure heart, one that was not ready to accept help. This was part of the plan, the natural law of the universe, the physics of things, which God placed into His wonderful creation, the plan which God gave to the inhabitants. And she read her poem to the people one more time.

<u>The Contemporary Woman</u>

The Contemporary Woman presents a capable facade,
and is what she presents, although there's more in that regard.

She is vulnerable and sensitive and unsure of her new role,
yet her courage to learn and grow makes her determined in her goal.

She offers her children understanding, her mate with pride and joy,
the business world with proficiency, but with life will not be coy.

She desires friendship with mankind, not born of dues or obligation,
rather one of equality and kindness, not as a result of subjugation.

She appreciates admiration for her intelligence, symmetry, and need,
But it's not nourishment to sustain her or on which her soul can feed.

As she plans her every action, she brings it first above,
praying to her Father that she does it all in love.

So she questions all she does and tries even harder to inspect
her log of daily accomplishments, because what she wants is . . .
your respect.

****

The inhabitants understood what the poem meant and were amazed! Treating one another with respect protected their relationships and thus their trust in one another. Trust and respect fostered love and helped them remain that way under all circumstances. God's plan was all encompassing; it was perfect. The plan kept the righteousness of God intact by not imposing His will upon the inhabitants. God could help, and His angels could help, but only if they were called to help by an inhabitant with a pure and seeking heart. The call for help was an exercise of the free will which mankind had been given. This free will also allowed the inhabitants to call upon evil if they chose this way for their lives. And they were to learn the many ways in which they did call upon evil. Their free will allowed them to choose between the two paths. As the inhabitants learned, they began to understand that treating one another with respect should be added to the growing list of lessons for them. Watching them work to incorporate this newfound wisdom into their lives made the angels rejoice. The prayers the angels heard were wonderful because now the inhabitants prayed in supplication, asking for help. They asked God to help them learn how to treat one another with respect and maintain peace and harmony between one another. They were also praying for protection so they could keep these gifts intact. God's heart was touched, and He was pleased to see His plan moving along with such perfection and such perfect timing.

Whenever the inhabitants chose good and sought to live their life according to God's righteous ways, the angels could see the crowns become wider with a much greater shine even though they were still of silver. The greater width of their crowns resulted from the inhabitants' decision to regain what God had given them and to learn how to protect themselves from losing those gifts again. The shine came because the inhabitants of the cold, bleak planet below the beautiful verdant land of the angels had finally realized that what God had given them was precious. And so a beautiful song erupted throughout the heavens because the inhabitants were making the godly choices. The poem which had inspired this new wisdom was recited often so even the little children could learn it and understand what it meant. Yet for the inhabitants, it seemed as if the learning process took a very long time. They wondered why it seemed to take forever to get it right, and sometimes they wondered if they ever would. But the angels knew. They understood that evil would not relinquish its hold on mankind easily, that evil was strong and could only be defeated by a stronger force than itself. The angels knew that the only force stronger than evil was love, and until love reached the right proportions within the hearts of the inhabitants, the trials and tribulations caused by evil would have to continue. They knew that the inhabitants had to keep their hope alive even when they were discouraged by the circumstances in their lives.

God wanted the inhabitants to know that He would rescue those who chose to follow Him from the evil and would do so in a timely fashion even though this was not according to men's time. To help the inhabitants understand this God explained in the Holy Bible, in 2 Peter 3:8, "But, beloved, be not ignorant of this one thing, that as one day is with the Lord as a thousand years, and a thousand years as one day." God explained this again in Psalm 90:4 when He said, "For a thousand years in thy sight are but as yesterday when it is past, and as a watch in the night." God went on to explain that the learning process took so long for the inhabitants because God wanted all men to be saved from the evil and wanted to give them the time they needed to understand. They needed to learn that though evil came with some rewards, in the long run, evil would bring them great harm. Men were slow to see this; and so God, with incredible patience and with immense love, waited and gave all men every opportunity.

In time, the inhabitants began to reap the benefits of what they had learned. Their hearts felt warm again. The emptiness they once felt in their hearts seemed gone. Their friendships blossomed, along with their renewed understanding; and they shared the harmony and peace which these lessons of prayer, of hope, of trust, and respect brought to them. And they were happy once again. But as their love began to blossom, evil was awakened; and when it saw that hope and love were developing in the hearts of the inhabitants, its anger was fierce. It determined to strike again and find a way to destroy the progress the inhabitants had made. Evil—which was the disease Satan had brought to their cold, bleak planet.....hated hope and trust, love and harmony—and moved again to annihilate everything that was good; to destroy love, to take hope from the heart of man. The evil could only thrive and multiply in hatred and jealousy, and in mistrust and dishonesty, so it slithered insidiously and with malevolent purpose, to invade the hearts of the inhabitants. The evil brought the inhabitants envy and competition which worked in their hearts to instill distrust and misinterpretation and thwarted the development of love by destroying hope and trust. Evil whispered of jealousy and lies; it placed doubt and worry, fear and anger into the minds of men, knowing that from the mind, evil could easily move, slippery, silently, slowly, yet inexorably, down into the heart. Once in the heart, the evil could begin to extinguish the warmth the inhabitants tried so valiantly to protect. The Holy Spirit which was sent to help protect God's work, could not live in a heart filled with evil, and as man gave in to evil, the perfect love and the warmth of the Holy Spirit had to leave the heart of man.

For the inhabitants, it was hard to understand why such simple acts of sin could cause this much upheaval. But the angels knew. They understood that the inhabitants had to experience evil to fully understand the value of goodness. The angels knew that it would be up to the inhabitants to choose between love and hate. Both the lesson and the decision were very important. From these experiences, the inhabitants could learn how to make the right choice on that day when they would be faced with the greatest decision of their life, when they would be incredibly tempted and misled by evil. It would be a decision which would determine their eternal life. God would equip them with the understanding; but ultimately, it would be their choice: good or evil, love or hate, trust or doubt, integrity or dishonor. They would be taught about these choices during their stay on the evil-filled planet below the angels. They would eventually have to make a choice and live by the rules of that choice. They would live for all eternity under the rule of either Satan or God. There were no other choices. There would be no fence-sitters in heaven either. In the end, the fence-sitters would belong to Satan because their names could never be written in the Lamb's book of life. This terrible day would come, and God wanted the inhabitants to be prepared, to be equipped to make the right choice. The inhabitants would either be a part of God's family, or called a lamb and have their name written in the Lamb's book of life and live with God, or..... they would be called a goat to be thrown into hell for all eternity to live with evil and to be evil. God had explained this to the inhabitants in the Holy Bible in Matthew 25:31-32: "When the Son of man shall come in his glory.....the holy angels with him.....shall he sit upon the throne of his glory. And .....he shall separate them one from another, as a shepherd divideth his sheep from the goats." God also explained in Revelation 20:15: "And whosoever was not found written in the book of life was cast into the lake of fire." The preparation for this day was a part of the plan God had created to help His children, a plan which had been lovingly incorporated into the natural law of the universe, the physics of things, to allow man to learn how to thwart evil. Someday, each inhabitant would be called on to make this choice between good and evil on their own. Sadly, when evil attacked again, many of the inhabitants fell prey to its deceit and its false claims. Chaos reigned, and trust was lost.

With the loss of trust, love and peace were also lost and so was the warmth in their hearts. It seemed as if the inhabitants simply could not hold onto what was good for them. This demonstrated the power of evil, for the inhabitants had not yet learned how to fight that power or how dangerous it was. The reason they fell backward again was because the power of evil was more than mankind could resist. The inhabitants had to fail until they learned how to fight. The angels knew that the beguiling nature of evil could blind the inhabitants and take from them their ability to see the truth but that while evil had won the battle, the inhabitants were learning and growing stronger and could still win the war! Through His words in the Holy Bible, God warned the inhabitants about Satan in his evil guises in Revelation 12:9, "Satan, who deceives the whole world"; and in Mark 4:15 explained that Satan can "take God's word from men's hearts". The angels knew that there was only one way for the inhabitants to become strong enough to resist the power of evil, and that God would teach them when the time was right, when they were ready to accept the lesson He prepared for them. The angels knew that the power of love was stronger than the power of evil.

Knowing this allowed the angels to have great hope for the inhabitants; they knew that at some point, things would change, and God's plan would move ahead. They knew that God's plan had everything in it to make sure that the inhabitants had the tools they needed to make a choice with their eyes open to what they were choosing and to maintain that choice. The magnificent plan created by the Father and the Son and the Holy Spirit would not fail. Those who would choose good would eventually learn. But it saddened the angels to see the misery in the hearts of these inhabitants because of their separation from God. It broke their hearts to see the inhabitants blinded by evil and unable to recognize what brought them their heartache over and over again. The inhabitants didn't yet know that a heart filled with evil always needed more evil to exist; it wanted to be fed; it wanted to grow and devour everything. It might start with something very small, but it always grew. But one day, a new prayer was heard. It was a prayer which sent a cry to God for help. One of the inhabitants had recognized how terribly empty they felt and how uncomfortable they were to live with evil. He also remembered how God had helped them in days past when they prayed with a sincere and repentant heart. He'd been able to retain enough hope to remember that God was always there and would help when called upon. And so he prayed the following prayer.

The Quest for Happiness

I long to find my happiness yet seem to always turn
to futile quests not ending the pain with which I burn.

I work and labor daily with turmoil in my soul,
knowing something's lacking in my life and in my goal.

I search for peace and harmony, looking for the way
to walk the path that satisfies, a way to live each day.

Yet nothing seems to work for me no matter how I try,
and my heart is close to breaking as I hear my anguished sigh.

I need to know what drives me, what I really seek,
and why I hope I'll find the way though life now seems so bleak.

I long to fill my emptiness, I long to feel fulfilled,
I long to have a peaceful heart so my restlessness is stilled.

Hear my plea, Oh Father, see the anguish in my heart,
send me what I'm lacking so from evil I can part.

****

The angels were so happy to hear this plea. They knew that this prayer went directly to the huge palace and that God's heart would be filled with joy. The angels knew that God suffered when those He loved so much suffered. The angels knew that God knew exactly how beguiling evil was, for His Son had been tempted by that same evil. In Matthew 4:3, God told the inhabitants: "Then was Jesus led up of the spirit into the wilderness to be tempted of the devil." In Matthew 4:10, God showed the inhabitants how Jesus responded to the temptation: "Then saith Jesus unto him, Get thee hence Satan: for it is written, thou shalt worship the Lord thy God, and him only shalt thou serve." Jesus had shown the inhabitants what to say when evil came, and He had shown them that they could resist. God knew the outcome of His loving plan and how these difficult times of learning would end for the inhabitants. God knew the joy which would come from choosing correctly on that great day when

His righteousness and mankind's free will would be tested. God had already created a special place for those who would be loyal to Him, would seek love and spurn evil. In fact God even gave each group a special name for the special place they would occupy in His kingdom.

Those who would remain stedfast and loyal would be called Bride, king, priest, lamb, sheep, overcomer, peculiar people, chosen, firstling, firstfruit, elect, and children of God and would live with Him for all eternity. Because of their repentant hearts, any sins these inhabitants had committed would be cleansed by the great sacrifice Christ had made for them. God also knew that others would choose evil, would not care about God's words or what He'd tried to teach them and that they would be called goats, and would live in the lake of fire with Satan for all eternity. As the learning process continued, through the plea for help which a seeking soul sent to the great palace, love and goodness slowly began to overtake the evil which for a short time had reigned. The prayers changed as the inhabitants gained back the ground they had lost. Hope and love formed again in their hearts as they strove to encourage one another to pray, to trust, to respect, and to help one another grow in these attributes. On the planet below the angels, with its evil still trying to corrupt everything which was good, the inhabitants continued the struggle to overcome. The inhabitants who'd found their way back to God worked hard to bring others back. They prayed day and night for one another. They asked God to draw every soul to them who also hungered so they could bring them testimony. God heard their prayers, and He answered.

Many flocked to these children of God who were succeeding in their battle against evil. Many hungered for their words of hope and a life of trust and goodness. Many learned and were brought into this precious fold where they too could have their names entered into the Lamb's book of life and where they too could have their thirst for God's words quenched through the Holy Bible. Many joined this group of "peculiar" people and it was a time of joy for this little group, a time when love flourished, and they sang praises in a new song which was cheerful and thankful and held the great promise of hope.

Love

Heartfelt joy! Such happiness! There's music in the air!
For when we're with our God of love, we forget our every care!

We walk on clouds, we smile a lot, we've energy to burn.
We see His loving nature, through His words for which we yearn

We recognize His care for us, so wonderful and sure,
a gift from Him so special, a love so very pure!

Care for it; it's precious! Let's protect it with our life!
Forgiving, loving, working at reducing any strife.

For love is an incredible blessing, a gift from God so true,
and every time we give it, it will give right back to you!

****

The angels sat back with a sigh of relief, realizing that another phase of God's plan had been completed. That not only had the inhabitants learned how to pray but they had also learned what it took to keep their hope alive and, through that hope, nurture the love in their hearts. The inhabitants were now ready to move on to the next phase of their development where they would learn how to deal with the times when evil would bring sadness into their lives. Evil wanted to destroy happiness and wanted sadness to dwell in the hearts of the inhabitants so they could not keep their hope alive and would not remember that they could trust God to help them. Evil was subtle, cunning, skillful, insidious, and patient. It whispered false promises, and it corrupted what was good. Evil loved to see sadness and depression in the hearts and minds of the inhabitants, for then it could conquer, then it could overpower hope. Then it could push from the heart all its warmth and any hope that God would or could help. The next lesson in God's magnificent plan was about to unfold.

Lord, lift up the light
of Thy countenance upon us.

Psalm 4:6

Chapter Three
The Temporary State of Sadness

The Poems of Chapter Three

But let all those rejoice who put their trust in You.
Let them ever shout for joy,
because You defend them;
Let those also who love
Your name be joyful in You.

—Psalm 5:11

Though the angels had rejoiced a short time earlier, they now had cause to worry. The inhabitants of the cold, bleak planet below had slowly been developing a sense of entitlement. The love they felt from their Heavenly Father felt so good that it prompted them to demand love from everyone around them. They didn't understand that God had gifted them with His love before they loved Him and that they were supposed to follow His example and give love to others before expecting anything back. In fact, the purest love was the love which could be given without the expectation of receiving anything in return at all. This was meant to be a great lesson to mankind, one which would help them develop pure love. It was a part of the natural law of the universe, the physics of things, the way God had engineered His great plan for the development of His peculiar people. The angels who lived in the beautiful verdant land high in the clouds above the bleak and dying planet understood this. They knew that the dynamics of love—how it grew, where it thrived, and what power it had—was of utmost importance to mankind as they waged their war with evil. Pure love was the only force which could defeat evil and give mankind the victory it needed over evil. But the inhabitants didn't have insight into the role they themselves would have to play to allow God's love to teach them how to love. They would have to learn to love others freely and not understanding this, they kicked and screamed and moaned about what they wanted and seldom looked at what they had. They felt deep sadness because they thought that they were being deprived of what they wanted. They behaved like children who were very spoiled by always getting their way. They allowed their discontent to move into depression which was a form of anger turned inward, anger which stole hope and reason from the heart.

It had been evil which had planted the idea that they deserved much more than they were getting from life and from those around them. Evil smiled as it did this, knowing that this would cause unrest between the inhabitants and make them became demanding; thinking that the world owed them adulation, and constant love and appreciation. They felt that God should do things differently; that God should make life easier; take away their troubles. They felt that God should cause those around them to recognize and acknowledge how special they were. Therefore, they complained. They became angry and withdrawn. They remained sad, and isolated themselves from one another, no longer sharing, no longer trusting. Confusion reigned in their hearts because of their depressed state of mind, taking away their ability to help themselves. Evil was pleased. It had done its work again knowing that even when Christ brought His teachings to the people, many did not understand the gift they had been given. They complained that they had trusted God to do things a certain way, their way...and He didn't.

At that time, many felt that if Christ was truly God's Son that He should have immediately conquered those who were against them. They murmured, angry that Christ hadn't done what they expected. Evil had blocked their minds and closed their understanding and made them discontent with God's actions. Evil blinded them to God's long-term goal which was to help the inhabitants find their way back to the forgiveness they needed when they disobeyed God. Even after Christ died on the cross to forgive their sins, many did not understand the sacrifice He had made for them and this caused Christ to ask how they could be sad after what He had done for them. The Holy Bible, in Luke 24:17 explains that before Christ rose to sit on His heavenly throne, He asked, *"What manner of communications are these that ye have one to another; as ye walk, and are sad?"* Christ was disappointed that those He had taught with such loving care had not developed to the point where they would trust God and accept that Christ's death was an incredible gift which would cover the sin of all mankind. They could only see the here and now and not the future. And this is just what evil wanted them to see.

But the angels knew that the inhabitants were children in the eyes of God and hadn't yet learned what they were supposed to learn. They didn't understand the mistake they had made when they allowed their minds to believe that God had let them down. They didn't yet realize that their judgment of the circumstances and the sadness this brought them had come from the doubts and uncertainties which evil had suggested to them. They could not yet defeat evil because they did not have enough trust to foster the faith needed to conquer evil. They were still takers, not givers. The angels cried this day for they understood the danger to the inhabitants when they did not trust God nor understand what He had given them in the incredible sacrifice of Christ, God's precious Son. To the angels, trusting seemed so simple....all the inhabitants had needed to do was to believe what God taught them. They had to decide whether they would trust God or not.....this was a part of what they needed to learn, a part of the decision they would have to make. It was the natural law of the universe, the physics of things, the plan to eventually save them from evil. Knowing the great sacrifice which God and Christ had made for the inhabitants, the angels were also aware of the love and patience which emanated from the beautiful palace. They knew that everyone in the heavens above were wishing that every inhabitant could recognize this precious gift. However, there were a few inhabitants who, when besieged by the doubt of those around them, didn't blame God for not doing what they wanted. They didn't give up and they trusted that Christ would return to fulfill His promise to them. These were the "peculiar" people who kept their faith, maintained their hope, and kept their minds from giving in to doubt. They seemed to understand that evil wanted depression to take away their hope and leave a debilitating sadness in its place. They somehow sensed that evil sends sadness; brings a loss of hope, a loss of trust, a desire to destroy all things good. Evil wanted them to trust in non-believers rather than in God and other believers.

But there were some who decided to trust God. They believed that God would do exactly what was right for them. Because they tried to do these things, they also prayed with a light heart which described how they trusted that their troubles would be resolved because God would help them. They did not pray in repetition, but they conversed with God in their prayers. They asked Him to keep them close and not let them slip into the doubt which evil wanted to instill in their hearts.

Troubles

When you're very deeply troubled, find a wood.

Take a walk and think things through the way you should.
Talk with God and try to open up your soul.
Let Him tell you what to do to reach your goal.

Learn control of every anger, don't give in.
Pray instead for those who harm and act in sin.
If we're patient and we keep our love alive,
God will bless us in the end if we but strive.

Thus we pray to build our trust and make us strong,
and we help each other when finding we've been wrong.
And we stay with God and love with all our heart.
Wait in patience, trust, and love and do our part.

Remembering time will heal our wounds, we count on this.
After the clouds, we're sure, our heart the sun will kiss.

****

Eventually, however, because sadness and depression spread so easily; even the inhabitants who held onto their hope, finally gave in to what evil sent them. For a time, it seemed as if evil had won. But God would not let them go; He knew that the goodness in these precious few lay dormant and would rise again, and the inhabitants would want to fight the evil, fight the terrible force which wanted to destroy them. So God allowed them to slip for only a little while so they could renew their desire for, and appreciation of, goodness. God knew that the inhabitants would want to satisfy their hunger for the warmth which hope and trust could bring them. This was the plan, and Heaven would wait while the angels whispered encouragement. However, the tide would turn only if the inhabitants chose to protect the seed of hope which lay quiet, hidden, in the recesses of their hearts.

God had planted that seed by loving them and giving them what they needed to develop. But for now with the seed dormant in the hearts of these inhabitants and in danger of being lost, the angels had to watch the sad fall of the inhabitants and could only pray for them and whisper of God's love to them. The angels wanted the inhabitants of the cold, bleak planet beneath them to recognize what was happening to them and turn their hearts of their own free will. The angels wanted the inhabitants to fight the evil so they could retain the seed of hope in their hearts, fight for love to grow despite the onslaught of evil. The angels could only hope that the inhabitants would learn quickly so they would not suffer for too long. But the sadness remained, and the depression clung; and the evil of that cold, bleak world, seemed to have finally found a way to keep the inhabitants from progressing. For a while, the prayers of the inhabitants stopped. It appeared that Satan had succeeded in keeping the inhabitants from reaching the goal which God had set for His children. The angels could do nothing. They had to keep the secret. They could only hope that the inhabitants would come to their senses and remember what it was like when love, trust and hope filled their hearts. The angels could only whisper to the inhabitants of God's love for them in the hope that this would encourage them to resume the fight against the evil which had trapped them.

When Satan was thrown out of heaven for his jealousy of mankind and he came to earth to bring harm to man, he brought with him other angels who had decided to join forces with evil and who were therefore also banned from Heaven. Each of these fallen angels specialized in the many different aspects of evil; some in lies, some in hatred, some in distrust, some in dishonesty and many others in all the things which displeased God. As the sadness and the depression grew, it attracted these many parts of evil which brought them all to the hearts and minds of the inhabitants. The birth of fear, also from a fallen angel had come to the inhabitants, and they knew great panic in their hearts. They could no longer find the warmth they hungered for. They suffered. They became slaves to the fear and anxiety in their minds and hearts which evil had planted.

In the Holy Bible, God had warned the inhabitants of the possibility of what was now occurring in their lives; for in Matthew 12:44-45, God explained what the evil angels of their world said: "Then he saith, I will return into my house from whence I came out.......findeth it empty....... Then goeth he, and taketh with him seven other spirits more wicked than himself, and they enter in and dwell there: and the last state of that man is worse than the first......." As evil entered man and multiplied, the inhabitants suffered even more with fear and depression until it had risen to the level of panic. The concerns in their mind debilitated them and kept them enslaved. The minds of the inhabitants conjured up terrible fears of the future and their suffering became unbearable. They gnashed their teeth and screamed from the agony of their worries and the thoughts which brought these fears. Finally when they could bear no more, some of the inhabitants cried out to God for help. They cried out in repentance for allowing themselves to be tempted, for listening to what evil offered, for not recognizing the value of God's protection and not recognizing the value of those who prayed for them, those God had so lovingly placed into their lives. Once again, they asked God for help, this time pleading with God in a way they never had before.

As these prayers for help rose to the heavens, and were moved by the natural laws of the universe, the angels could hear the prayers which traveled to the magnificent palace. The angels asked God if they could whisper into the ears of the inhabitants once again. They wanted to remind them that in the days when they prayed, hope and trust lived in their hearts and with these, lived love..... and love always cast out fear. As the angels whispered, they reminded the inhabitants that in 1 John 4:18, God had comforted them with the words: "There is no fear in love: but perfect love casteth out fear; because fear hath torment. He that feareth is not made perfect in love."

The inhabitants realized when they read these words that they had indeed been tormented by their fears. They also realized that when their love grew from their hope and trust, it didn't contain fear. As God saw that the inhabitants had developed a new understanding of the power of love and that their pleas for help were so sincere, God answered their prayers. He also told the angels to go to work and bring good thoughts and reminders to the inhabitants about the days when the inhabitants found peace through prayer. Eventually, these good thoughts fought their way through the evil, through the doubt and the fearful imaginings. As the inhabitants remembered what love felt like and remembered how gently God had cared for them, hope blossomed again, giving them the power to fight the hold which evil had on them. As the angels' whispers of God's love took hold and the inhabitants recalled the benefits of prayer, they began to hope that all they suffered would not be in vain, and they prayed a prayer filled with a greater understanding of the value of God's love. They rose from their fear, and prayed. They trusted God. And because of this trust, the angels whispered to remind them of God's warning from the Holy Bible about what evil had done: "......with lies ye have made the heart of the righteous sad: and strengthened the hands of the wicked." (Ezekiel 13:22). As the inhabitants pondered these truths and tried to make sense of their suffering, they began to understand more about the power of sadness and that its power came from evil—came because they had not trusted God with their circumstances and had not appreciated those who prayed for them and loved them always. Because they had learned a little more, they now prayed a new prayer which reflected their new understanding.

Sadness

Are we blue and downcast, discouraged and upset?
Do we wonder why our Heavenly Father let
these very difficult circumstances fill our life with pain?
Do we wish to understand so nothing's been in vain?

Yet has the spirit of unhappiness entered to prevail?
Even though we know that these thoughts lead us to fail?
And even though we do believe all passes by God's throne
that He allows these moments even if we groan?

God wants for us great wisdom and a trust in Him so strong
that though the days of sadness seem very, very long,
we'll learn beyond a single doubt that God has a perfect way
to teach us to be patient; pray, and wait for a sunny day.

But we must work and labor, must do our part to thrive
by protecting the love God gave us, and by keeping it alive.

****

Thus the natural law of the universe, the physics of things, began to work their miracle. Trust in God came back into the hearts of the inhabitants and helped them push the fear aside. The angels reminded them what had worked for them in the past, how powerful their prayers were, and how good hope and love felt in their hearts. Therefore, as the inhabitants prayed, they meant what they said, and began to fight the evil. They cherished God's love and cherished other children of God who they now loved as they did their own family. They remembered that when they came together in prayer, they felt less fear; and as they shared their concerns, they began to trust one another again. They listened to the burdens each carried, and they prayed for one another, not just themselves. They remembered God's words in Roman's 12:9,10: "Let love be without dissimulation. Abhor that which is evil; cleave to that which is good. Be kindly affectioned one to another with brotherly love; in honour preferring one another."

As these words warmed their hearts and they regained what they had lost, they saw that they learned a valuable lesson from their terrible bout with sadness. And because they had learned this lesson well, they were thankful for what had happened in their lives even though it had been so difficult because it meant that they had made it through a very important lesson. This became a time when there was rejoicing in the beautiful verdant land where the angels lived and where

God's palace glowed like a beacon, where the light was extraordinary and the colors vibrant and love and joy overflowed every heart. As the inhabitants prayed and asked God for help, they grew stronger and wiser; they appreciated what God did for them and helped one another. The evil angels had to flee from the inhabitants because the inhabitants now understood that when there was love in their hearts— real, unselfish, fearless love—they had the power to throw off evil's cruel yoke. This too was a part of the great engineering feat, the plan, the natural law of the universe, the physics of things which God put into place for the inhabitants. The inhabitants had even begun to understand that they would hinder the spirits which sought to discourage them if they heeded the words from 2 Corinthians 6:14-18 where God said, "Do not be unequally yoked together with unbelievers. For what fellowship has righteousness with lawlessness? ....Or what part has a believer with an unbeliever?......For you are the temple of the living God.......'I will dwell in them and walk among them. I will be their God, and they shall be my people.' Therefore 'Come out from among them and be separate......Do not touch what is unclean, and I will receive you. I will be a Father to you, and you shall be my sons and daughters......'"

These words helped the inhabitants understand that they could overcome evil if they ran from it when it first appeared. It seemed that if they could do this, they would not have to work so hard to fight it later on. They saw that there was extraordinary power in being with other believers, others who also protected their trust in God and His love for them. They learned to nurture those relationships where God was first and foremost in those lives, and where they would pray for one another. The angels recognized that the people were reinforcing what they'd learned. They renewed their hope, and now miracle of miracles, they finally recovered from the sadness and loss of hope and regained their precious joy and renewed goal to love. They realized that God had used the evil of the world to bring them these losses so the lesson would stay with them and they would want to fight against evil when it came to claim them once again. "After all," the angels asked, "didn't the inhabitants realize that this is part of the natural law of the universe, the physics of things which God arranged for them because He loves them? Don't they know that love will help them? Don't they realize that God will always be there for them and give them those believers who will also help them? Don't they realize that goodness brings joy?" The angels helped by whispering of love and assuring them they were not alone, that God was with them.

There came a flicker of hope in the hearts of the inhabitants that maybe this time they could retain what they had learned and put it into practice. They began to realize that even when they had given in to the evil, God was there, ready to help them out of it when they repented of it. They realized that they were responsible for bringing so much suffering on themselves and sent another perfect prayer to heaven. They wanted to let God know that they trusted Him and still longed for His love and guidance, His words and His ways, despite their many failures. They were beginning to recognize that bad times would come as evil tried to reclaim them but that God cared for them and would see them through. They were trying to keep in their hearts the fact that they could always trust God. And so they prayed.

Someone Cares

If a time has come when inside we feel there's none to really care

and in our heart an ache has grown and we think our future's bare.
When the hurt we feel and the tears we shed, it seems we do alone,
and it seems that not an ear can hear the agony of our moan.

But be assured there's Someone there, there's Someone by our side
whose heart just breaks with ours, for one day we'll be His bride.
He deeply cares about our life and feels our inner pain;
He wants us to know He's with us and that our life is not in vain.

Christ loves us very much indeed and awaits God's sickle thrust
that will harvest to the Heavens the ones who've shown their trust.
Let's lift our hearts and be assured that Someone really cares
and have the faith to tough it out, for Someone fully shares

the trials and tribulations that we carry through this day,
which help us learn and grow in trust 'til Heaven comes our way.

****

These prayers demonstrated that the people now seemed to understand that God cared deeply for them and about what happened to them. Knowing that the inhabitants had recognized this and understood His love for them made the angels happy. The heavens were filled with their joyous song, the melodious sound of harps, and the happy words the angels spoke to one another. The people were happy too and tried to follow those things which they had learned. They did not want to give in ever again to the fear and the terrible sense of panic they experienced when evil had overcome them. Nor did they want to experience another separation from love. They were tired of constantly slipping back. They had suffered so much under the mind control which evil was able to exert over them. They didn't want to go through that pain again. They wanted to remember that they could trust God, but also that they needed to pray and learn and practice His words to stay close to Him. They wanted to remember that sadness did not come from love......it came from evil, and evil came when they didn't pray, when they didn't ask for God's protection and when they sinned. They wanted to remember that when they didn't have hope and trust and when they didn't love one another, they lost the warmth they so desired.

The inhabitants had also learned that when they did not study God's words, they would not know how to protect themselves from the evil which stalked them. Sadness had come because they had opened the door of their hearts to evil. They had sinned and given in to something other than loving and trusting God with all things. When the evil came, they hadn't fled from it, they hadn't fled from the ungodly, they hadn't heeded the words God told them in the Holy Bible. They had given in to the fear because they had lost their connection to God, sinned and thus lost their trust in Him. They themselves had allowed the evil to enter their minds and then their hearts, and finally their actions. They realized that they needed to learn how to recognize evil when it came again in the future so they would not be enticed by it. But to do this they had to be watchful and know how to escape from the evil when it came. They could only do this if they knew God's words, if they studied what God taught them and did what He asked. When they studied the Holy Bible, they found scripture which helped them learn what they should do when evil knocked on their heart's door. They read where God said, "But thou,

O man of God, flee these things; and follow after righteousness, godliness, faith, love, patience, meekness" (1 Timothy 6:11). They realized that they hadn't been diligent in avoiding the traps which evil laid for them. They had been curious, and what evil asked of them seemed so inconsequential. They had looked at evil, and it had enslaved them. They had been lazy and hadn't kept God first in their lives. They asked themselves if they had forgotten to be thankful. They remembered that God always blessed a heart which was filled with thankfulness for what He had done for them. In Psalm 30:4 in the Holy Bible, the inhabitants read, *"Sing unto the Lord, O ye saints of His, and give thanks......For His anger endureth but a moment; in His favor is life; weeping may endure for a night, but joy cometh in the morning."* When they read these words, the inhabitants wondered if they prayed correctly. They asked themselves if their prayers were complaints and selfish pleas for help, for now they saw that this type of prayer was lacking in love and appreciation. They saw that they were selfish and this made them accept the temptations which evil placed before them.

They also realized that they enjoyed being told that someone loved them and that perhaps they should tell God how much they loved Him. They had not told their Heavenly Father how much they loved Him and also hadn't thanked him in appreciation for His care and protection and for all He did for them. They had not thanked Him for how patient He was with them as they continued to make mistakes. They hadn't told Him how much they valued the forgiveness of their sins and the sacrifice which went into providing this great gift for them. They hadn't thanked him for the people in their lives who supported their faith. As they pondered these faults and failings, they realized that they could never be too thankful, that every prayer should thank God for His incredible love and the future He prepared for them. They realized that God did not need them but that they needed God and needed to understand the good that God had in mind for them. And, miracle of miracles, they finally realized that they needed to let God know that they were sorry for the mistakes they made and would try to do better in the future. They knew too that they had to be sincere in these desires, or God would never hear these prayers. So they prayed.

Say Thanks

We so often let the bad things override all that's good and true
and worry and feel hopeless and thus become so blue.
But it's at this time our efforts should turn to thankfulness,
and on our knees to God we should, confess our selfishness.

For even in a time of loss or pain or even fear,
we've much to thank our God for, things we hold most dear.
So thank you, Lord, for all Your love and the fact that You still
provide for all our future care if we accept Your perfect will.

Please forgive us in our sins and help us overcome
so we can finally show our love, be worthy when the days are done.
Please accept our gratitude and know we love you too
and long to be more like You in everything we do.

****

This prayer pleased God. His heart was touched. Evil had been given time to prosper because man had come under the control of evil in the Garden of Eden. But God used these times when evil reigned in the hearts of man to help the inhabitants learn how to make the choice between good and evil. This was the natural law of the universe, the physics of things, the plan which God had engineered to help the inhabitants break the claim which evil had on them through inherited sin. The plan was to help the inhabitants not only learn the difference between good and evil but how to protect themselves from evil by having the proper tools to use if they chose to follow good. Evil had already staked its claim on the inhabitants when mankind ate of the tree of the knowledge of good and evil. This act of disobedience had introduced inherited sin into the lives of men and gave evil its legitimate right to fight for their souls.

However, God had prepared a way to free men from the tentacles which evil used to imprison their hearts. This had been accomplished through the sacrifice of Christ as He died, perfect... and unblemished by sin..... for each of us who are imperfect. Christ died in full atonement for our sins...for us. Only with such forgiveness could the inhabitants hope to spend eternity with God. Only with the proper preparation of their soul could they hope to make the right choice; one which would remain with them for all eternity. They would someday have to choose between good and evil. If they claimed to love and choose God, the inhabitants would have to be tested in their love, tried like gold is tried in the fire. Only pure love could conquer evil. Only love and repentance through Christ's sacrifice on the cross could pay the debt of the inherited sinful nature man had and break the claim Satan had on them. This was a mystery which God would unfold for the inhabitants over time. The key for success was in learning God's words through scripture, trusting them and following them. The angels wished that they could explain all these mysteries to the inhabitants. but they could not. In God's righteousness, evil would hold God accountable if He interfered with man's ability to make his own choice and use his free will. Man had brought this upon himself when he gave in to evil and the first man disobeyed God and brought sin to all men who followed. Mankind added to evil's claim on their souls by every sin they committed thereafter which had not been forgiven. Sins which were not forgiven could impact even future generations.

Evil wanted the inhabitants to believe that certain behaviors didn't even matter to God and also that other behaviors were simply a disease and not see these as the sin they needed to address. In Numbers 14:18, God told them, "The Lord is longsuffering, and of great mercy, forgiving iniquity and transgression, and by no means clearing the guilty, visiting the iniquity of the fathers upon the children unto the third and fourth generation." To protect themselves but also to protect their children, the inhabitants needed to repent their sin...every sin.... and ask for forgiveness. God's great plan of salvation—the one he'd laid into the foundation of the earth as the natural law of the universe, the physics of things—would help mankind. God had given His promise to send one who would crush evil's head. In fact, right in the beginning, in Genesis 3:14-15, God spoke to Satan when he appeared in the Garden of Eden as a serpent to cause mankind to sin and disobey God. God said, "Because thou hast done this thou art cursed . . . and I will put enmity between . . . thy seed and her seed, it shall bruise thy head." With these words God described Satan's future and the birth of Christ and His work of redemption. The seed of mankind would eventually bring the miracle of Christ's birth to the world, and Christ would bruise the serpent's head by breaking the bond of sin which allowed Satan to own the souls of men. Through the sacrifice of Christ, which paid the debt of sin, men could now choose to be free of Satan if they repented and followed Christ's teachings. Now man would at least have a choice. Out of love and compassion, God had provided everything man needed to find his way back to God and live with Him for all eternity. Each one would make his own choice, and if he chose God, he would have to follow God's statutes.

In James 2:14 God warned, "What doth it profit, my brethren, though a man say he hath faith, and have not works? Can faith save him?" God's incredible plan—the natural law of the universe, the physics of things, the magnificent and all encompassing plan God created to help man—could help men do the works which God asked of them. But even given all the opportunities God provided, mankind would still have to make the choice between good and evil themselves; and God, in His righteousness, could not allow into heaven those who carried the evil of sin, **any sin**, or a complacent heart. Just as one needed a passport to enter another country, men needed their names written in the Lamb's book of life to enter heaven. There were strict rules governing whose name could be written in this wondrous book. To continue on this path of learning the difference between good and evil, the inhabitants would have to enter the next phase of this incredible plan.

The inhabitants needed to embark on yet another lesson meant to prepare them for the day when their choices in life would determine whether they would become goats or sheep or the Bride of Christ in eternity. As part of His plan, God would inspire role models who would grow in faith and who would retain their faith and obedience to God in the face of evil. Thus, they could teach and encourage others. But the inhabitants would have to learn how precious these role models were, to them and to God, and learn how important it was for them to nurture and protect those relationships. The inhabitants were to learn that being a role model for God touched God's heart and brought a blessing to the household of the role models who would become the catalysts to help many make that great and important choice to prepare themselves for the First Resurrection. If they did not.....they would be left behind on that great day. Before they could begin this new lesson, the inhabitants needed to remember the lessons they recently learned of respect, of love, of trust, of hope, of obedience, and of remaining constant in prayer. When God saw that they honestly tried to keep these alive in their hearts and supported this effort with their good works, the new phase of God's magnificent plan began.

O Lord our Lord,
How excellent is thy name in all the earth!
Who hast set thy glory above the heavens.

—Psalm 8:1

Chapter Four

The Gift of a Role Model

The Poems of Chapter Four

And you shall teach them the statutes
and the laws, and show them the way
in which they must walk
and the work they must do.

—Exodus 18:20

The angels who lived in the heavens high above the cold, bleak planet of the inhabitants burst forth with joy as the great plan—so masterfully engineered by their Heavenly Father and His Son, the Lord Jesus, and the gently guiding Holy Spirit—was working, and was right on schedule. Of course that schedule was not by the time frame of the inhabitants, but was according to God's masterful timing. The inhabitants—though they didn't understand time as God had fashioned it, nor understand the natural law of the universe, the physics of things as yet, nor know about the plan God had instituted for them—were indeed beginning to learn. This was a joy to those in the heavens above them. As evil continued to work and was the source of all discontent, the inhabitants grumbled about how it seemed to take forever to resolve the problems they faced and to fill the void in their heart that so often dominated their life. They didn't want to do the work to fight the constant and unbidden anxiety they felt when they hungered for something more and felt driven to keep searching for ways to fix their problems quickly. They felt that time was an enemy, moving too fast when they felt good and too slowly when they were upset. But in reality, time was moving at a perfect speed. In fact perfect timing for the learning process was a part of God's plan.

Scripture explained that one thousand years for the inhabitants of the cold, bleak planet was like one day for the angels who looked at time through the eyes of eternal life. This phenomena was similar to reading a book in only a few hours even though the book described the lives of the characters over a period of many years, sometimes many generations. The inhabitants didn't understand this, but it was, again, just the natural law of the universe, the physics of things, and part of God' great plan. It was just the way things were, the way God wanted them to be.

The inhabitants entered a period of time where they trusted God, prayed, and recognized that sadness came from a loss of hope, trust, and love and had learned that the evil spirits of the world continually sought to harm them and destroy their relationship with God. They realized how good they felt when they were with others who also prayed and trusted, those who worked to avoid evil. They had discovered that they had much to share with other believers, other seekers of the warmth. This, the angels knew, was a good thing. It was progress. But still...to the inhabitants time moved slowly....it was time consuming to read the instructions which God gave them through scripture. They understood that written into their magnificent book, the Holy Bible, were the words of God which said, "Therefore be imitators of God as dear children . . . and have no fellowship with the unfruitful works of darkness, but rather expose them" (Ephesians 5:1,11). But the inhabitants had yet to learn that they had a responsibility to pray and trust God, and also had to take responsibility for maintaining their spiritual life. This hadn't occurred to them and sometimes evil whispered to them about how long these lessons seemed to last. Evil caught them unawares, making them sad or angry, making them react rather than act, making them think that their sins were of little consequence. Nevertheless those sins could affect their attitudes and their mood. The inhabitants allowed their moods to cause a reaction which damaged the work of the Holy Spirit within them. The angels saw this and recognized that here was yet another lesson which the inhabitants would have to learn. After all, the inhabitants were still children in the eyes of those who lived in the beautiful land above the cold, bleak planet and needed to be nurtured into adulthood so they would be ready when the God's plan was complete. They would not be allowed to join Christ for all eternity, to be forever with God and the angels, without exercising personal responsibility over their spiritual lives. This meant that they themselves had to watch for the whispers of evil and stop them before they could bring them into harm's way and would have to take the time to study God's words and self-control to be obedient.

Impatience can be a danger and open the door to evil. The inhabitants had to learn that their emotions and their reactions to those emotions and their impatience caused them to hurt one another. Sometimes these reactions came from their personal heartache, but nevertheless when they reacted from impatience, they lost something important. They lost control, and then they lost the ability to pray as they wanted to, and they lost the friendship of those they had hurt through their inconsiderate behavior. They were no longer role models to one another. They no longer cherished their relationships with other children of God. Thankfully, there were some who seemed to understand the lessons of the past and hold onto them. God was pleased with them and made them the teachers. In Ephesians 4:11-13 in the Holy Bible, God explained that He would provide these special teachers to the inhabitants saying: "And he gave some apostles; and some prophets; and some evangelists; and some pastors and teachers; for the perfecting of the saints, for the work of the ministry......" In Ephesians 4:14-15, God went on to explain that with this perfection, mankind would no longer be children who could be fooled by deception, saying, "That we henceforth be no more children, tossed to and fro, and carried about with every wind of doctrine......" As the inhabitants saw the staunch faith of those whom God had chosen to teach them, they flocked to these people and listened to them and were inspired to make changes in their lives and hold on to what they had learned. When they did this, they began to feel the warmth wash over their hearts again. Through the teachers and role models whose hearts seemed so joyful, the inhabitants began to feel a new harmony in their lives because they were learning more about the word of God and what He asked of them.

The inhabitants found that they could trust what they were being taught. As this trust grew, they began to share their burdens and their troubles and when they did, they would pray together to ask for God's help. They learned that when they did this, their prayers were answered sooner and more abundantly. They felt the comforting presence of God in their heart and it stayed with them for longer periods of time. This meant that they were in fellowship with one another; that they were with like-minded people who were trustworthy and who worked together toward the same goal. Not everyone had learned this, but those who did talked together and decided that this was so important that they needed to share this newfound knowledge with others. This way, everyone could avail themselves of the benefits of learning, of praying together, of sharing one another's burdens, of asking for God's help. They noticed that as they shared their wisdom, again the warmth they longed for came into their hearts with an even stronger force. As others saw this happen, they too wanted what the wise had gained, what those who had become their role models and teachers offered them. Many inhabitants sat at the feet of their role models to hear of experiences of faith and how those in scripture learned to conquer evil and find such joy. These teachers became a great gift to the inhabitants; and as they flocked to listen to them, to learn and to gain strength in fighting evil, they grouped together into little congregations of learning. They learned and better understood God's words and referred to the scripture which supported their teaching. They were learning to do good, to be role models themselves, to share this gospel with others, and draw to themselves the incredible benefit of love and fellowship with other believers. God's plan was working; and the angels marveled at how God's engineering, His great plan, had made this a part of the natural law of the universe, the physics of things. The inhabitants still had much work to do to move from being the children of God to becoming the Bride of Christ, but now they understood the godly responsibilities of being a trusted friend and thus a role model themselves. This newfound understanding became evident in their prayers.

A True Friend

Dearest Heavenly Father, thank you!
You have sent me such a special friend.

One who is always available to me
and has a wonderful memory for what I like,

yet has a terrible memory for what I said about
someone who angered me.

My friend is easy going about sharing
those things I enjoy doing,
and is adamant about my not doing
something that would bring harm to me or to others.

My friend loves me and understands me;
sympathizes with me and guides me,
doesn't hold a grudge against me
when I've had a bad day, and not been kind.

My friend delights in my accomplishments,
and isn't jealous of me,
loves my children, and respects my spouse.
My friend stays close in times of pain and sadness.

Thank you Father, for bringing this friend
into my life to keep me
from loneliness and to be my role model.
Because of the gift of friendship that you have given me,

I realize that I must ask myself,
"Am I these things to my friend?"
I resolve now Father to be a better friend to others.
Help me to do so.
****

When the angels heard this prayer, their hearts sang with joy to witness the relationships which developed between some of the inhabitants and their recognition of how precious these relationships were. This would enable them to grow into role models who could always be trusted and who would help one another in times of need. These inhabitants asked themselves, "Is this how Jesus would have acted in this same circumstance?" As trust grew between friends and they appreciated one another's attributes and deemed their relationship worth protecting, they could teach one another without hurting one another and even point out their errors. The angels knew that this was a great breakthrough, for it opened the way to show one another their faults and failings as well as their good qualities. Once the inhabitants were made aware of what they still needed to do, they could choose of their own free will whether or not they wanted to overcome that which was wrong in God's eyes.

Sometimes it hurt to learn, it always hurt to be told about the mistakes that one makes, but accepting admonition demonstrated that they were humble and wanted to be more pleasing to God. God understood this and had given His role models a gentle heart and the ability to forgive so they would not sit in judgment of the mistakes they saw in the inhabitants they wanted to help. The role models had decided to do their best to obey God rather than men and used prayer to help them teach. From Acts 6:4, they learned that the apostles said, "But we will give ourselves continually to prayer, and to the ministry of the word." They also wanted to continue stedfast in the apostle's doctrine and fellowship and in breaking of bread because they read in Acts 2:42 that this was what the apostles did: "And they continued stedfastly in the apostle's doctrine and fellowship, and in the breaking of bread, and in prayers." They wanted to help those they could. They were determined to help because they understood that the sacrifice Christ made on the cross provided the only way to the forgiveness of man's sin.

The teachers also realized that others watched how they conducted their own lives and how they handled the adversities they faced and, through this, would learn how to handle similar circumstances and become role models themselves. True role models didn't just talk about God; they walked in God's instruction so they could set the right example. God especially blessed those who stood shoulder to shoulder with the inhabitants who were trying to find the right path as they struggled with an attack from the evil one. This made a lifetime impression on those inhabitants who had found a true friend in need. So once again, a special prayer about the friendships which existed between those who were called teachers and role models and those who were seeking God was sent to the great palace high on the mountain. And heaven sang!

A Friend in Need

Dear Heavenly Father, I have a friend I love so much,
for her soul is a noble one.
She stands so firm and weathers Satan's
thrusts until he's finally done.

I've watched her as she's dealt with life,
with joy and sadness too.
I've seen she never loses faith
in what You will finally do.

That's not to say it's been easy,
in fact it's hurt so much,
yet from her pain she reaches out
the heart of Christ to touch.

She's a wife, a mom, and a grandma
with plenty of love to spare.
She's a friend, a neighbor, a counselor,
who teaches us how to care.

Yes, she may cry, and feel the pain
of worry and concern,
but soon she's up and fighting again,
for the devil she can discern.

She knows he wants to draw her from
her faith and prayers and love,
but she also knows she'll find her help
in You, Father up above.

I'm blessed in having met her,
I love her and her beautiful soul
and cherish her as a special gift,
this friend with a Godly goal.

She's an example to all who know her,
especially to You and me.
When she's holding the hand of others,

Your kingdom they easily see.

One of the reasons I love her
is the way in which her spirit grows;
forgiving those who hurt her,
another precious gift she sows.

So I long to see the hard times
change for those that bring a smile
and watch this lovely person
thrive from having walked her mile.

I want her to reap Your Blessings
for all the wonderful things she's done.
This special friend who's loved,
whose noble heart is loyal and fun.

Please bless and keep her always,
Please, Father, cover her with love.
Protect her lovely family
and bless her from above.

****

In this prayer the angels saw love; unselfish love and appreciation. The inhabitants could now care deeply for others and ask God to help someone other than themselves. They could now recognize the value of their friendships and recognize a true role model in their friend. The angels knew that those in the beautiful palace would rejoice too, would be so happy for the progress of the inhabitants and the further development of love. For only pure love could defeat evil when evil raised its ugly head and came to devour the love which had begun to blossom in the hearts of these inhabitants. The angels knew that when evil entered the serpent to cause man to sin in the Garden of Eden, sin passed to all other men. But, by His sacrifice on the cross, Christ made possible the forgiveness not only of that sin but also of all men's personal sins if they were remorseful. The angels knew that God had explained this to the inhabitants in the Holy Bible in Romans 5:18-19 when He said, "Therefore as by the offense of one judgment came upon all men to condemnation; even so by the righteousness of one the free gift came upon all men unto justification of life. For as by one man's disobedience many were made sinners, so by the obedience of one shall many be made righteous." This was the first lesson of a continuing blessing. Not only would the sins of the individual be forgiven but also the sins which had been passed along to them from their forefathers. God also said that the good works of an individual would be blessed and that future generations would also receive a blessing from the good works of their forefathers. This helped the inhabitants understand why it seemed that some were always blessed and others had such difficult lives and often could not free themselves from sin.

But both of these gifts, the gift of forgiveness which Christ purchased with His life and the gift of inherited blessings which God had given the inhabitants, had to be opened, had to be accepted, had to be understood, and had to be used properly in order to work. Apostle Paul asked the people in Romans 6:16, "Know ye not, that to whom ye yield yourselves servants to obey, his servants ye are to whom ye obey; whether of sin unto death, or of obedience unto righteousness?" This clearly indicated that the people could choose whether they wanted to serve God or serve the evil which Satan brought them, and that these two choices were their **only** choices. God's role models taught this to the inhabitants so they would understand the battle in which they were engaged and the choice they would have to make. To accept Christ's gift and be forgiven of their sins, the inhabitants would have to forgive one another and to esteem one another higher than themselves. As they did this, they began to understand one another's differences. They learned that they all carried sin and should all learn forgiveness and understanding and learn not to judge. They learned that when they did judge one another, they often made a mistake because they did not know the circumstances which caused someone to act as they did. They also learned that if they judged others, they themselves would be judged.

The inhabitants began to recognize that when they were burdened, their burden was lightened when others cared for them and prayed for them and assured them that they were loved. This made them flock to those who had this empathy and understanding in their hearts, and in this process, they themselves learned these attributes. Many brought thanks to God for the people they met who demonstrated the love which had brought them so much joy and taught them about goodness by their example. When they had passed through their times of trouble, they in turn wanted to help others in this same manner. Through this exchange, many of the inhabitants became role models for one another, and their appreciation of this was manifest in their prayers. These role models amassed blessings not only for themselves but for their children and their children's children.

Bearing One Another's Burdens

Dear Heavenly Father, Thank You for those who care for me
in the congregations that I love.
Thank You for bringing these friends
to me who've been touched by angels above.

The ones who look into my eyes
when they take my hand to shake,
looking for grief or happiness,
for the difference they could make.

And when they see a tear or frown,
their grip holds a little longer,
for they want to let you know they care
so one can be a little stronger.

Their faith is sure, yet quiet
with an inner type of calm;
and when they see someone in pain,
they search to find a balm.

And then one knows a Child of God
has reached into your heart
and offered to share your burden
so you only carry part.

When I leave such a Godly encounter,
feeling lighter and feeling less pain,
I know I took some love with me

and now can make more gain.

****

Little by little, the inhabitants were learning and beginning to emulate one another. The love between them began to grow. Each inhabitant was given the opportunity to become a role model, and each was making their own decision about how to live their life, using their free will. But as this lesson began to take root, evil sneered and wrung its hands in glee, making plans of destruction once again. The angels hoped that the inhabitants would use their free will to resist the evil and overcome the temptations in front of them which could cause them to fall. The angels knew that those who rose to become the role models for the inhabitants, would stay faithful to God and would flee the evil. Thus, God's plan, the great and magnificent plan which covered every move which evil could make, was again put to the test. The natural law of the universe, the physics of things, as God had engineered it, would allow the inhabitants to use their free will. But this time, they were better equipped to flee the evil…. if they chose to serve God instead of evil. The angels wanted, with all their hearts, to see everyone resist the evil and come forth unscathed by the heartbreak which evil left in its wake.

Sadly, many inhabitants fell to the evil; but many others did not fall when evil slithered—cold, malevolent, insidious, sneering, sure— into the minds of the inhabitants. The angels rejoiced when some resisted by saying NO! in a loud voice and filled their minds instead with the word of God. These inhabitants were saved from the evil and did not fall, for evil had to flee when the word of God and the sacrifice of Christ remained in the minds and hearts of men. Those who did not fall to this new attack continued to help others resist, to remind those who began to fall of what they could lose. They prayed day and night and rejoiced when they pulled some back from the attack and into God's word once again. This time, when evil struck, the evil encountered three different groups of people.

There were those who succumbed to the evil. There were those who resisted completely. And there were some who slipped at first but then resisted because while the evil had begun to fill their minds, the prayers of the faithful helped stop the evil from moving from their minds to their hearts. This was because the ones who had resisted right in the beginning worked hard to help those who were weak but wished they could resist. The weaker ones were finally able to push the evil from their minds, not letting it invade their hearts. This resistance meant that they had become the overcomers which God wanted them to become. God said that if they resisted evil, they would be called overcomers. Therefore they prayed in thankfulness for those who had helped them become what God wanted them to become.

Angels in the Congregation
Dearest Heavenly Father,
Thank You for those who helped me,
those who keep me from sin.
Thank You for those whose forgiveness
touch my heart and help goodness win.

These are the people I admire who are willing to reach out to me. Their prayers pull me back from evil, and their love is really the key.

They always wear a wonderful smile and never hold a grudge
and greet me with a hug and kiss, regard not lipstick smudge.

They're close to You and gentle and restful in Your love;
they trust You so completely to take us home above.

They assure me that You love us regardless of our mistakes,
and because they're so forgiving, they understand my human aches.

Their faces, not young, are beautiful for the character they show;
their heart is filled with kindness because the pain in life they know.

Thus, I'm so very grateful for the chance to call them friend
and grateful for the kindness that helps my heart to mend.

I'm grateful that You sent them to help me grow and learn,
so I, through them, can love You and the clutches of evil spurn.

****

Thus, those who were to become teachers, role models and overcomers were developed. And those who were learning how to resist evil and to do so of their own free will were learning more day by day as they leaned on the role models to help them. This group of seeking inhabitants, whose hearts yearned for the warmth of love, clamored to learn more about resisting evil and gaining forgiveness. They wanted to be more like their role models and be free of the terrible struggles which resulted when they fell prey to evil. While it seemed to be a happy time in heaven where the harps played and the angels sang and the palace rejoiced, there was another lesson which lay on the horizon for the inhabitants. They would still have to learn the responsibilities of a child of God so they could strive to become worthy for that which God wanted to give them. To have their names written in the Lamb's book of life and become a worthy Bride for the Lord Jesus, they would need to live by God's rules of love. To live by God's rules meant that first the inhabitants would have to know what these were and then understand what their personal responsibilities were to fulfilling those rules. This is what the role models were teaching and doing, and as a result of their loyalty to God, these role models and what God could work through them were mentioned in the Holy Bible as a treasure in earthen vessels. In 2 Corinthians 4:7, the apostle Paul said, "But we have this treasure in earthen vessels, that the power may be of God, and not of us." And thus the learning process was taking effect, and the next lessons were to begin.

Your word is a lamp to my feet
and a light to my path.

—Psalm 119:105

Chapter Five

Responsibilities of a Child of God

The Poems of Chapter Five

Behold, I set before you today a blessing and a curse:
The blessing, if you obey the commandments of the Lord
your God which I command you today; and the curse,
if you do not obey the commandments of the Lord your God,
but turn aside from the way which I command you today, to
go after other gods which you have not known.

—Deuteronomy 11:26, 27, 28

The learning process continued for the inhabitants of the cold, bleak planet which lay below the heavens. Satan however was very subtle and since the inhabitants life seemed to be going so well, Satan caused them to become lazy about their spiritual life. They forgot how terrible they felt when they were engulfed in evil and began to think that they no longer needed any help from God. They didn't understand that this was because evil had come again....this time in the form of pride. Pride gave them the false sense that they knew all there was to know and were safe in their own knowledge and ability. This was the subtlety of evil and how it whispered into their minds that their own strengths were exceptional and that everything God asked them took away their fun and was a waste of time.

These whispers fed their ego, made them feel important. And with these destructive thoughts came another, for evil was not content to do a little damage; evil wanted to destroy all that was good. Evil wanted to win their souls and **own** their hearts. Thus the whispers kept telling them that they were special individuals, more important than those other inhabitants who were not as talented; not as self-sufficient, not as smart. In fact, evil told them that they were as powerful as God and that this power was built inside them and all they had to do was use it. Evil told them to follow their own thinking and treat others as this dictated. Evil said they did not need to esteem others higher than themselves or honor their mother and father, or ask themselves if Jesus would really care what they did. As evil whispered into their minds, some of the inhabitants began to believe that they did not need prayer or God's love, or even the warmth and support they received in fellowship with other believers. Evil whispered that they should be proud of themselves because they did not need anything from anyone and could always retrieve what they might need spiritually after they visited evil for just a little while and drank of its delicious temptations. The inhabitants had forgotten that God had warned them that pride is very dangerous and had been what caused Satan to be thrown out of heaven.

Pride removes humbleness from the heart and leaves in its place....arrogance. Arrogance leads to judgment, breeds cruelty, jealousy and envy. And these lead to rebellion. Pride and jealousy had been the downfall of Satan. This is why Satan could easily suggest these actions to men. Pride was the weapon which evil knew could be used to draw men from their pursuit of love and then to sin and then to their destruction. Therefore, some of the inhabitants fell away from the comforting presence of God, believing themselves to be self-sufficient, believing in their own power, believing that they did not need God, nor the teachers who had helped them. They rationalized away their sins making them seem little and not worth worrying about...they had forgotten the warnings they'd read in the Holy Bible: "The fear of the Lord is to hate evil: pride and arrogancy, and the evil way, and the forward mouth, do I hate" (Proverbs 8:13). They'd forgotten that God warned: "And I will break the pride of your power" in Leviticus 26:19. But the angels knew the danger of pride, and they saw that the inhabitants had opened their heart to Satan. The angels knew what would come to pass because of this and knew that the natural law of the universe, the physics of things, and the engineering placed into God's magnificent and all-encompassing plan called for a perfect, humble and obedient heart. The inhabitants had opened the door to evil through their pride and had thus lost their humbleness.

Soon life no longer went as the inhabitants had hoped because with their pride, the inevitable separation from God occurred. To make matters worse, evil had nurtured the inhabitants' pride to the point where the inhabitants rebelled against God. They no longer wanted to learn God's words, nor follow His statutes. They felt that they were strong enough and wise enough to choose between good and evil whenever they wanted or even if they wanted to do so. They started to believe that all they had to do was believe that Christ had come and died for their sins and they would be saved and that how they acted did not really count especially when their sins were so small. But the angels knew that when pride took hold of the minds of the inhabitants, rebellion would enter their hearts, and make it difficult for them to return to God. They knew that rebellion would make them stubborn and that God had warned of this when He said in Deuteronomy 32:27, "For I know thy rebellion, and thy stiff neck."

It became a terrifying time for some of the inhabitants because the evil spirit of pride and the evil spirit of rebellion brought other spirits—more evil than these first—and they gained access into the lives of the inhabitants. These spirits had not only entered the inhabitants' minds to make them think highly of their own abilities and become arrogant, but now because of their acceptance of this evil thinking, these spirits could enter them so forcefully that they pushed the Holy Spirit from their hearts, destroyed love, and the warmth it brought, and lived in their hearts for a very long time. Their arrogance made it difficult to even recognize that they may have sinned, or to ever apologize or repent. Sadly, as these inhabitants attended to their daily lives and busied themselves with the chores and distractions of their chosen schedules, they purposely....and arrogantly.... neglected their spiritual life. Caught up in the rigors of their quest for self-importance and lulled by the complacency which made them think they did not need to invest in their spiritual life, these inhabitants no longer stayed close to God, no longer gave their time or effort to the Lord.

They also neglected to meet one of their most important responsibilities. This was to teach their children about God. They were terribly wrong in their thinking, but this is what evil wanted. The names of these inhabitants would not be entered into the Lamb's book of life if they failed to honor God or failed to teach their children about God. Sadly, because of their deadly decision, their children's names would not be written in the Lamb's book of life either. Teaching their children properly was one of the statutes which God **required** them to follow. If they had done this, their lives would have been blessed, and their children's lives would have been blessed. But because of their arrogance and their pride, they neglected to do this and began the spiral into complacency which would lose them their blessing, and perhaps the blessing for many generations to come. Those who had worked to teach these inhabitants of the terrible risk they were taking and how their choices would impact their lives and the lives of their children felt terrible. They had done their best to teach the people, to warn them against leaving God and believing they could live with evil. They had also tried to teach these inhabitants that they needed to be a good example to their children.

The Example

Set the right example; be careful what you say;
show, by all your actions, the very Godlike way.
For children learn from parents; they copy what you do
and often keep forever the way of life you view.

Don't tell them to act one way when you act in another;
let them see you showing love to every brother.
Give them understanding, love, and hugs, and all,
especially some encouragement as they answer life's trying call.

For you can make a difference in happiness and pain
to how they will respond to life in sunshine and in rain.
You can teach them of the evil, teach them how to fight;
so when the Lord returns again, they'll be in raiment white.

****

Those who had been role models and teachers to these inhabitants tried to remind them that God had clearly instructed them through the Holy Bible by telling them to learn His words and walk in His instruction through Proverbs 4:20-22: "Give attention to my words; incline your ear to my sayings. Do not let them depart from your eyes; keep them in the midst of your heart for they are life to those who find them, and health to all their flesh." Further, the inhabitants had been instructed to teach these words to their children through

Deuteronomy 6:7, *"You shall teach them **diligently** to your children, and shall talk of them when you sit in your house, when you walk by the way, when you lie down, and when you rise up."* Sadly, the neglected children never saw their parents praying or learning God's words or treating one another with love. They only saw their parents' pride in their own strengths and their complacency about all things regarding God. Because of their parents' neglect in these things, the children suffered. They learned only that which the actions of their parents taught them. Sadly, even though they too hungered to fill the void in their heart, they had never been taught how to fill it.

So as the children grew, they searched in all the wrong ways, in all the wrong places, to stop the pain of having an empty heart. The actions of the children brought them great sorrow and was dangerous to their soul. It brought chaos to the household. God had warned the inhabitants of this in Matthew 10:21 where He said, *".......and the children shall rise up against their parents; and cause them to be put to death."* The children hadn't been taught properly and only knew that they were driven to find what was missing in their life even though they did not know how or what that was. Their parents had neglected to teach them, so they suffered and turned to those things which evil told them would be satisfying to them. But nothing evil whispered into their hearts was good for them. Later, because the parents had caused this to happen to their children, they had to watch their children endure terrible circumstances and they and their family members also suffered. They were experiencing the consequences of their actions, the consequences of not nurturing their spiritual life and not seeking God's protection. The children did not have anything good with which to sustain them in their time of need except their pride, their arrogance, their stubbornness and what they thought was their great ability to handle their own lives. They had learned this from their parents and evil only pushed them further into defiance and anger. Some turned to drugs and alcohol to ease their pain, others to medicines that never seemed to work. Even while walking in their pride and not following any of the suggestions made by the role models God had given them, the role models still tried to reach out to them, still tried to help them and continued to pray for them. Their conversations with these inhabitants told them about their responsibility to God so they might mend their ways. To this end they developed a little poem which they hoped would help the inhabitants understand what God wanted them to know about raising children.

Children

Children are on loan to us for such a short, short while;
a piece of clay to shape and mold and send out with a smile.
A good heart, a moral conscience, and a definite feeling of worth
is what we hope we've given them in the short time since their birth.

For they too fill God's special plan and have reason here for being,
and we must let them go in time, even when we are not seeing
that it's time for them to test their wings, a time for tempting too,
a time when they alone must stand, deciding on all they do.

They'll make mistakes but hopefully grow, and then have to decide,
for when they lose their way, we'll wish we'd been a better guide.
We need to have made them ready, taught them how to perform,
for we also lived as children and were given our own chance for reform.

So let's try together to do our best; then hopefully we can say
we helped our children love God first so they would find their way.
Let's never have to look at the past in sorrow for what we've done.
Let's give our children instruction so heaven they will not shun.

****

The angels knew that evil was gaining in strength, but they had
to keep their silence. They hoped that soon these inhabitants would
get back on track and knew that it would be more difficult for the
inhabitants to break the hold which evil had on them and harder yet
for them to save their children. It was far harder to break free of a
spirit which had comfortably lodged in the heart. It was far better
when these spirits were not allowed total access to the heart in the first
place. It was very difficult for these inhabitants to break away from
evil. They were now older and set in their destructive patterns and
their children had never heard of God's statutes. They had chosen to
distance themselves from those who tried to help them; had closed their
ears to God's words. Worse, it was close to impossible for them to rid
themselves of the spirit of arrogance, complacency and pride which had
come to live in their hearts and had hardened their hearts against
God. They had been warned but despite these warnings, they had
chosen to ignore God, ignore His statutes, and spurn those who tried
to keep them from the precipice of evil. They mocked those who were
faithful, spurned their words and chose evil. It seemed that they had
given up their desire to leave evil and find God. Their children
rebelled, and their lives too were filled with evil. All around them evil
reigned; and their friends, their colleagues, their children—sometimes
their entire family—all walked in indifference to what God asked of

them. They did not put any effort into learning of God's Plan of Salvation and sought the things they shouldn't. The evil spirits had access not only to their minds but to their hearts and came to dwell so they could continue their whispers of envy and jealousy, of complacency, of disparaging those who loved them and prayed for them.

But in time, because of the prayers of God's faithful, many of these inhabitants began to realize that they were steeped in sin. They saw that their children suffered from the sins of the parents; the children suffered because they had not been given the right example, they hadn't been taught about God. The parents began to see their own lives for what they really were and how far they had moved from love and honesty and goodness, far from God. They began to see how they lived to satisfy the evil spirits of greed and self-aggrandizement and hadn't concerned themselves about the welfare of their children. Some of the inhabitants remembered that they had read this warning in the great Holy Bible which God had given them to help them make the right decisions. Yet because they had allowed the evil free access to their hearts, they had to struggle to grasp what was truth. They had difficulty remembering what they once had with God and comparing that to what they now had with evil. They felt that they had been blinded by the evil, trapped, and now were unable to find their way out. They began to worry that they would be trapped forever. They seemed to have no willpower to break free of the spirits which held them hostage. But these consequence were just part of the natural law of the universe, the physics of things. They came from the evil of Satan's spirits and the disobedience of the inhabitants. God's righteousness had to allow these consequences to occur. What the inhabitants did not understand was that God's righteousness had to follow the natural law of the universe, the physics of things. God's righteousness had to allow them to suffer the consequences of their disobedience just as Adam did when he ate from the tree of the knowledge of good and evil. God could not interfere with what evil had done until man cried for help, until man asked God to help him. Satan had ownership rights to every sinful inhabitant. The angels knew this, but the inhabitants who had fallen to evil and their children who hadn't been taught didn't know these natural laws. The suffering of these inhabitants lasted for a very long time, and generations of children came under the influence of evil because of the sin of their parents. One man's sin in the Garden of Eden affected all men, so it could easily be understood that one man's sin would affect his children and his children's children. This was a consequence of what Satan had done and how man had responded. This was a part of the natural law of the universe, the physics of things. The angels felt sad when they watched the suffering of these inhabitants, but finally, one day they heard a plea to God for help. They heard the prayers and supplication of the parents, hoping that the Father and His Son and Holy Spirit would respond to their pleas to help them free themselves of evil. However, for what seemed a long time, the prayers of the inhabitants seemed to go unanswered. This was because their hearts were still too filled with pride. God knew that if He answered their pleas right away, they would only fall back again as they had done so many times before. God would wait. This was a part of the plan, the natural law of the universe, the physics of things, put into place to help mankind and to allow the inhabitants to break the bond of evil which held their hearts. In time, God saw that their suffering had tempered their arrogance and had put a rift into their pride and He felt that it was time to try again to help the inhabitants learn how to escape their captivity. God knew everything: past, present, and future. His incredible engineering feat had already taken into consideration what would happen in every circumstance, and that's why He knew that now the time was right. The suffering of the inhabitants made their hearts ready to accept His help. So God sent an inspiration to those who prayed fervently, those whose hearts were attuned to receive His answer. He commissioned the angels to whisper to these parents and bring into their minds the remembrance that they hadn't taught their children, they hadn't been an example to them, and hadn't passed along to them the wisdom which God had so lovingly and painstakingly provided for them. "This was wrong," the whispers admonished. "This resulted in great heartache and chaos, but more importantly, this caused a separation from God for you and for your children." Many of these inhabitants pondered these new thoughts which were entering their minds, and wanted to change their ways. The role models, who prayed for those inhabitants had fellowship with them and conversed with them and broke bread with them. They told them a story to help them understand and choose... of their own free will... what was needed. They wanted these parents not to give in to the evil, not to give up on themselves, or on their children. They wanted them to remember how difficult it was to be a child and to have so much to learn. These role models did not want the parents to punish the children for what the parents had caused but rather to understand, teach, guide, and gently lead them to God and that God would help.

Remember

Can you remember how crushed you were
when the one you liked didn't call?
Can you remember how ugly you felt
when you really weren't ugly at all?

Can you remember how deeply
your emotions seemed to go?
And how you felt that everyone
wasn't a friend, but a foe?

Can you remember all these things,
the struggle at home and at school?
Can you remember how it hurt to learn,
and often feel the fool?

Can you remember when some in your life
just let you run so wild?
And how you wished they showed their love
since you were really still a child?

Can you remember? Oh, you can?
Then you'll surely see
that you need more understanding
when guiding them to be

alert and strong to do God's will
as you were sent to do.
For who has been appointed to prepare them?

Yes, my parent . . .
God chose you!

****

When the parents heard the words in the poem which their role models read to them, they were afraid and they repented. They asked how they could undo the harm they had already done. The Lord explained that maybe, for some, the evil could be undone, but others might have to suffer for a lifetime. What they had done to their children out of their pride and complacency, out of their laziness and lukewarm attitude toward God, might not be undone if they could not evict the evil which had power over them. Because of what they neglected to teach their children, it would be difficult to bring about change. But nevertheless, to those with a truly repentant heart, God gave another chance. God was kind to the inhabitants and wanted to help them instill into the hearts of the children what should have been placed into their hearts much earlier in their life.

These inhabitants had learned a lesson, but had almost lost their future with God and any chance to make amends. They may have to watch their children suffer if they could not reach their hearts. They really needed to get it right this time. Thus, God watched those who had not instructed their children and not paid attention to how husband and wife, parent and child, child and grandparent and others were to treat one another. God knew that this had a great impact on the family. Just as children learned by example how the parents interacted with others and how they chose how to live their lives, they also learned by how the parents treated one another. This too was the responsibility of those who loved God and hoped to become a part of His new kingdom. In fact, God had instructed in Philippians 2:1-5, "Fulfill ye my joy, that ye be like-minded, having the same love, being of one accord, of one mind. Let nothing be done through strife or vainglory; but in lowliness of mind let each esteem the other better than themselves." Vainglory was like pride and arrogance. Lowliness of mind was humbleness. Love was healing, and it was gentle. These words explained that living by the word of God and practicing love would help them immensely in what they needed to accomplish. The role models also showed these inhabitants another part of scripture where God said in 1 Peter 3:8-9, "Finally, be ye all of one mind, having compassion one of another, love as brethren, be pitiful, be courteous: Not rendering evil for evil, or railing for railing: but contrariwise blessing; knowing that ye are thereunto called, that ye should inherit a blessing." Here, God told them that by practicing love toward one another they would obtain a blessing.

The inhabitants needed these blessings for the huge chore before them in regard to the children they had neglected......the children whose hearts had been invaded by evil because their parents hadn't taught them properly. Doing as God suggested would provide the right example to their children. They were also to teach from the Holy Bible to help the children regain trust in, and respect for, their parents as they taught them of God. In Romans, Chapter 12, they read such things as: give with simplicity, rule with diligence, show mercy with cheerfulness, hate what is evil, cleave to good, rejoice in hope, be patient in tribulation, constant in prayer. Bless those who persecute you, weep with those who weep, live peaceably. When they had done these things, when those inhabitants had placed these instructions into their heart and mind and worked to fulfill them, their hearts began to fill once again with the wonderful warmth which made them so happy. As they taught their children with words and deeds, their children began to change. Love came again to these families. This was the blessing God granted them because they were so deeply repentant, and striving with all their heart to please Him, to regain what they had lost. The heavens sang when one of these inhabitants read the others what he had written about the relationship between husbands and wives. All of these repentant souls loved the poem and took it into their hearts with thankfulness.

Husbands and Wives

Marriage means different things to different people,
and our expectations for our spouse is often unreasonably high.
A spouse may be a friend most of all
and perhaps is lots of fun and makes us laugh.
Maybe our spouse is a wonderful listener or wonderfully loving,
very nurturing or perhaps even a terrific parent.

A spouse may be wise and philosophical
or simply make us feel appreciated and needed.
A spouse can be that person who is 100 percent in our corner.
and maybe a wonderful provider as well!
If our spouse is sometimes what we need; tries to be what we need
or even is everything that we need, the love we feel
for our spouse grows greater every day.
But have we ever asked ourselves, "Am I what my spouse needs?"

****

Once again, God's magnificent plan to save the inhabitants from the natural consequences of falling prey to sin and then choosing to remain in sin was working. God knew that some would eventually move back to what Satan offered, and therefore spend eternity in the lake of fire. But God also knew that many would choose of their own free will to follow God and leave evil. These would live with God in the beautiful new heaven and earth He would create for them where there would be no more sorrow and no further temptation from evil. God had promised in James 4:7 in the Holy Bible: "Submit yourselves therefore to God. Resist the devil, and he will flee from you." But God also warned in Ephesians 4:30: "Grieve not the Holy Spirit of God, whereby ye are sealed unto the day of redemption." For it was only when the Holy Spirit lived in man's heart that he could resist the devil. The Holy Spirit would not live in a heart which entertained evil in thought or action but only one which would strive to serve God and repent of evil. As the inhabitants repented, God saw the next phase of His plan to help the inhabitants begin. Here, God would teach them the benefits of being a child of God and what God wanted to provide for those whom He would call His children and those who would become the Bride of Christ.

I will praise thee, O Lord,
with my whole heart.

—Psalm 9:1

Chapter Six

Promises for Our Future

The Poems of Chapter Six

I will bring the one-third through the fire,
will refine them as silver is refined,
and test them as gold is tested.
They will call on My name,
and I will answer them.
I will say, "This is My people";
and each one will say,
"The Lord is my God."

—Zechariah 13:9

The angels were saddened when the inhabitants of the cold, bleak planet below almost lost their halos of silver. The halos were still there but had less shine. This meant that the inhabitants had a lot of work to do to regain the ground they had lost. The great and wonderful plan engineered by the Father and His Son to increase the wisdom of the inhabitants through the natural law of the universe, the physics of things, had been put into place to guide the inhabitants toward making their choice between good and evil. The angels knew that the inhabitants needed to think about their future, for there was more to life than just the few short years the inhabitants were to spend on earth. There was their eternal future to think about. The choices they made while on their cold, bleak planet would impact their eternity. Every soul who had been created by God would have a future which would last for all eternity... but where they would spend that eternity was up to them.

The angels hoped that the inhabitants would make the right choice; that they would long to spend all eternity wrapped in the warmth of perfect love. Love would blossom from being with the Father of love as a part of the new heaven and earth which God was creating for those who chose Him over evil. The inhabitants had been frightened when their children rebelled. They realized that it could easily have been too late for them to make things right again if they hadn't seen what they'd done in time to change. All would have been lost, not only for them but for generations to come. They realized that they needed to make a commitment to God, to make the goal of their life to follow God's statutes, and to raise their children to know these rules and to know God. They themselves needed to be the right kind of role models to provide this to their children. They needed to learn God's statutes themselves in order to teach them to their children. They needed to have a positive and godly attitude to pass along to their children. They needed to love their children the way God loved them and teach their children about this love.

But the angels also saw that the inhabitants who had fallen away and had finally called upon their Heavenly Father for help could now begin to see the fruits of their labors. They were now not only learning God's words and following them but also teaching them to their children. They could move toward the recognition that they would need to have not only faith in God but also do those works which His words asked of them. They began to understand that God had been teaching them when He allowed them to experience those difficult times. He'd wanted them to learn. He knew that their suffering helped them recognize and then understand the importance not only of protecting against evil when it came but also of teaching their children the importance of this protection. But could they continue to do it? Would they do it? Did they know how? Would their children listen to them? And what about the older children who had slipped into sin? In Ephesians 6:13, God explained, "Therefore take up the whole armour of God, that you may be able to withstand in the evil day, and having done all, to stand." They learned once again that prayer and fellowship, learning God's words, giving to Him the Holy Day He asked of them when they could dedicate the day to a church service and to praying and bringing God their tithe of 10% to say "thank you".

From God's inspiration, born from the inhabitant's pleas and supplication in prayer, and what they learned from their ministers the inhabitants also learned that children needed encouragement and learned from the words, actions, attitudes, and struggles of their parents. They were also inspired to understand that children needed love. From love would come their desire to please their parents and to also please God. Through love they would **want** to learn. With love they would be willing to accept their lessons. To develop the new bond which the parents wanted to have with their children, they injected fellowship and fun into the children's lessons to reinforce that love and encourage their participation. They formed a plan and shared their ideas with other believers and brought their children into their fellowships where the children would see that others were striving to do what was right in God's eyes. They made their fellowships enjoyable by playing games, by providing good food, by sharing their experiences of faith, and by telling stories of the times when they struggled. They told of how difficult it had been to pick themselves up when they fell and how others in the group encouraged them when they had fallen. From watching and listening to the adults, the children learned and the adults felt the warmth of hope and love move into their hearts again. Their halos of silver gleamed, and the angels rejoiced. But then wasn't that all part of the plan, the great engineering feat of how to bring love into the awareness of God's children so they would desire love for all eternity and strive for that joy? God knew that the inhabitants' own desire for love would help them learn to love others, that their own desire for respect would teach them to respect others, and that their own thankfulness for the help they received would teach them to help others, extending the gift of friendship. He knew that they would cherish the godly friendships they received and be thankful for those friendships. He also knew that the inhabitants would come to value peace and seek ways to be peacemakers themselves after they experienced life without peace for a time. That was just the natural law of the universe, the physics of things, which God had developed and placed into His plan.

The parents made up some songs for the children to sing. There were songs of joy, songs of thankfulness, songs of praise, and little songs which taught the children of the goals which should be placed before them such as attending Sunday school, reading the Bible, learning about their faith. They taught the children to try each day to be good and to do good to others, to be patient, to be peacemakers, to be thankful, to honour their parents and grandparents, and to become all that God wished for them to be. When the parents sang these songs with their children, they learned too and hoped that they would never again forget to teach their children God's words or allow God's words to slip away from their hearts. That had been a terrible mistake on their part and had lost them many years and caused them so much heartache. It was now a greater struggle to prepare their hearts and their children's hearts for the day when God would send His Son for those whose hearts were ready, those whose hearts had been purified in the fire of pain and heartache. The angels rejoiced to see these inhabitants try to do what was right. They too sang songs of praise to their Heavenly Father when they saw the shine increase on the halos of the inhabitants and the joy in the hearts of the children. In fact, for a while, the planet didn't seem quite as bleak and cold as it had been. But wasn't all this just the perfection found in the natural law of the universe, the physics of things, the plan which God had engineered so carefully so His children could thrive? Wasn't it God's love for mankind which caused Him to want to provide a way to thwart the evil which wanted the children of God to fail? Wasn't it to prevent evil from stealing the hearts of the children? As the inhabitants worked to do what was right, God rewarded them by blessing them. As they cared for one another and loved one another, they shared their faith, and shared what they learned each day. They also shared their experiences of faith with one another, for they found that this helped sustain them when they were troubled. Their faith grew from these good works, and God was pleased.

What Is Faith?

Faith is being willing to step out from all we know and love,
wondering what the unknown tomorrow holds,
not knowing how or when or where yet trusting
that God will provide all.

Faith is accepting what appears to be loss in the sureness
that even out of despair comes good
for those who love the Lord.

****

The inhabitants began to study the word of God with greater purpose. God opened their understanding and showed them the many blessings He'd promised to those who followed His statutes. The inhabitants read in James 1:12, "Blessed is the man that endureth temptation: for when he is tried, he shall receive the crown of life, which the Lord hath promised to them that love him." And in 1 Peter 5:6, they read, "Humble yourselves therefore under the mighty hand of God, that he may exalt you in due time." These were beautiful promises. God was pleased and the palace rang with the sound of harps and the singing of those in the beautiful edifice high on the mountain. As the angels looked toward the palace, they could see prisms of light dancing through the windows in a tapestry of color, causing a rainbow to stretch its shapely and beneficent arms over the huge building. They could feel the joy and the love pouring from the palace, uncontainable, beautiful, perfect and they were so pleased. The angels also saw the currents which swirled above the cold, bleak planet below reach for the conversations of the inhabitants and carry them up to the heavens. They saw many of these conversations go to the great palace and be stored in the great computer and knew that these were the prayers of the faithful. They knew that God was pleased to receive so many prayers, and so they were pleased.

Blessings flowed from the Father in heaven to His children on the cold, bleak planet and God showed the inhabitants even more of the wonderful promises He'd given them about their future and inspired them to read in the Holy Bible in Romans 2:7: "To them who by patient continuance in well doing seek for glory and honour and immortality, eternal life." God did this so the inhabitants would know that He would look after them and bring them with Him into the new Creation. Thankfulness filled the hearts of the inhabitants as they read God's promises. They recognized God's perfect love. and fell in love with righteousness. They fell in love with the beauty they found in God's heart from the love He carried for them. They were touched by what He wanted to give them, by what He wanted to do for them if they would only listen to His words of guidance. The inhabitants longed to be like the apostles of Christ and develop the strength of faith they had. They'd read of the apostle's commitment to God in the Holy Bible in Romans 8:38-39 where the apostle Paul said, "For I am persuaded, that neither death, nor life, nor angels, nor principalities, nor powers, nor things present, nor things to come, nor height, nor depth, nor any other creature, shall be able to separate us from the love of God, which is in Christ Jesus our Lord."

The inhabitants longed to have that same commitment but knew that evil would come again to stalk them and that they needed to be ready to fight. God knew that His promises would give the inhabitants hope, and along with their prayers, help them hold onto their trust in Him. These gifts would keep them safe and these gifts would prevent Satan from gaining a stranglehold on them.....at least for now. But God also knew that later, as evil grew in strength, just as love grew in strength, the inhabitants would have to learn about and put on the armour which God would provide for them so they could fight the much stronger evil which would come for them. For now, God was pleased by the progress of these inhabitants and pleased by how His plan was working. Over time, those with beautiful hearts would follow God and resist evil for the inhabitants were growing in faith and sharing their thoughts and feelings and their hopes and dreams with one another. And best of all, they spoke of the things of God.

The Things of God

Hope is always of God; hopelessness is of evil.
Honor and morality are of God; justification of wrongdoing is not.
Faith and trust are of God; fear and despair never is.
Sincerity and a kindly nature are of God;
hypocrisy and stinginess is evil.
Humbleness and childlike faith are of God;
arrogance and aggression are not.

A yearning for righteousness is of God;
envy, gossip, and malice are from Satan.
A desire to comfort others is Godly;
to comfort only ourselves is selfish.

Believing in God's protection and the power of prayer is Godly.
Surrendering our will to the promptings of the Holy Spirit is of God
and brings joy to God's heart. And these things of God shall gain for
us a place in Heaven and eternal joy.

****

God continued to teach the inhabitants what He wanted for their
future by providing them with many wonderful revelations through
His Holy Bible. In Revelation 2:26, the inhabitants discovered
the words of Christ which told them: "And he that overcometh, and
keepeth my works unto the end, to him will I give power over the
nations." And in Revelation 3:5, Christ said, "He that overcometh,
the same shall be clothed in white raiment......" The verse that the
inhabitants liked the best was in Revelation 3:21 where Christ told

them, "To him that overcometh will I grant to sit with me in my throne......." The inhabitants discussed what was meant by the word overcomer. They understood that this meant those who could resist temptation; push evil away when it attacked. This meant that they should hold fast to God's words, do good always, and strive to resist all things which God abhorred. These words gave the inhabitants hope and inspired them to try harder. They wanted to become overcomers and learned that through God's grace, if they slipped in this endeavor but were immediately and sincerely repentant, they could still be overcomers.

As the inhabitants learned these truths and began to read the promises God gave them for their future, they began to desire to give something to God and wondered what they could give. They knew their limitations; but they also knew that when you loved someone, you wanted to give back some of the love and goodness you received. While it was important to offer godly love without thought of receiving something back, love was best when it was not a one-way street. Love, it seemed, was the most rewarding when it was reciprocal. When love was given, those receiving love were often inspired to return love. That was the magic and what the inhabitants needed to grasp. This was why God wanted them to love their enemies. Thus, as they felt God's love, they understood why they wanted to give love to God.

What Can I Give to God?

What are my talents, what gifts did God give to me?

What do I like to do?

How can I use the gifts God gave me to serve him?

Perhaps we love to write and open our hearts to all the wonders and
emotions, the mysteries and evidence of the joys and pain of life.
Perhaps we can learn how to use this gift
by expressing our thoughts on paper.
Perhaps then we will learn why things are the way they are.
And perhaps our eyes will be opened to the
work of God in everything.
Perhaps this will help others see the wonder of God.
Perhaps writing is feeling
and expressing God's love intellectually.

Perhaps we can dance or sing, play an instrument,
listen to music, and move to its rhythm.
With each sound or movement comes an expression of joy or sorrow.
Perhaps we can transmit joy to others through our dance or our song.
Perhaps dancing and singing are feeling
and expressing God's love physically.

Perhaps we can paint as here we might capture in color and form,
the beauty in all the things of God's creation,
its great magnificence, power, and majesty
and bring to others the beauty of the creation
through our paintings.
Perhaps painting is feeling and expressing God's love visually.

Perhaps we are limited in outward gifts, but inwardly, we can love.
Perhaps we can smile and encourage, hug and reassure.
Perhaps send a card or two; Perhaps we can call and visit

to show the love we have for others.
Perhaps loving is feeling and expressing
the wonder of God emotionally.

But if I could choose but one, it would be to write.
For the movement of dance, the excitement of paint,
and the gift of love can be described, thus felt by
expressing these things in the form of words.
The emotion of joy, of sorrow and anguish, of love or pain,
of thankfulness and hope are parts of the rhythms of life;
parts of the whole which describe life;
and parts of those things that teach us of God.
And these too can be portrayed in words

To survive the deepest valleys of life we must have hope.
Words can provide hope to others when they are God's words.
Hope is our mainstay. Where would we be without hope?
Where would we be without the promises of the Bible?
Where would we be without the miracles of faith and the love of God?
All these sustain us. All are a part of the miracle of life,
and they all come from God.

God loved us first and provided miracles so we could learn of Him,
so we yearn to serve Him in whatever capacity we can,
and we yearn to share with others the gifts He's given us.
Because of what we see and touch, feel and know,
we are, most of all, in love with God.
And because of all He has given and taught of these things,

We are, above all, Thankful.
And because we are thankful, we want to give something back.
We want to serve God.
Giving of ourselves, our love, our time, our talents pleases God.
But do we do this?

****

The angels marveled at these words and saw that the hearts and souls of the inhabitants were maturing into a love which could sustain them in times of trouble and prepare them as a worthy Bride when Christ returned for them. The angels hearts were touched by what these inhabitants said, and knew that if anything could make God shed tears of joy, this poem would. They knew it would touch the Father's heart as none other had. These words from the inhabitants rose from the planet below and were caught by the currents and sent to the palace. The angels recognized that the inhabitants were developing a true and lasting love for God. Pure love was unconditional, long-suffering, trusting, and patient. True love sacrificed for others by looking to their best interests. God's love for the inhabitants was the purest, most unadulterated love which existed in all the planets and in all the heavens above.

The angels knew that every soul which God created wanted to be loved, just as God's soul did. God's love for mankind was greater than any love that ever existed. Because God loved so deeply, He longed to wipe away all the tears which the inhabitants had suffered at the hands of evil. He longed to prevent evil from harming those He loved. And He longed for the inhabitants to love Him of their own free will. But God's righteousness had to allow evil to continue until man knew both good and evil and would make the choice between them of his own free will. The rules of God's righteousness in the face of what Satan had brought to all mankind demanded that God could only present His case for good as evil would present its case and allow men to choose between them. But love was powerful. Actually, love was more powerful than hate; so if the inhabitants could love, they could conquer evil. But there were rules to follow, prerequisites for neutralizing man's sin, for if they remained in sin, Satan could claim them. God promised in Revelation 7:16-17 in the Holy Bible: "They shall hunger no more, neither thirst anymore; neither shall the sun light on them, nor any heat. For the Lamb which is in the midst of the throne shall feed them, and shall lead them unto living fountains of waters; and God shall wipe away all tears from their eyes."

The inhabitants were comforted by these loving words and were strengthened as God had hoped. Those who put God first served Him with all their heart even in the face of great adversity. They prayed every morning and every night, and when they left their homes and when they ate, they gave thanks. They trusted and appreciated their Heavenly Father and His Son and kept their hope alive. They read Their words in the Holy Bible and tried diligently to share them with others. They pondered them so they could understand them and do as God asked. These souls wanted to give of themselves to God; and began to serve others, to sit under the word of His teaching, and to tithe as a way of thanking God for His great gifts. They honored their teachers and the wisdom of the elderly and took admonishment well so they could change what needed to be changed. They kept God's day, the Sabbath day, holy by going to church to repent with a sincere heart when they failed and determined to try harder to resist the evil thoughts which came to them unbidden. They taught their children as best they could, and they spent time in fellowship with one another to share their faith and their experiences of faith. God was pleased with His people.

The inhabitants had fun when they were together too. Sometimes they played happy little games, other times they shared thoughts about what they had read or written. Sometimes they spoke of the wonder of the fruits of the Holy Spirit, which God had taught them in Galatians 5:22-23: "But the fruit of the Spirit is love, joy peace, longsuffering, gentleness, goodness, faith, Meekness, temperance: against such there is no law." From these words they learned of their responsibilities and how to hold themselves in love. But also from these words, the inhabitants learned about the heart of God and Christ, for the Holy Spirit emanated what came from them.

God was a Trinity of the Father, the Son, and the Holy Spirit. This beautiful heart, taught by the Spirit, was something the inhabitants were striving to develop in themselves. As they continued in fellowship with one another, even the littlest children realized that if they too practiced those things which pleased God, they would be blessed; and it would, of course, also please their parents and those around them. The children watched the adults and they learned. The adults were being excellent role models and setting the right example. The children knew that they too could participate in the conversations which took place in their fellowships and delighted in everyone's response to them. It was a time of joyful sharing and wonderful learning. One day, a little child asked if she could read everyone a poem she had written. The inhabitants were touched by the little girl's enthusiasm and joy. The eagerness in her heart to share her thoughts brought joy to everyone, young and old. They were pleased to hear the words in her poem, for in her words, they could recognize her understanding and her striving. They were enthralled by the lilting words which sounded so cheerful.

I Think I Can

What must I do today? Well, perhaps I can be kind all day.
Could I? I think I'll try!
I did it!

What will I do today? Yesterday, I was kind all day.
Today, I'll be kind and loving.
Can I? I'll Try!
I did it!

What can I do today? Yesterday, I was kind and loving all day.
Today, I am so sure that God loves me,
and loves what I did yesterday.
that I know I can accomplish wonderful things today!
And I will!
I love You, God!

****

The angels also heard the words this little child spoke, and recognized the child's innocence, her desire to please, her understanding of the need to try every day to do God's will; and they heard the enthusiasm in her heart. The parents were doing a good job. The congregations were providing the right example. The children were learning. This too was a part of the great plan, the natural law of the universe, the physics of things, as it had to be played out on this battlefield between good and evil. With the children learning and the adults striving, love grew, and the love protected their hearts from evil. The inhabitants knew that at some point, evil would come again to knock at their heart's door; but this time, they would be better prepared. They spoke often of God's promise in Luke 12:32 when He told them, "Fear not, little flock; for it is your Father's good pleasure to give you the kingdom." Since evil would grow as love grew, God wanted the inhabitants to learn more about the power which evil would use against them. Thus began the next phase of the magnificent plan of love which God the Father, His Son, and the Holy Spirit had engineered for the people. They were now to learn more about evil, the instigator of all heartache.

Happy is he . . .
whose hope is in the Lord his God.

—Psalm 146:5

Chapter Seven
The Evil Instigator

The Poems of Chapter Seven

Take therefore no thought for the morrow:
For the morrow shall take thought for the things of itself.
—Matthew 5:34

And shall not God avenge his own elect,
which cry day and night unto him, though he bear long with
them? I tell you that he will avenge them speedily.
—Luke 18:7, 8

The angels who lived in the heavens far above the cold, bleak planet saw that the inhabitants had learned about the power and benefit of love and were therefore being equipped to make their great decision. The inhabitants did not yet understand that they were being prepared for this; they assumed that it would be easy to make such a decision if they ever needed to make it. They did not yet know that even now, before they fully understood, before they were fully able to resist evil, Satan was already keeping score. Satan was keeping track of their mistakes, and their failures, and every sin they committed. Satan believed that he could break their spirit, disrupt their desire to keep on trying by reminding them of their sins. He believed that this would help him own their hearts completely in the end. However, God knew that evil was keeping a scorecard. He knew that for every failure of man, a mark against him was registered on that scorecard. God also knew that Satan would bring this to judgment day so he could claim as his own every inhabitant who had broken God's statutes. Satan knew that God wanted all men saved, but he also knew that their sins could keep them from being saved. Satan wanted to prevent God from achieving His goal and wanted all the inhabitants to fail. Satan knew he would be cast into the lake of fire when God had reached the hearts of the number of inhabitants He longed for, so Satan had to stop God from obtaining that number. Satan knew every word which was written in the Bible; thus, he knew of God's plan and knew of his own demise. Satan could only hope to prevent that day from arriving by thwarting God's progress with the inhabitants. Every soul gained for Satan was one less that God could obtain. Every soul gained for Satan gave Satan that much more time to stop God from completing His work of redemption for mankind. Satan kept a scorecard of all the sins the inhabitants committed, so he would know their weak points and be able to point his finger at these inhabitants if God tried to say they were worthy. Satan knew that God could not claim that any inhabitant was worthy if he was an unredeemed sinner. Sadly, the inhabitants didn't know about the scorecard Satan kept, but they did know that evil was gaining in power and that they had to struggle continuously to keep him out of their hearts. Satan was fighting for his freedom, so this fight for the souls of the inhabitants consumed him. God hadn't wanted this battle. He'd wanted, literally, a Garden of Eden for all eternity for His children. This battle for their souls was the fate of mankind because of their disobedience when they ate of the tree of the knowledge of good and evil. Because of what they did, they had to learn of both good and evil. Because of Satan's rebellion and his desire to obtain mankind for himself, the temptation had occurred and mankind had succumbed. Offering mankind a way to free themselves from their sin, if they made the choice for good of their own free will, was the reason God brought His wonderful plan of salvation into being. All mankind had to struggle with evil because man had disobeyed God and gave in to the temptation Satan brought them, therefore they had to deal with the consequences which resulted from their disobedience and the compounded consequences of the sins of their forefathers. Despite the fall of mankind, God granted a way out for them. This was all a part of the great plan, the feat of engineering which God had created to help every inhabitant. Thus, the plan was incorporated into the natural law of the universe, the physics of things, just as God had orchestrated that the seeds of pure love could grow. Man now had the opportunity to learn of both good and evil and learn that goodness and love could overcome evil.

The angels knew that God's kingdom could only open its doors to those with love in their hearts, real love, not the fake or conditional or selfish kind of love. Only pure, perfect love. Love would work in the life of men similarly to the way a passport or visa gave him permission to enter another country. When men achieved this degree of love, desiring to make restitution for their sins, obtain forgiveness through the sacrifice Christ had made for them, and had a sincerely repentant heart, their names were written in the Lamb's book of life. This became their visa, their passport to enter heaven. This was a required part of the natural law of the universe, the physics of things, which God in His righteousness would not put aside under any circumstances. No man could enter heaven without it. This was why God had developed such a marvelous feat of engineering to bring forth a plan of salvation which would bring love to the hearts of man and provide them with the opportunity to have their sins forgiven. God wanted them to enter His kingdom.

But not all the inhabitants accepted the fact that God had prerequisites for entering heaven. They stubbornly rejected this concept and didn't understand that only through His plan could God ensure that His kingdom and the new world He would create would be free of sin and evil, free of spirits which brought harm and sorrow. These prerequisites assured that heaven would **only** be filled with the pure love of forgiveness, understanding, empathy, and kindness. This was the natural law of the universe, the physics of things, which God had created to help men, to prepare a bride for His Son, and to fill His kingdom for all eternity with those who truly loved. It was out of love that God had made these preparations and had developed this plan to save the inhabitants. Someday all who entered God's kingdom would know this and understand the many great sacrifices and tremendous effort God had made for their sake. But the angels already knew, and they marveled at the incredibly pure and sacrificial love in the heart of God. The angels knew that just as an inhabitant needed a passport to move from one country to another, such a passport was also needed to enter into the kingdom of heaven. The passport the inhabitants needed could only be obtained by a repentant and forgiving heart ruled by pure love and developed by following God's statutes. Those were the rules. Anything less and Satan could claim that God was not a righteous God.

Behind the scenes, in the lower parts of the cold, bleak planet, evil too was planning the fate of mankind. The evil one (also known as Satan, the devil, the serpent, Beelzebub, and Lucifer) was planning and plotting. He watched mankind, looking for weak points, seeking where they were most vulnerable. Inherited sin, the sins committed by the forefathers of the inhabitants, left certain weaknesses in the inhabitants; and the evil one wanted to find these and exploit them. He wanted to stop God from claiming their souls. Satan wanted to remain free; but if he couldn't, he wanted these souls for himself, for all eternity. The evil one had many helpers. These were the fallen angels who Satan had taken out of heaven with him. They were called spirits and powers and principalities. They plagued mankind by whispering of the joys of committing sin, and they laughed gleefully to see men fall prey to their whispers. They especially liked to capture an inhabitant who was struggling to follow God. This caused the most havoc in the lives of the other inhabitants who were living alongside the sinner, those who were also struggling against evil. But God, being omnipotent and all knowing, knew that this would happen and had prepared the hearts of the inhabitants for this eventuality.

In Romans 8:38, the apostle Paul assured the children of God that if they continued stedfast in loving God, they would be all right despite what was happening in their lives. The apostle Paul said, "For I am persuaded, that neither death, nor life, nor angels, nor principalities, nor powers, nor things present, nor things to come, nor height, nor depth, nor any other creature, shall be able to separate us from the love of God, which is in Christ Jesus." He could say this with assurance because he and those with whom he spoke had followed the statutes God laid down for them. As the inhabitants of the cold, bleak planet below began to learn the basics about true and godly love, something new stirred their hearts. They had always been concerned for those who thought as they did, for those under their care, for those related to them. But suddenly they found themselves concerned about those who would not seek God, those who continued to sin, those who were possessed by evil spirits, even those who had brought them harm. This concern was an expansion of their love. It was the beginning of godly love, but they didn't realize this at first. The prayers of these loving inhabitants demonstrated how sincerely they wanted to understand and wanted to stay faithful themselves.

These inhabitants continued working in God's vineyard and did not become pawns to evil. Their prayers told God about their concerns for their personal battle against evil and for what tomorrow would bring to them. Their prayers asked God for help so they could remain strong and faithful. But their prayers also asked God to look after those other inhabitants who were weak or who did not yet understand. This demonstration of true love pleased God, and the angels smiled.

What About Tomorrow?

Dearest Heavenly Father,
I don't know what to do
and so I come in humble prayer to give it unto You.

There are so many problems because a searing fire burns,
looking to destroy me, keep me from the path I yearn.
But, Father, You have taught me where I need to go
when tears erupt and problems seem to overflow.

I've always turned to You, Lord, in patience and in love,
knowing that my help will come from heaven up above.
In the past You've saved me, and I know You will again.
It doesn't matter how it seems to any other men.

You'll rescue me in time, and You will never let me down.
You'll make of me the finest gold and make for me a crown.
If only I will trust You, know you're always there
to give me everything I need with gentle loving care.

So thank You, Heavenly Father, for listening to my plea,
for filling up my heart with trust and being there for me.
But, Father, let me add one thing so You will also hear
that I ask You to look after all the souls I hold so dear.

For many have not understood, many do not know
that You are what they hunger for, not their evil foe.
So help us all, My Father, help everyone to be
found worthy when Christ returns to bring us back to Thee.

Amen

****

As their strength improved and they prayed for others, the inhabitants wondered if those who had died without ever knowing God were forever condemned not to know love, and unable to enter God's kingdom. They understood that many of these people simply had not had anyone to teach them or, worse yet, had the wrong influences in their life. Even as children, some had been taught to follow evil. As the inhabitants pondered these new concerns, they also realized that if they felt badly for these people, surely God did too; and if God did, then surely He had a plan for them. The inhabitants wondered how they could learn what that plan was. The angels were pleased that now not only the role models but many of the other inhabitants had enough love in their hearts to care for others and that they sought a greater understanding of God's plan for unbelievers as well as for themselves. God therefore allowed the angels to whisper to the inhabitants to tell them to pray for the answer to their question. For the inhabitants to learn of this was a part of the natural law of the universe, the physics of things, which God had put into place. Therefore, the inhabitants prayed for answers and God heard them and sent the Holy Spirit into their hearts to tell them of His great and mighty plan for all souls, all who lived and all who died. God filled their hearts with wisdom and asked them to pray for those who had died without gaining an understanding, those who died never having the opportunity to find forgiveness, know the truth, understand pure love as it could exist only through God. God guided them to Romans 14:9 where He explained, "For to this end Christ both died, and rose, and revived, that he might be Lord both of the dead and the living."

The inhabitants began to pray for those who never knew about God, those who fell away, those whose hearts were seeking but not finding God because of the work of the evil spirits. They not only prayed for those living but also those who had died under these circumstances, those in the realms which held the unredeemed dead. Because of their prayers, these realms opened for the remorseful seeking souls to come to grace, and there was great rejoicing because these souls found redemption through Christ. They were helped by the prayers of others. These souls were drawn by the love they sensed in these prayers and they learned where and how they could find grace. God was pleased, and the angels rejoiced....and because of this love from others, many came to God. Many hearts were purified and some to become a part of the Bride for God's Son. The inhabitants read in Revelation 19:7, "Let us be glad and rejoice and give honor to him for the marriage of the lamb is come and his wife hath made herself ready." From these words they recognized that those who were faithful, helping others, and striving to become overcomers were making themselves ready for the return of Christ. As the inhabitants asked questions and conversed with God, coming to Him with a pure heart, and the loving desire to help others, God was pleased. Love was growing, maturing, and strengthening. Evil also saw this and was not happy. So evil attacked because evil hated to see this progress being made. The evil spirits of Satan tempted the inhabitants once again, knowing when they felt hurt or tired, and where they were weak and vulnerable. Evil slithered, cold, cruel, malevolent, across their eyes and into their mouths, filling their heads, to reach their thoughts.

Evil battered the minds of the inhabitants trying to move into their hearts. The spirits hit and hurt; they lied and they hinted that God had lied. They whispered that God was no longer with the inhabitants, that they were all alone. The evil spirits wanted to take away the good from men. They caused fear to rise in them and fill them with sickness and exhaustion. Evil tried to bring the spirits of envy and jealousy into their hearts. But many inhabitants held on and did not let their trust in God waiver. They remembered that evil would have to flee if they resisted. So they stood firm and they resisted. Finally, evil was thwarted because these inhabitants said NO! to these spirits who whispered of cruelty and jealousy, of lust, anger, and rebellion against God. The inhabitants stood their ground knowing that the evil would have to move on if they could just stand strong in God's love. The inhabitants trusted God to bring them through. And God did just that. Again the heavens sang, and the angels rejoiced. The inhabitants' hearts were filled with love and thankfulness because God had done exactly as He promised. The inhabitants had stood firm, had resisted the evil, and trusted God. They felt the warmth in their hearts grow, and they prayed for those still struggling against the evil. Everyone was pleased to see the outflow of this precious love and concern and to see this new strength of conviction. The prayers of the inhabitants changed to reflect this new understanding of how they could trust God when times were bad and how their trust would assure them of a victory against evil. These prayers were music to God's ears.

This Too Shall Pass

When others ask me to pray for them, I always want to say
that all the trials we go through will soon pass away.
But what I say is "wait awhile, and see how God loves you,
for in this He will show himself as loving, good, and true."

How wonderful to think and know that with every awful trial
the end result will come one day when we will wear a smile.
For if we really know this, believe it, trust it, wait,
there's nothing that the evil one can do to change our fate.

For we are here just a little while, a moment in God's time;
and then for all eternity, we'll spend life so sublime.
We'll be the Bride for Christ, God's son, and love His gentle heart,
we'll never ever once again feel Satan's cruel and fiery dart.

We'll eat of milk and honey, we'll walk on streets of gold,
we'll always be protected, we'll never age too old.
We'll sit beneath God's throne of love and listen to His word,
and it will be the sweetest thing that we have ever heard.

The birds will sing a song so sweet, and trees will line the waters;
we'll live in a home Christ built for us; be God's sons and daughters.
We'll live where the sun shines brighter than we've ever seen before,
we'll never shed another tear or go through sorrow anymore.

The angels will sing the most beautiful songs which we can also sing,
flowers will bloom, prophets will speak and death will lose its sting.
We will sit on a throne, wear white robes and carry a beautiful palm,
we will praise God in thanksgiving, and the harps will be our balm.

So thank You, dearest Father, for the seeds that you have sown.
When bad times come again, we'll have Your thoughts, not our own.
We'll remember Your beautiful promises to help us through this day,
to walk through this winding maze, which we know shall pass away.

****

The inhabitants were learning that all their troubles, every care and concern they had, every heartache and disappointment they experienced, came from evil. Evil wanted to destroy them, take from them their faith in God, steal their hope, harm their family relationships and their friendships; so there would be no one to turn to except Satan. If this didn't work, Satan instructed his evil spirits to take the inhabitants' homes, their jobs, their money, their possessions, even their health, so they might blame God for their losses. There wasn't anything that evil would not do. There were no boundaries to evil's cruel nature. It was malevolent. Evil had become stronger, more determined to win and had developed lethal strategies for attacking mankind. It spread across the planet bringing unrest wherever it went, stirring hate in men's hearts whenever it could. Greed became an excellent tool for evil to use, and so the lust for money and possessions was planted in men's hearts, and many men cheated one another and laughed doing it. Power was another tool which evil used as a lust in men's hearts. Many in the world fell to Satan because Satan gave them power in exchange for following him. The lust for power and money ruled many men. These inhabitants could no longer find God, nor could they find or give love. Their hearts grew cold and they didn't care. They had money, and they had power and believed that they didn't need God. God had warned the inhabitants that this could happen and said in Matthew 24:12: "And because iniquity shall abound, the love of many shall wax cold."

The consequence of iniquity and the consequence of a cold heart which held no love was eternal separation from God. Satan was pleased. Evil's cruelty expanded to actions which God said in His Holy Bible was an abomination to Him. But many did not have any concern for this and made excuses for those actions. The evil spirits found those who would succumb to their whispers of power and money, jealousy and hate, cruel acts of retribution to those who disagreed with them, and to actions and activities which God hated. Terrible wars broke out all across the cold, bleak planet which spun in its agony beneath the land of the angels. Hatred abounded and plotting and theft were committed within families and communities. Many inhabitants were murdered, many tortured and abused. Husbands mistreated their wives, children disobeyed their parents, and men turned upon one another in a frightening hatred. Evil inspired these inhabitants to commit some of these atrocities in the name of God. Evil was overjoyed when God was blamed for the tragic and evil things that were happening in the world. The battle between good and evil was in full force, and evil clapped its hands together in glee. Some of the inhabitants became very frightened when they saw these deeds. They wondered what they should do, asked where they could hide. Many wondered why God allowed these terrible things to happen in the world. Many even demanded to know how a God of love could allow such atrocities to occur. Their questions caused some of the inhabitants to fall away from God because the whispers of evil made them doubt what God said. When they began to doubt God, doubt that this was the end times which God had warned them about, they listened more avidly to the whispers of evil and evil entered their hearts. They hadn't grasped the fact that they had brought this on themselves. They had opened the door for Satan to show them what evil was when they ate of the tree of this knowledge and the inherited sin of their ancestors added to their troubles as did their own sins. Evil had gained a stronghold in the hearts of many, but others remained faithful to God, understanding that what was happening was separating good from evil.

The faithful understood that a great battle was raging for their souls. They understood that God would see them through, that He had a plan for their long-term redemption. They believed that no matter what happened to their environment or to their bodies, God would make it right in the end. They dug in their heels, and decided of their own free will to trust God and wait. They knew that they needed to pray and to support one another through these evil times. Many of God's prophets died at the hands of evil, never denouncing God, always trusting Him. Joyfully, many inhabitants held onto their love for God and for one another and keep it firmly and safely in their hearts. They kept their trust in God alive. They also hung onto their hope that in time God's promises would be fulfilled. They believed that, though life's circumstances were grim, God would make everything right for those who loved Him. They read in 2 Esdras 2:14 in the Apocrypha, "Take heaven and earth to witness; for I have broken the evil in pieces, and created the good: as surely as I live, saith the Lord." Their prayers reflected their loyalty to God and how fully that loyalty lived, unconquered and undiminished, in their hearts.

Whom Shall I Fear?

There is a choir song we sing about the Lord's protections
even when others are plotting to hurt us by their transgressions.
It tells us that we need not fear, the Lord is by our side
even when the waters threaten from an ever-rising tide.

Joshua and David met their foes and the Lord helped them win,
For God was on their side as they went to fight against sin.
Even when the odds seemed slim and success seemed far away,
at just the perfect moment, God stepped in to save the day.

Thus what we must remember and keep within our heart
is that God is always with us to the finish from the start.
He may seem slow in coming, for impatience fills our soul;
but come He will and just in time, for that's His stated goal.

He'll mold and love and lead us, keep us safe inside His hand
so we will be together in His perfect promised land.

He'll redeem us as His children, forever in His heart,
We'll be the bride for Christ His Son and never have to part.

****

The angels could read between the lines of these prayers and see that the inhabitants were doing their best to reinforce their faith. Many inhabitants were being uplifted by what they read of the role models in the Bible, of the battles that they too had endured. So the angels whispered to these faithful inhabitants to read the Holy Bible so they would be strengthened. Thus the inhabitants found these words in Revelation 2:10, which said, "Fear none of those things which thou shalt suffer: behold the devil shall cast some of you into prison. That ye may be tried; and ye shall have tribulation ten days: Be thou faithful unto death, and I will give thee a crown of life." These words helped the inhabitants immensely. They turned to the Holy Bible for additional help so they could repeat it's words and stories to as many as would listen. In Revelation 3:10 they read, "Because thou hast kept the word of my patience, I also will keep thee from the hour of temptation, which shall come upon all the world, to try them that dwell upon the earth."

All of this was a part of God's plan, the one incorporated into the natural law of the universe, the physics of things, to bring His people through the days of evil. The inhabitants met in fellowship as often as they could so they could uplift one another. They understood that this time of tribulation had to occur as the forces of good and evil battled for their souls. They prayed and asked God to help them safeguard their trust in Him. They prayed for one another, and they continued stedfast in the apostle's doctrine for what they should do to please God and obtain His protection. They found another text in

Revelation 7:13,14 which helped them: *"And one of the elders answered, saying unto me, What are these which are arrayed in white robes? And whence came they?...... And he said to me, These are they which came out of great tribulation......."* The inhabitants understood God's words. They realized that the power which evil had would bring great troubles to them, but the power of their love for God and the trust they had developed in God would sustain them through this time of evil. If they held fast in their faith, repented their sins, and took Holy Communion to forgive them, they would remain safe. They would emerge as tried in the fire, pure and precious like gold. Now with their new understanding of why they had to suffer and convinced that God would bring them through this time of tribulation to eternal love, they sought to help as many others as possible to understand this.

How Can I Help My Family?

Sometimes a loved one will choose to walk in a very dangerous way.
I don't know how to help them, prevent them from going astray.
When I speak they won't listen think I don't understand their need;
it's just that I see the danger, for to God's word they pay no heed.

While I know there are times when no matter how hard I may try,
circumstances come no matter how many tears that I cry.
But I trust God has a solution; will guide them in all that they do,
for I taught them correctly when their innocent hearts were new.

And if I've laid the proper foundation, offered for them and I pray,
I know God listens and watches, protects my loved ones each day.

He will prompt the longing to return to His precepts, His love,
and a longing to seek the altar, find forgiveness, and Heaven above.

My job is to continue to trust God, to teach through my example;
so when loved ones leave the altar, they won't like the evil they sample

May I never grow weary of praying, continue to love above all,
and believe that God will not fail them even if sometimes they fall.

May joy fill my heart with God's love and all His promises too
that God desires all to be saved and His word is perfect and true.

****

The inhabitants didn't yet know it, but some of them were very
close to finishing their training. They were only a few short steps from
the finish line when God's words would be firmly embedded in their
hearts along with the promise that God's Son would come for them.
When Christ returned at the First Resurrection, He would show
them the mansions He had built for them. They would be given
celestial bodies free from pain and sorrow. They would be taken from
the cold, bleak planet to experience the perfect love of the Father, the
Son, and the Holy Spirit for all eternity. These thoughts were not
only their hope but now their firm belief. These were thoughts and
wisdom which God had placed into their hearts. They were the
promises God had written into His Holy Bible so the inhabitants
could learn and become God's peculiar people. The inhabitants longed
for the great day when all their hope and all they believed would be
fulfilled. The devil, Satan....who had once been the highest angel in

heaven before he rebelled out of jealousy and was thrown out of heaven......wanted mankind for himself. But all who followed Satan would live in constant disobedience, envy, hate and lies. They would be banned from heaven forever. Spiritual death would come to those separated from God. This was called the second death, and it was for all eternity. There were only two choices open to mankind: to follow Satan and evil, or to follow God and good. There was nothing else to choose from. If some inhabitants were "lukewarm," they would eventually have to follow Satan, for God could not let these "fence-sitters" enter the kingdom of heaven. In Revelation 3:16 God warned, "So then, because thou art lukewarm, and neither cold nor hot, I will spue thee out of my mouth." It was arrogant of these men to think that they did not have to make a commitment, to think that they were okay as they were. Satan made them think: "Who is God to tell me what I have to do? And why should I take the words of the Bible literally?"

Sometimes, in their arrogance, men could not grasp that good and evil were their only choices and that there was a firm line between them. But God, in His infinite love and His understanding of the difficulty man had as he fought evil, was patient. He would wait until men had a greater understanding of both good and evil before He sent His Son to end this time of training. God wanted all men to be saved, so He would wait until all could have the opportunity to learn. In Timothy 2:3-4, they learned, "For this is good and acceptable in the sight of God our Savior; who would have all men to be saved, and to come into the knowledge of the truth." Here God was explaining His patience and His desire. But this did not mean that God would wait forever. There was a deadline. In the meantime, while men learned, God gave them great blessings so they could recognize His love and know that He was with them through everything. The blessings of God were found in their families, their friends, their homes and congregations, even in their countries.....especially those that saw peace. The blessings were in everything they saw and touched and ate if they would look for them and appreciate them. God gave them an extraordinary creation to enjoy despite the fact that because of Satan, it held the ugly evil which lived in the bowels of their planet. God opened men's understanding to see His love and the majesty in His creation, but Satan would use this too in his efforts to hurt the inhabitants. This was what the inhabitants were to learn next in the great and magnificent plan of salvation which God had put into place in the natural law of the universe, the physics of things.

For with God
nothing will be impossible.

—Luke 1:37

Chapter Eight
Elements of the Creation

The Poems of Chapter Eight

Look at the birds of the air,
for they neither sow nor reap
nor gather into barns;
yet your heavenly Father feeds them.
Are you not of more value than they?

Matthew 6:26

The inhabitants followed the word of God, resisted evil, and helped one another through good times and bad. Love grew in their hearts, and God was pleased. But during this period of time, evil had been planning its next attack. Evil had grown even stronger by carefully plotting its next move. Its hatred was kindled as it watched the progress of the inhabitants. It was true that love begat love, but it was also true that evil begat evil, and so evil strengthened itself to ready itself to wage a battle and win. Evil's hatred was therefore at its peak and waiting for the right opportunity to strike. When it saw that the inhabitants were thankful for the blessings God had given them, it saw that here was an opportunity to turn those blessings to its own advantage. If evil could twist the inhabitant's thankfulness to its own purpose, it would succeed in its quest to distract the inhabitants from their godly purpose. Slowly—like a snake slithering through the brush, hidden, sly, subtle and deadly—evil turned the inhabitants thankfulness into something that God abhorred.

The inhabitants grew crops of corn and wheat, vegetables and fruits. Some they kept, some they sold, and some they traded. They depended upon these crops for their livelihood and were thankful that God provided the crops for them and thankful when God sent the rain and the sun to nourish them. It was through this need that evil saw an opportunity to turn the inhabitants thankfulness into a great admiration for the sun and the rain because these elements were necessary to the successful harvest of their crops. Therefore, slowly, ever so slowly, insidiously, slyly, subtly, evil worked to turn the inhabitant's thankfulness for of the elements of God's creation into adulation. Before evil began its new attack, the inhabitants had rejoiced about the power of God and what God had created for them. They wrote stories and poems about the magnificence of what God had created.

Dawn

Arise, awake; see the beautiful dawn,
the glistening dewdrops upon the lawn.
Drink in the beauty that lies thereof
and remember that God made this with His love.

The flowers, the trees, the beautiful earth,
all these were given to us at birth.
A gift and a promise from God to thee,
is all nature's beauty for us to see.

The deer in the forest, the lamb in the glen,
lions on the plain, and the bear in his den.
These wondrous creations, amazing to me,
touch my heart with the glory of God that we see.

As we arise with the dawn; note God's gifts all around;
we can witness the miracle and let it astound.

For this brings to our hearts What God sends from above,
to help us discover the depth of His love.

****

Evil knew the thoughts of men and knew how much they appreciated what God had given them. But evil had a plan to turn this appreciation into something more, something evil. In fact, evil knew exactly what would upset God and turn God's people away from Him. So it stopped the rain for a time and sat back, gleefully wringing its hands in pleasure as the inhabitants watched their crops die. The inhabitants prayed for rain, but it did not come because Satan held it back. Evil whispered into the hearts of the inhabitants that God had left them. Evil told them that the rains did not come because they had never honoured the rain for what it gave them. In time, the inhabitants forgot to trust God, they forgot to be patient and wait for Him. They began to worry about their crops. They began to listen to the whispers of evil. At first they resisted what the evil told them to do, not feeling quite right about honouring the rain for what it brought their crops. The inhabitants knew that God controlled the rain. In fact, they knew that God controlled everything on their planet and more. In Psalm 33:6 they had read, "By the word of the Lord the heavens were made, and all the host in them by the breath of His mouth, He gathers the waters of the sea together as a heap; He lays up the deep in storehouses. Let all the earth fear the Lord; Let all the inhabitants of the world stand in awe of Him. For He spoke, and it was done; He commanded, and it stood fast." But as the inhabitant's anxiety level rose from the failure of their crops and evil whispered more often, the words which evil brought them seemed to make sense until finally the inhabitants capitulated. Desperate to save their crops, they praised the rain, and they sang and danced to the rain asking for its favor. Evil smiled its cruel, malicious smile and danced its own gleeful dance of triumph. This was only the beginning of what evil planned to do. Evil whispered again, and man began to perform rituals to please the rain god. Evil whispered once again, and man also praised the sun and the moon and the stars for helping the rain. Man began to pray to the rain asking the rain to bless their crops, and soon many of the inhabitants had adopted many gods to whom they prayed. The creation, with which God had blessed His people, became a subject for worship. Evil had once again broken into the minds of men. Men had forgotten that they once praised only God for the wonder and gifts of the creation.

Ocean Depths

The sea is a wonderful thing to watch; have you ever wondered why?
Where the crests of waves stretch to the awesome heights of the sky.
In this wonderful creation we can easily see
what God has created just for you and for me.

We can ponder the sea; its soothing scenes; see God's power in this.
Accept the gifts He's provided for us, in joy and total bliss.
But even through this incredible feat there's power, danger, and fear.
We learn from God's Creation, He's in control of all we hold dear.

We have our concerns and worries which seem acted out by the sea,
in its never-ending motion and the threats of its depths for its fee.
As we feel the fear of the storms, we run and cringe and cower.

For our stress and tension seem so like the sea's churning power.

Is the anger we feel represented by waves crashing upon the shore?
Are fears parallel to the ocean depths where danger lurks and more?
When the storms of life seem burdensome like storms upon the sea,
time always fights in the battle, and the sun makes the clouds flee!

Then we turn only to God the Creator to help us in times of need,
we turn only to God for everything, in praise, in word, and in deed.

****

The angels watched as great turmoil erupted on the planet below their heavenly abode. They watched as the inhabitants began to worship the creation instead of God despite what they had once written about the creation. The angels were concerned when they saw that the inhabitants had accepted evils lies and believed that the sun blessed their crops of its own accord, not by God's command, and that the rain watered their crops, also of its own power, not by God's power. The inhabitants had forgotten that God powered all the elements and that while their planet was beautiful in many aspects it was bleak and cold from lack of love and lack of understanding and from the evil which destroyed everything God loved. If only the inhabitants could see the land of heaven and how beautiful it was, how its beauty was perfect because of the love which emanated from God and from His Son. If only they could realize how life without evil could be? the angels thought. How could they even think that their sun and stars and rain were worthy of worship? This was a sad day in heaven. God had warned the inhabitants not to worship the creation. In Job

36:27 of the Holy Bible, they'd learned that only God could make the rain, for scripture said, "For he maketh small the drops of water; they pour down rain according to the vapour thereof; which clouds do drop and distil upon man abundantly." And in Job 37:3 and in Job 37:14, they learned, "He directeth it under the whole heaven, and the lightning unto the ends of the earth."

Nevertheless, the inhabitants set up altars at which they worshipped the sun and the stars and those elements they desired to favor their lives. They sought an easy and tangible way to control what they wanted and when they wanted it. They had become arrogant and spoiled, once again, because of the whispers of evil. They had listened to the words of evil, the words which broke their trust in God. They had been tempted, and they had succumbed to that temptation. They conceived of many gods, they built altars and statues, they chanted, and they brought offerings to these created things. And their enemy smiled. Their enemy—the sly, wicked, and subtle Satan—smiled in glee and danced in circles, laughing. He knew that it would take a long time for the inhabitants to find their way back to what God had been trying so hard to teach them. Satan, the enemy of mankind, was happy with what the inhabitants were doing and hoped that they would forget God. Satan was pleased, but God was angry. Psalm 78:58 described what the inhabitants had done that made God angry: "For they provoked him to anger with their high places, and moved him to jealousy with their graven images." The inhabitants had not only brought danger to their souls by what they were doing, but they had angered God and greatly disappointed Him. In Isaiah 47:13, God had warned the inhabitants about worshipping the stars or moon or sun: "Thou are wearied in the multitude of thy counsels.

Let now the astrologers, the stargazers, the monthly prognosticators, stand up, and save thee from these things that shall come upon thee."

There were many other areas in the Bible which warned of this as well. Despite these warnings the people continued to worship other gods for many years. They did much that was wrong in the sight of God, and their enemy rewarded their misconduct with earthly treasure. But the enemy could not restore the heavenly treasure of love to their hearts. That only came from God, from the purity of their loving relationship with Him. As the inhabitants fell further away from God, they seemed, for a while to have all they wanted. Their crops had the sun and the rain they needed to grow. The inhabitants were well fed and everyone seemed content. Except for one thing. The warmth they once knew was missing. They realized that a deep and bitter emptiness had invaded their hearts, replacing the warmth which had been so special to them. They remembered that in the past they had been cold and isolated when the warmth of love left their hearts and that this happened only when they left God. So some began to question what they were doing, why the warmth had left. They tried to see more clearly where they had gone wrong and what needed to be changed. They began to understand that by worshipping idols they had left the statutes of God and had lost their love by being separated from Him. Deep in the recesses of their heart, they knew that God was displeased. They knew they had done wrong. In time, the enemy began to lose his foothold because the inhabitants recognized that their hearts were empty. So....many turned back to God. They recognized what they had lost and their worship of idols and their offerings diminished until they seemed unable to appease the sun or the stars or the moon or the rain or to guarantee the crops.

But most of all, the inhabitants began to recognize the unrighteousness of what they had done. They realized that they had to make a choice, that to have God's blessing they had to heed His words, and many prayed the words they'd read in Psalm 79:7: "Turn us again, O God of hosts, and cause thy face to shine; and we shall be saved."

Finally, the sly and coveting evil which had been living in their hearts became evident to the inhabitants. As the evil spirits screamed their anger at the new prayers which the inhabitants had begun sending to the heavens hoping again to reach God, evil could no longer hold the hearts of the inhabitants. Many began to see that the spirits they now served and the new gods they worshipped didn't care about love or virtue. They began to see that the few rewards they had received from worshipping other gods had come from Satan, from evil, and were certainly not worth what they had lost. They wanted the warmth back. They wanted the goodness of God in their hearts. Then the inhabitants began to recall what they had learned about the spirits of their world and how these spirits could enter the hearts of the inhabitants to turn them away from love and from God, and they became afraid. They recognized that they had not placed God first; they had succumbed to the other gods they'd been warned about. They had forgotten that they had been commanded in Exodus 20:3: "Thou shalt have no other gods before me. Thou shalt not make unto thee any graven image, or any likeness of anything that is in heaven above, or that is in the earth beneath; or that is in the water under the earth: Thou shalt not bow down to them, nor serve them; for I the Lord thy God am a jealous God, visiting the iniquity of the fathers upon the children unto the third and fourth generation of them that hate me." They wondered if God would forgive them. They saw that they had done a terrible thing and had angered God and that God was silent. Even when they prayed in repentance, they did not hear Him any longer in their hearts. He no longer whispered His love and direction into their hearts. They heard no inspiration from God's Spirit.

With this gone, with no guidance, no goodness, no warmth, they were frightened; and they weren't sure what they should do. Those few who had remained faithful and had seen what had happened to the hearts of many of the inhabitants, gathered them together, and explained that they had done just what God had warned them not to do. They showed these inhabitants how they had followed other gods and had allowed evil spirits into their hearts. The inhabitants who had remained faithful told them that they must go immediately to break apart the new altars, scatter the offerings, and pray fervently for forgiveness for what they had done. When God saw that they did this, saw that they tried to make restitution for what they had done and heard their prayers, He looked into their hearts for sincere repentance. And when he saw their sincerity and their remorse, He forgave them and told them to remember the lesson they had experienced. But in His loving kindness, God told them that they did not have to feel guilt after they repented because God's grace was sufficient for them. Sadly however, there were some who did not repent and would not destroy their altars to other gods or scatter their offerings. Their hearts were hardened against God's word. These separated from the others and were now used by the enemy to harm the ones who had returned to God. The angels saw this too and wondered what the inhabitants would do to protect themselves from the terrible spirits and from the inhabitants who followed these spirits. The angels knew that these spirits of Satan were the tempters, that they belonged to evil. They knew that allowing them to continue to work their evil was a part of the righteousness of God and the warning God had placed in His great engineering plan which was His way to help the people learn of evil so they would hunger for good. The angels also knew that those who continued to follow these spirits were capable of hate and would instill rifts between the children of God to bring hurt to them. These inhabitants could become what would be termed the "goats" on judgment day and be cast into the lake of fire with Satan. This was, after all, just the natural law of the universe, the physics of things, as God had foreordained to bring to His son a perfect Bride and to Himself a perfect people.

Those who had repented grew in wisdom and began to write down all the things they had learned so they would not make so many mistakes in the future. They started at the beginning with what they'd learned of prayer and of hope, of trusting God, of helping one another and striving to be an example to others. Now they could add the warning not to seek other gods. They realized that if they wanted to follow God and not succumb to evil, they needed to immerse themselves in God's words. They needed to study the great book which God had inspired the prophets and apostles and others who had been the role models in earlier days, to write and hand down through many generations to help mankind. This was a part of the great engineering plan written into the natural law of the universe, the physics of things, which God had set up to protect and provide for those who would love Him. Because they had prayed with a sincere heart for forgiveness, God had forgiven the inhabitants, and they began to make progress again. God watched them as they grew in maturity and began to understand and determined in their hearts to learn more about God's words and follow them. The plan was moving ahead and would satisfy God's righteousness and ensure that Satan could never again make a claim on mankind. In time, evil would be confined for all eternity and love would prevail. The inhabitants shared their thoughts and continued in fellowship with one another so they could help one another remain strong in faith.   The angels loved these new conversations and laughed when they heard the lighthearted conversations of the inhabitants, which demonstrated their newfound happiness

Did God Create the Hot Fudge Sundae?

God gave us animals and crops to harvest, He gave them out of love.
Berries from the ground, fruits from trees, He sent us from above.
We also learned from the gifts God sent how to make special treats.
And best of all, we've also learned to make the most delicious sweets.

There is one that is our favorite, one with which we are impressed;
this is the tall, cold and creamy one; yes, sundaes are the best.
The flavor doesn't seem to matter; it's the rich, dark chocolate fudge.
That's what makes the sundae great and the choice of any judge.

We wish we had the nerve to eat more than one, maybe two or three;
but perhaps we'd be glad we didn't, for how awfully sick we'd be.
What a special treat to really splurge, and maybe even taste
one topped with nuts and lots of cream, which would not go to waste!

Yes, we are chocoholics, and weaken every time
we see a hot fudge sundae, but is that such a crime?
For when God gave wonderful food, didn't He plan for sundaes too?
He let us glimpse what Heaven holds so we'd want to be there too!

****

God smiled and often chuckled to hear the light hearts of the inhabitants speak with so much joy and thankfulness. The inhabitants entered another period of reflection, a time when they searched the Holy Bible for everything that could help them learn and help them rebuke the evil when it came for them again. They knew it would come again. They realized that their tests would become more difficult, and there would also come a time when they would have to make this great and final choice between good and evil on their own. The inhabitants read about how God would try men's hearts and that this process would purify their hearts so they would be ready to enter the kingdom of heaven. Job 23:10 taught them, "But He knows the way that I take; when He has tested me, I shall come forth as gold." The inhabitants spoke to one another and to their children and when they had fellowship with others. They discussed what they would need to be found worthy. They wondered what would help them withstand the days of temptation, the days when they would be tried by God to see what they were made of.

God wanted a Bride for His Son who would love Him and be loyal to Him and do so with all her heart. Loyalty was very important to God because it meant that you would never leave or forsake someone you loved no matter what happened. The inhabitants whose hearts had now returned to God wanted to be ready, wanted to be prepared so they would not fail. They wanted to please God, give something back. They longed to do good, and they also wanted to be a part of heaven. They wanted to see the streets paved with gold and feel themselves enveloped in perfect love. There were a multitude of reasons why they wanted this, and they each gave and sought help and encouragement from one another. They were keeping one another's hope alive. Then when evil came again and knocked upon the heart's doors of these inhabitants, evil would have to leave if it could find no way to enter. The Holy Spirit resided in the hearts of the inhabitants because of the goodness they tried to espouse and because when they did sin, when they made their mistakes, they were sorry and they repented. They took Holy Communion with a humble heart asking God to forgive them and thanking Him for the sacrifice He made for them which enabled them to have this gift of forgiveness. Evil was angry and tried over and over again to gain access to their hearts, but for now, evil could not. But evil knew that it would have another chance to tempt and possibly win these souls, for the days of refinement were not finished. Evil waited to grow in strength again for that terrible day when it could attack with fierce determination and with great, horrible power, hoping to break man, hoping to make him renounce God. The inhabitants tried their best to prepare for that day. As they talked with one another and listened to their teachers, the wisdom of their elders, and read the word of God, they spoke of what it meant to be tried like gold in the fire. The angels could see that the inhabitants did understand what this meant. The angels could see how God's great and magnificent plan was working, the plan which God placed into the natural law of the universe, the physics of things, to help the inhabitants triumph through the dreadful days of refining; the end times.

Diamonds and Gold

Gold is highly valued, beautiful, durable, and sought by many.
But gold can only be produced after suffering intense heat.
Diamonds are also highly valued, durable and very beautiful.
But these can only be produced after intense pressure and shaping.
Our Heavenly Father is creating a Heaven, which he wants to fill
with beauty and perfection, with things durable and valued.
And those things are us. We gain compassion, learn of love and
have an understanding heart after we are molded and developed.
Because of sin, we are difficult to mold and cannot do it alone.
We can only be developed through the grace of God and when He
directs the intense heat and the pressure to help us reach this goal, we
can rest assured that He never gives us more than we can carry. He
gives us victory over the circumstances we have endured. Thus we can
be thankful for times of pain, knowing that this is when we grow.
We can ask our Heavenly Father to help us learn quickly.
We can tell Him that we are thankful for the pain, the lesson, the
growth, the opportunities, the failures which lead to victory.
For without these things would we be the person we are today?
Without God's love and His promise not to give us more that we can
bear, we would not have successfully been tried and made into
something of great value. Perhaps, without our experiences of pain,
we would not have needed, would not have sought, and found, God.

****

As the angels heard these words, they rejoiced. They knew that finally, the inhabitants were truly preparing themselves and seeking success in overcoming evil. Their understanding seemed so much greater now. But there would come another phase in God's great plan for the inhabitants which allowed the inhabitants to use their own minds and hearts and their own free will, to ask questions, to ponder the work of salvation, to understand it. Then they would have to decide to whom they would be loyal; God and goodness or Satan and evil. The inhabitants now embarked on a time when they would converse with one another and with their ministers, and form questions which could be answered from the wisdom they would find in the Holy Bible. Their questions would come from their imperfect mind but would be answered by God's perfect wisdom if they had an open and seeking heart. God wanted them to want to learn. He did not want fence-sitters, those who were lukewarm.

The inhabitants were to learn that not every question had an answer which they were capable of understanding, that some things would remain a mystery which God would reveal to them only when they reached heaven. They would have to take some things on faith and that this could only be accomplished if they truly trusted God. But God would reveal incredible truths to them as they studied His words. He would remove the veil from their eyes and open their understanding. They would learn many things. Only a few things would remain unrevealed. They read in 2 Corinthians 3:14, "But their minds were blinded: for until this day remaineth the same vail untaken away in the reading of the old testament; which vail is done away with in Christ." The inhabitants realized that the Bible was very precious yet a mystery to many, but that God would open their understanding of the mysteries in the Bible to those with a pure and truly seeking, loving heart. The prophet Esdras had asked God to give him understanding, asking in 2 Esdras 4:22, "Then answered I and said: I beseech thee, O Lord let me have understanding." In 2 Esdras 4:26 God answered, saying, "Then answered he me and said, The more thou searchest the more thou shalt be astonished." And in 2 Esdras 9:25, God said, "And if thou will implore the Most High without ceasing, I will come and talk with thee."

For where your treasure is,
there will your heart be also.

—Matthew 6:21

Chapter Nine
The Answers to Our Questions

The Poems of Chapter Nine

Now we have received not the spirit of the world,
but the spirit which is of God:
that we might know the things
that are freely given to us of God.

—1 Corinthians 2:12

As the inhabitants grew in faith, they had many questions to ask. They believed that if they could have their questions answered they would grow in understanding and that a greater understanding would help them when their enemy attacked again. They understood that the enemy was more angry and powerful than ever before because they truly loved God and asked His help to find a way to turn evil away. They realized that evil was determined to plague those who followed God. Now they wanted to understand why this enemy had such an evil agenda. They knew that Satan was fighting for his life and had to stop God from obtaining the number of souls He wanted. But they wanted to know how such evil had come into Satan's heart and what would happen to him if they could defeat him. God saw that the inhabitants were ready to learn; they were ready to have their questions answered. So God opened the inhabitants' understanding of His words in the Holy Bible.

He also opened the understanding of their ministers, those who taught these words to the inhabitants. And they began to learn about evil. This was an important step for it was difficult to fight what you didn't understand. Thus, as the inhabitants asked their questions of their own free will and God answered them. Again, this was just a part of the progression of the natural law of the universe, the physics of things. It was still the magnificent plan God had put into place so the inhabitants would learn what they needed to know to be prepared for the First Resurrection. God revealed the story of evil to the inhabitants by way of the Holy Bible which explained that evil, the enemy of all mankind, had been cast out of the beautiful verdant land way above the cold and bleak planet because evil and goodness could not be allowed to live together. They learned that evil always tried to corrupt what was good and that evil had begun in the heart of the most beautiful angel in heaven because that angel became jealous of Christ, the Son of God. The angel's name was Lucifer, and he had lived in the heavens with the Father, the Son, and the Holy Spirit and all the angels. The Bible explained that there was a hierarchy in the realm of the angels, and Lucifer held one of the highest positions. He was extremely beautiful, and because of his beauty, he was called the son of the morning and was given the great privilege of sitting on the left side of God's throne. Christ, the Son of God, sat on the right side of God's throne and Lucifer began to envy Christ because the right side of God was the most esteemed position. Lucifer was at first covetous of Christ's position, then envious, and finally jealous. His jealousy ate at him and brought anger into his heart.

And thus was born an evil heart, a heart filled with covetousness, envy, jealousy, and anger. These evils had filled Lucifer's heart so full that it pushed love completely out. With love gone and these evil emotions in place, hate could increase. Lucifer was also angry because God had said that He planned to exalt mankind to a position above the angels. This too had made Lucifer jealous. As Lucifer's mind and heart raged against what God had given Christ, and what He planned for mankind, Lucifer plotted to overthrow God and Christ, and exalt his own throne above the stars of God. To further explain this to the inhabitants, God directed them to a portion of the Holy Bible which explained what had happened in heaven. In Isaiah 14:12-15, the inhabitants read, "How art thou fallen from heaven, O Lucifer, son of the morning! How art thou cut down to the ground, which did weaken the nations! For thou hast said in thine heart, I will ascend into heaven, I will exalt my throne above the stars of God; ....I will be like the most high. Yet thou shalt be brought down to hell, to the sides of the pit." As Lucifer's jealousy and personal ambition grew, his hatred toward God also grew. As his heart hardened toward all things good, Lucifer formed a plan to overthrow God and become the ruler of heaven and of mankind and of all the angels and of all the creation. Pride filled his heart and rebellion filled his mind. Soon he was whispering his ambitions to other angels telling them that if they left God, he would give them a high position when he became ruler. Lucifer had been the most beautiful angel of all. God had loved him and had given him many blessings. But Lucifer could not accept being in second place, being second to God's Son, Jesus Christ. Envy of Christ's position in God's heart ate at him. This made him discontent with the position God had ordained for him and Lucifer lost his love through his envy. God had placed that love in his heart by loving him first, but Lucifer threw it away in his discontent. Without love, his heart filled with anger and jealousy, and these emotions began to rule his life.

So Lucifer began to garner the help of some of the angels by promising them that they would rule with him when he overthrew the power of God. He was so exceedingly beautiful, strong, and winsome; and he was so eloquent and beguiling in his speech that these angels believed his lies and were persuaded to follow him. Therefore when Lucifer waged war against God, one third of all the angels in heaven joined his rebellion. But God easily defeated Lucifer and the rebelling angels and because of what he had done, God told Lucifer that he had to leave heaven forever along with those angels who had sided with Lucifer. They, along with Lucifer, were cast to earth, to the cold, bleak planet below the land of the angels, below the great palace upon the high mountain in the heavens. Michael, the archangel was given the responsibility of seeing that Lucifer and the angels who had rebelled left heaven and were cast down onto the earth where they were to remain until they would be placed into the lake of fire. The Holy Bible explained this in Revelation 12:7-9: "And there was war in heaven: Michael and his angels fought against the dragon and the dragon fought and his angels, and prevailed not; neither was their place found any more in heaven. And the dragon was cast out. That old serpent, called the devil, and Satan, which deceiveth the whole world; he was cast out into the earth, and his angels were cast out with him."

When Lucifer and his evil angels reached the cold, bleak planet below the heavens, they lost their angel status. They became evil spirits also called evil powers and principalities and dominions, and Lucifer's name was changed to Satan. Satan was also called serpent, Beelzebub, the evil one, and the devil. It became Satan's goal to destroy the children of God who lived on the earth because he knew that God planned to develop a Bride for His Son from these inhabitants. God also planned to create a new heaven and a new earth and destroy the old earth when the bride was developed. When those plans came to pass, Satan and the evil spirits would be cast into the lake of fire. Therefore, Satan needed to prevent God from reaching His goal. But God had already put a plan into place which would prevent Satan from destroying those God chose. Even though Satan knew God's plan, knew the natural law of the universe, and the physics of things which God had instituted, he plotted ways to stop God's plan from moving ahead. Satan knew that he could not change what God had put into motion, but he could work to prevent or at least delay its completion. He knew what had been written in the Holy Bible about God's plan of salvation and therefore he knew about his own end. His only option was to delay God's plan so he could put off.... for as long as possible.... what would happen to him. For when God's plan of salvation was completed, Satan and his spirit helpers would be thrown into hell for one thousand years.

Revelation 20:1-2 explained Satan's end by saying: "And I saw an angel come down from heaven, having the key of the bottomless pit and a great chain in his hand. And he laid hold on the dragon, that old serpent, which is the Devil, and Satan, and bound him a thousand years." Satan did not want to be bound, nor locked into the bottomless pit for a thousand years, so he had to fight God's plan of salvation by preventing mankind from accepting God and following His will. He had to stop God from obtaining that special number of inhabitants which He wanted for the bride of His son and for His kingdom. When God obtained that number, God would send Christ to fetch them from the cold, bleak planet; and Satan would be bound into the pit, the lake of fire. It was interesting to the inhabitants to finally understand why Satan fought so hard to stop them from becoming children of God. But this brought more questions to their minds. What was the great tribulation which would begin three and one half years before Christ returned for His bride? Who would Christ take when He returned, and where would they go? Why was Satan going to be released after the thousand years was up? What would be happening during that thousand years when Satan would be bound? What would happen when he was loosed again? God moved to answer all their questions by directing them to scripture and opening their understanding of His words. They began to read about how deceptive Satan was and found that even the scriptures identified Satan as a deceiver of all of mankind. In Revelation 20:3, God explained that Satan had even fooled entire nations. "And . . . cast him into the bottomless pit, and shut him up, and set a seal upon him, that he should deceive the nations no more."

As the inhabitants realized what was to happen to Satan, they understood so much more about why Satan attacked them with such force. God continued to open their understanding, and soon they also learned that there were two periods of time when God would allow the inhabitants to be made ready to inhabit the new heaven and earth. The first period would end when the First Resurrection occurred and Christ returned for the inhabitants who had prepared themselves, the ones who would become the Bride of Christ, the kings and priests, to rule with Christ and help Christ bring testimony during the thousand years when Satan would be bound. These were called the overcomers, the firstfruits of God's harvest. When Christ came for His bride it would be called the First Resurrection. The inhabitants who would be taken by Christ on that day were, according to the Bible.... to number 144,000. These would be the firstfruits of God's labor.

Revelation 7:4 explained: "And I heard the number of them which were sealed; and there were sealed an hundred and forty and four thousand.........." And in Revelation 14:3, "And......no man could learn that song but the hundred and forty and four thousand which were redeemed from the earth." Some of these would govern and teach during the thousand-year kingdom of peace when Satan would finally be bound. Some would be kings and were described in scripture in Revelation 20:4: "And I saw thrones, and they that sat upon them . . . and they lived and reigned with Christ a thousand years." Those who sat on these thrones would be the kings who God would appoint from his firstfruits, the overcomers taken by Christ in the First Resurrection. Some would be the priests of whom God foretold in Revelation 20:6: "Blessed and holy is he that hath part in the first Resurrection; ......they shall be priests of God and of Christ, and shall reign with him a thousand years." And in Revelation 7:16-17, "They shall hunger no more, neither thirst any more . . . For the Lamb which is in the midst of the throne shall feed them, and shall lead them unto living fountains of waters: and God shall wipe away all tears from their eyes."

But before this great day came and the number God longed for was fulfilled, great tribulation would come to the earth and it would last for seven years. Those faithful to God would be persecuted, the earth would shake, mountains would fall, seas would turn red, a third of all marine life would die, and a third part of the sun, and the stars, and the moon would be blotted out. One third of all mankind would die. The inhabitants were directed to Revelation 8:7 where the Bible described what would happen: "And the third part of trees was burnt up, and all green grass was burnt up." And in Revelation 8:12,

"And the third part of the sun was smitten, and the third part of the moon, and the third part of the stars." And in Revelation 9:11, "And they had a king over them, which is the angel of the bottomless pit." But God also told them that Christ would return before the greatest destruction took place so His faithful—the Bride, kings, and priests—would be spared. God explained this in Revelation 11:2-3: "The holy city shall they tread under foot forty and two months . . . they prophesy a thousand two hundred and threescore days." When half of the seven years of destruction had passed, Christ would return and take with Him "they which follow the Lamb whithersoever he goeth. These were redeemed from among men, being the firstfruits unto God and to the Lamb" (Revelation 14:4). After this, grace would no longer be available on earth. Neither would the voice of the Holy Spirit, or Christ or the goodness of God's elect. God explained this to the inhabitants in Revelation 18:23 where He said, "And the light of a candle shall shine no more at all in thee; and the voice of the bridegroom and of the bride shall be heard no more at all in thee; for thy merchants were the great men of the earth; for by thy sorceries were all nations deceived."

When this seven-year period of the end-time began, a beast in the form of a man would appear and reign on earth. The beast would receive his power from Satan who hoped to break the faith of those who followed God by giving this beast great authority and ability. Because of this power, the beast would cause many to worship him and thus worship Satan. Revelation 13:4 explained: "And they worshipped the dragon which gave power unto the beast: and they worshipped the beast, saying, Who is like unto the beast?" Revelation 13:5 explained that for forty-two months before the First

Resurrection took place, the beast would come into power and would reign. "And there was given unto him a mouth speaking great things and blasphemies; and power was given unto him to continue forty and two months." Those who succumbed to worshipping the beast were described in Revelation 14:9-10: "And............... if any man worship the beast and his image, and receive his mark in his forehead, or in his hand, the same shall drink of the wine of the wrath of God . . . " At the end of this forty-two-month reign of the beast, Christ would return to take the Bride, kings, and priests from earth; and the wrath of evil would bring a great battle to the earth. Revelation 16:14 told the inhabitants: "For they are the spirits of devils, working miracles, which go forth unto the kings of the earth and of the whole world, to gather them to the battle of that great day of God Almighty."

This would occur after Christ took his elect to heaven for the wedding feast, and there would be no more grace or pure goodness left on earth. These passages in the Holy Bible made the inhabitants work harder to learn God's words and live a life pleasing to Him because they desired to be among the overcomers who were taken by Christ at the First Resurrection. The inhabitants continued to learn, yet when one question was answered, there seemed another to take its place. But now they understood why Satan's wrath was directed at them. Satan was literally in a fight to the death, and he used some of the inhabitants to help him break the children of God! The inhabitants learned that the evil beast and the false prophet would also be cast into the lake of fire burning with brimstone, and this would occur just before Satan was cast into that lake. They read in Revelation 19:20, "And the beast was taken, and with him the false prophet that wrought miracles before him, with which he deceived them that had received the mark of the beast, and them that worshipped his image. These both were cast alive into a lake of fire burning with brimstone." The inhabitants continued to learn from scripture and discovered that once the beast and false prophet were thrown into the lake of fire, an angel came from heaven with a great chain and bound Satan into the lake of fire where he would remain during the thousand-year kingdom of peace when Christ would reign. Revelation 20:1-3, "And I saw an angel come down from heaven, having the key of the bottomless pit and a great chain in his hand. And he laid hold on the dragon, that old serpent, which is the Devil, and Satan, and bound him a thousand years. And cast him into the bottomless pit, and shut him up, and set a seal upon him, that he should deceive the nations no more, til the thousand years should be fulfilled: and after that he must be loosed a little season." During the thousand years when Satan would be bound, the inhabitants who had been taken by Christ at the First Resurrection would help Christ bring testimony to all men who had ever been conceived, ever lived, or ever died. This was God's righteousness, His perfect plan which would allow **all** of mankind—even those who had not been taken in the First Resurrection—to receive equal testimony of God's plan and Christ's sacrifice for them. All would be told of the free will they had to choose between good and evil. All would learn, understand, and believe because there would be no evil to distract them. However, all of these inhabitants would have to be tested just as those other inhabitants, the overcomers who Christ took at the First Resurrection, had been tested. This was why Satan would be loosed again for a little while. God explained this in Revelation 20:7: "And when the thousand years are expired, Satan shall be loosed out of his prison." When he was loosed, Satan would go out again to deceive mankind and try again to gain them for himself. Except for those taken in the First Resurrection, (the Bride, kings and priests), all of mankind who was ever conceived, ever lived or ever died would be tested. This period would end in the final great battle on earth. The inhabitants found this in Revelation 20:8 where God said of Satan, "And shall go out to deceive the nations which are in the four quarters of the earth, Gog and Magog, to gather them together to battle the number of whom is as the sand of the sea." This second opportunity for redemption would take place after Satan had been bound for one thousand years and then loosed for a while and would come to an end on Judgment Day. When this day came, all of mankind would have had the same opportunity to live forever with God that the Bride, kings, and priests had been given. They would also have the same responsibility to withstand Satan when he came to turn them from God even though they could not be the Bride of Christ.

When this final testing and battle were over, the devil would be cast forever into the lake of fire and with him would be all those inhabitants who did not have their names written in the Lamb's book of life, those who had not followed God's statutes. This time, Satan would be bound forever. The inhabitants read the words in Revelation 20:10 which said, "And the devil that deceived them was cast into the Lake of Fire and brimstone, where the beast and the false prophet are, and **shall be tormented** day and night forever and ever." This was clarified again by God as they read in Revelation 20:12: "And I saw the dead, small and great, stand before God; and the books were opened: and another book was opened which is the book of life; and the dead were judged out of those things which were written in the books, according to their works." The inhabitants also read in Revelation 20:15: "And whosoever was not found written in the book of life was cast into the lake of fire." This would be called the Last Judgment; and the inhabitants now knew that all the inhabitants who had ever lived or died, who had not been taken in the First Resurrection would be judged by their deeds; by what they did and how they treated one another throughout their entire life. The lambs and sheep, those who did have their names entered into the book of life on Judgment Day, would go to heaven; and the goats would go to the lake of fire and brimstone with Satan—and the beast and the false prophet—to be tormented day and night for all eternity.

It was not easy for the inhabitants to think of those who would not follow God and would spend eternity with Satan, tormented forever and ever. But they knew that God's plan of salvation was perfect and that He willingly shared it with all men by opening their understanding of scripture and giving them the role models who would teach them. God did this in the hope that men would listen and had hearts ready to accept. But not every inhabitant was able to accept, or understand at the same time, and this was why God gave so much time to the inhabitants. Their hearts had to be ready, pure, loving, accepting, and repentant. Those who carried sin, those who would not repent, those whose hearts were hardened or lukewarm were addressed in Revelation 21:7-8: "He that overcometh shall inherit all things; and I will be His God, and he shall be my son. But the fearful, and unbelieving, and the abominable, and murderers, and whoremongers, and sorcerers, and idolators, and all liars, shall have their part in the lake which burneth with fire and brimstone: which is the second death." The inhabitants knew that the Holy Bible was complete. It told men all they needed to know if their hearts were right, and they sincerely asked God to show them His plan and guide their lives. Some who did not ask God for help and therefore could not learn the words written in the Bible became fixed in their unbelief. This further hardened their hearts, stole their ability to love, and made them lukewarm toward God. Some became hard hearted in their misconceptions and arrogance. God's plan called for a certain number of the inhabitants to reside in His kingdom and become the Bride, kings, and priests for His son. The kings would help Christ rule, and the priests would teach and counsel the people.

But for the time period in which the inhabitants were now living, all Satan had to do was to stop that number from being reached. If he could do this, he would live as he always did and never have to enter hell. For that was just the natural law of the universe, the physics of things, the way God's plan had been developed. God's righteousness demanded that every man have an equal opportunity to become a part of the Bride of His Son, a king, a priest, or a lamb in God's kingdom. However, God's righteousness also allowed Satan to tempt mankind, for man had sinned. That gave Satan the right to condemn them and take them for himself. Man had listened to Satan, disobeyed God; and when he had eaten of the tree of the knowledge of good and evil, man had to obtain that knowledge. He now had to taste the sweetness of good and the bitterness of evil. This too was just the natural law of the universe, the physics of things, which fulfilled God's righteousness. If Satan could prevent love from ruling men, he could prevent the number God longed for from being found. Therefore Satan and his evil spirits worked day and night to cause even godly people to stumble. If Satan could build a following, he would have others to help him prevent God from reaching that number. God had answered the questions posed by the inhabitants. Now they knew what was happening and why. But so did Satan. And so Satan worked on the inhabitants, day in and day out, roaring like a lion, looking to devour the children of God and turn them from their goal. He'd warned his evil cohorts that they too would be thrown into the lake of fire if they did not prevent the children of God from learning and developing love and compassion. Satan did not want the inhabitants to learn forgiveness and develop a loving heart, and obedience to God which they could use as a passport to enter the kingdom of God. As Satan and his evil spirits attacked mankind, they hardened many hearts and caused great lies and false information...and complacency..... to bring harm to the inhabitants.

Again the angels hoped that the children of God—those who would be called the Bride, kings, priests, lambs, firstlings, firstfruits, overcomers, the elect, peculiar or chosen—would be strong and recognize and thwart the enemy's attacks, especially now that they understood what Satan was trying to do. By now the inhabitants had been given the resources with which to fight against evil, but they had to be willing to put them into practice. This effort which the inhabitants would have to put forth was just a part of the natural law of the universe, the physics of things, as God had planned. And many did not want to give God what He asked of them and so they struggled against their enemy, they continued to question God, sometimes wondering why they seemed so alone, why they didn't always realize He was with them, why they had to suffer. Sometimes their feet stumbled as they lost their love and loyalty, their compassion and they could no longer forgive. Their fear over their many failures overwhelmed them, and sometimes when they failed, they questioned whether or not they were still okay with God. They often lost their ability to understand the grace which was available to the pure, humble, and truly repentant heart. It was difficult for them to understand how great and powerful grace was; how the sacrifice of Christ took away their sin if they repented sincerely and forgave others. The sacrifice of Christ had been so perfect that it covered every truly repented sin. But their questions and their fears sometimes filled their days and robbed them of their peace and their energy. So they prayed to find peace.

Where Were You?

Lord, I saw some footprints impressed upon the ground,
and recognized a pair was mine; the other, Yours, I found.
I saw then that You walked so close and shared my joyous days.
I felt assured of kinship and of all Your loving ways.

But then there came another day, one filled with great despair;
I asked of God, "Where are You?" for the footprints were one pair.
"Do I really walk this path alone? Where are You in my pain?
"What did I do to make You leave; How can my soul make gain?"

And, gently then, the Lord said, "I never left you, child,
I carried you safely in My arms, those are My prints through the wild."

****

These struggles were part of God's plan to teach and strengthen the inhabitants. God knew that when the going got tough, the tough got going. He wanted the inhabitants to learn to trust not only Him, but themselves as well. He wanted them to know that they had developed good hearts and tried to be faithful to Him. He wanted them to know that they had been forgiven and were the children of God and possibly a part of the Bride, kings, priests, firstlings, or firstfruits. It was for them that Christ had made His sacrifice and had given His life. It was for everyone who would strive to please God, learn of Him, and follow His statutes. That was why God offered them grace. They might fall, but if they admitted their sins, had remorse for them, and truly desired to do better in the future, they would be forgiven. God knew the power of Satan, and He also knew the sincerity of the inhabitants' hearts.

Therefore, many inhabitants trusted God and stayed the course, and God was pleased. It was, after all, just the natural law of the universe, the physics of things, which God had put into place for their benefit—to help them win His kingdom, to give them victory over the evil which stalked them, to give them freedom from their sin. Christ had given them grace, the precious commodity which Satan could not take away from them. The inhabitants developed their questions and tried to find the answers. With their ministers' help, with the great book God had given them, and with God opening their understanding, they obtained wisdom and insight. They rejoiced and thanked God with a pure heart. The heavens sang with the songs of the angels, and the harps played, and the palace glowed with joy! And miracle of miracles, the inhabitants even began to thank God for the bad times, the times when they had to endure heartache, because they now understood how the bad times refined them and made them like pure gold which had all its impurities removed by fire. God would use the refining process to make them into the temple they would become as children of God. The inhabitants spoke of their fears and how they struggled to stifle those fears with the knowledge that God was with them in these difficult times, so they really had nothing to fear. They read in Proverbs 4:20-27: "My son, attend to my words; incline thine ear unto my sayings . . . For they are life . . . and health . . . Turn not to the right hand nor to the left: remove thy foot from evil." And in Proverbs 3:25-26, "Be not afraid of sudden fear, neither of the desolation of the wicked, when it cometh. For the Lord shall be thy confidence, and shall keep thy foot from being caught." They were learning, so when they suffered and asked God why, eventually they would find the answer......and this was because God's wisdom and understanding now filled their hearts. And they prayed.

Why?

Why can't we all be kind, Lord, why is there so much pain?
How can I grow in love, Lord, how can I make gain?
Why is there a Satan, and why have you given him power,
why let his influence cause the children of God to cower?

Why didn't you make us perfect right from the very start?
Why did You allow the evil to enter into men's hearts?
These were my many questions, Lord, until I read your word
and listened at the altar where I knew You could be heard.

From these blessed words I learned the wonderful love you serve;

that laws of righteousness bind You, laws that even You observe.
And that within the laws of the universe, for pure love to win,
the battle must be won against the enemy called sin.
I know now that man decides his fate, for he has his own free will
to choose the path that leads to life or one that will kill.
And until we all can accept this, commit to making the right choice;
the evil one will stalk us with his lying, seductive voice.

God's own and perfect righteousness and the laws this creates
we know will prevail in the end to seal the evil that He hates.
For in the law of the universe, love must defeat,
for only through a perfect love can the evil one be beat.

****

These prayers were music to God's ears. And Christ, His Son, danced with the joy of knowing that His Bride would soon be ready even though only God knew the hour and the day He would send His Son for the Bride. But the time was fast approaching and all of heaven waited, and those on earth who waited also watched, hoping every day that the lover of their soul would come soon. God wanted the inhabitants to open their hearts to one another, to make themselves vulnerable, to seek to be close, to share their hopes, dreams, and wishes; to be loyal to one another. But God also knew that this was difficult because the inhabitants were afraid of being hurt. Being open allowed one to be rejected, and rejection was very painful. Christ himself had experienced many rejections, and God knew that it took courage for one inhabitant to reach out to another this way. So He was proud of them and thought: *These are my people,* my children, the Bride for my Son! The angels rejoiced to hear the conversations of the inhabitants because they now rang with love and innocence, with hope and excitement. Everyone wanted to be loved, so they weren't surprised by these conversations. In fact they were pleased. Christ also heard the words some of the inhabitants spoke to one another, and He too smiled. After all, those who spoke these words were to be His Bride, and He wanted a Bride who could speak words of love openly and show her willingness to be vulnerable and trusting and loyal. These conversations were carried to the heavens and sent to the great palace, for while they were not actually prayers, they were words which those in the palace wanted to hear.

Fears

Can I trust you or will you hurt me? Do you like me?
Do you want to know me, know what and how I think?
Will you like me even then? I like you.
I'll forgive you for being human, making mistakes,
if you'll like me.

And if you'll like me and can forgive me when I need forgiveness,
then I tell you that I love you.
But if I love you, then I'll need you; can I trust you?
And if you'll love me too,
we will need each other and be vulnerable together.

****

The plan was working; the people continued to wait for God to take them to their home in heaven where warmth and love and trust could thrive, and where there would be no evil. The hearts of these special people were so beautiful that the angels wondered if Christ asked His Father each day, "Can I go to fetch My Bride today, Father?" They smiled thinking of the anticipation Christ had in His heart for His Bride. But it was not yet time. There were still lessons to be learned. To become the Bride of Christ, the inhabitants had to have faith in themselves and faith in the grace Christ provided for them. When evil came again, it would try to instill doubt; not only the doubt that God was with them or that He would fulfill His promises, but doubt which worked inside the inhabitants about themselves and whether or not they were truly forgiven.

Evil wanted them to believe that they could never be worthy and doubt that God's grace was sufficient for their failures. If evil could do this, it might cause the inhabitants to doubt the validity of the sacrifice of Christ and its power to forgive their sins. They had learned in 2 Chronicles 6:36: "For there is no one who doesn't sin." And in 1 John 1:7, "But if we walk in the light as He is in the light, we have fellowship with one another, and the blood of Jesus Christ His Son cleanses us from all sin." Satan had not been idle over these many years and many failures. He had grown in strength because he had grown in cunning. He was a liar and a deceiver from the beginning. This is why God had warned the people in Ephesians 6:11 to "put on the whole armor of God, that you may be able to stand against the wiles of the devil." The devil thought that if he could make the inhabitants believe that they weren't good enough and never would become good enough to be a part of the Bride of Christ, they might give up. He thought that this would be an excellent way to separate them from God. So Satan, though he had difficulty penetrating their hearts, worked on their minds. He whispered to the inhabitants of their many past failures, of future failures of the same kind, of their pride and ego, their wrongful thoughts, their many steps backward. This took away their self-esteem and made them wonder if they could ever be found worthy. They weren't perfect after all, so how could they be worthy? They wondered if the sacrifice of Christ was never ending, if it could possibly cover so many sins committed day after day. They remembered how angry they were when a car cut them off on the highway. They remembered what they said to their computer when it lost the copy they had been creating.   They remembered when they felt dislike for someone who snubbed them. They remembered when they yelled back at someone who yelled at them. They remembered a jealous moment and an angry moment. They remembered that they did not seek the forgiveness of someone they had hurt even though they knew that Christ wanted them to do this. How could Christ's sacrifice cover so many things? How could Christ cover them when they would probably commit these same sins again tomorrow? These were the questions which Satan whispered to them hoping the words would travel to their minds to plague them.

But they turned to one another for help. They asked if they were okay with God. Their role models and ministers reassured them that God loved them no matter what if they were truly sorry for what they did and sincerely did not want to do the same things again and if they would work on themselves to change for the better and if they could forgive one another and ask those they harmed for forgiveness, then God would forgive them always.

Am I Okay?

Don't be so hard on yourself, you're really a very nice guy.
You've learned from your mistakes, so don't waste time and cry

for something done and over or for lessons learned then lost.
For if your steps are two ahead and only one re-crossed,

you're making gains to your reward and have God to help you grow.
So put on all your armour and do better tomorrow!

Christ's sacrifice is meant for all, it's a gift unlimited;
so if you're really sorry, your sin is always shed.

Then will come the great reward when the tempter leaves your side,
for then you'll be the conqueror and with God you will abide.

****

The tender heart of God was touched. He was pleased to see the concern of His children, knowing they wanted to do good, wanted to be a worthy child of God. He had made provision for what Satan would do to these little children who He loved so much, and He was filled with joy to see them come through as He had hoped. His plan was working. They would soon be ready! The angels heard these conversations, and were delighted because these words showed them how much these inhabitants had learned; they were developing caring hearts and they were filled with love for others. Their love was becoming pure and perfect. Now was the time when the inhabitants were ready to learn that what they felt toward God and the aspirations they had for their eternal life was perfect. God did not want them to worry; He wanted them prepared, wanted them to know that He saw their beauty, and what they aspired to. He would help them, and they would not fail. The magnificent plan which God had put into place for the inhabitants was well worth the effort. God was glad that He had worked these lessons into the natural law of the universe, the physics of things, to help these inhabitants find their way.

Open thou mine eyes
that I may behold wondrous things.

—Psalm 119:18

Chapter Ten

Beautiful Aspirations

The Poems of Chapter Ten

*For ye are the labourers
together with God,
ye are God's husbandry,
ye are God's building.*

—1 Corinthians 3:9

With their new understanding and their questions laid to rest, the inhabitants were content. So much of what happened to them and around them made sense now. Finally, it seemed easier to stay on the path of righteousness because they understood what, how, and why there would be an effort to force them from it. They were grateful that God had answered their questions and had helped them learn why they had to go through their trials and tribulations. Because so much worry and speculation had been removed from them, they were now free to dream of their future, of better days, of the streets paved with gold, of a time when there would be no more sorrow. They began to recognize where they could make improvements in themselves and how this would benefit both them and those around them. They saw that they needed to make some changes, especially in their level of patience and in reminding one another to seek the higher road and appreciate what God was doing for them. They aspired to be better people, to be overcomers. They realized that this would help them when evil came again to tempt them. But most of all, they aspired to become children of God, the overcomers who would become the Bride of Christ, kings, priests, firstlings, firstfruits, the elect, the chosen, a peculiar people, the lambs who God would gather to live with Him for all eternity. Then when that great time of redemption occurred at the First

Resurrection and at the Last Judgment, they would go with Christ and spend all eternity with Him, and with their Heavenly Father and the Holy Spirit. This hope filled the inhabitants with awe. They spoke to one another about their aspirations and their dreams of a future with God and what they could do to please Him. They shared their thoughts with one another and discussed what should live in their heart. They knew that though they had already learned so much, more would be required of them before that time would come. God had said in Luke 12:48, "For unto whom much is given, of him shall be much required."

They read of some of the things God asked of them in 2 Esdras 2:20,23-25 in the Apocrypha of the Holy Bible: "Do right to the widow, set aright the matter of the orphans, give to the poor, shelter the forsaken, clothe the naked, heal the wounded and the sick, laugh not a lame man to scorn, protect the infirm, and let the blind come before me into light. Keep the old and young within thy walls....... and I will give thee first place in my resurrection." As they read the words do, give, shelter, clothe, heal, protect, and nourish, they recognized their selfishness. They saw how little they did. They recognized that they had to move from the emptiness of a selfish heart to the fulfillment found in the giving of oneself. This required that they love others as they loved themselves. But sometimes they had to struggle against both their tendency toward inaction and their impatience to do everything God asked. They wanted to develop and overcome immediately, but this wasn't possible. They tried to remember that some things took time and effort. Even one simple act of kindness each day toward their fellow man was an act of kindness toward God. And if they gave to God even a little each day, they were pleasing God, and they were developing into the overcomers God longed for. Sometimes in fact, God asked them to do something which became that which God would reward the most. The inhabitants remembered the beautiful words in Matthew 25:21, "Well done, thou good and faithful servant, thou hast been faithful over a few things, I will make thee the ruler over many things: enter thou into the joy of the Lord." As the inhabitants studied the word of God, God opened their understanding even further. He led them to a number of places in the Holy Bible where God explained why some might have to suffer more than others. Numbers 14:18 said, "The Lord is longsuffering, and of great mercy, forgiving iniquity and transgression, and by no means clearing the guilty, visiting the iniquity of the fathers upon the children unto the third and fourth generation." The inhabitants found similar references in other parts of the Bible, such as Exodus 20:5, Deuteronomy 5:9, Isaiah 14:21, Titus 2:14, and Acts 13:41.

As they studied these words, they realized that just as the sin of Adam and Eve had caused mankind certain struggles, the sins committed by their ancestors could also be the cause of the specific struggles they were now enduring. But God had placed into his wondrous and merciful plan a way for those now seeking His word to escape from the consequences of the sins of earlier generations upon their generation. Holy Baptism could remove not only the consequences of the original sin of Adam and Eve but also provide them with the strength to overcome the consequences which the sins of their forefathers had on their lives. Suddenly, the troubles they lived through made sense. They realized that an inhabitant might be suffering in a very difficult marriage because their father or grandfather or great-grandfather committed unrepented sins against his marriage and marriage partner. Just as Adam and Eve's sin brought consequences to all who were their descendents, so then would the inhabitant's forefathers cause the consequences of their sin to affect them. Then they realized that their own sins would affect their children and this made them seek forgiveness more quickly. As they studied God's word, they also learned that Holy Baptism represents the rebirth and the essential prerequisite for receiving the Holy Ghost, allowing man to enter into a covenant with God. This opened the way to communion with God so they could achieve the salvation of their souls and allow all future divine blessings. They recognized that God's blessings could help them overcome the sinful tendencies they inherited from their forefathers and also give them the strength to bear the consequences of those sins. They now no longer blamed God when tragedy struck. They now understood that there were consequences in life which had to be endured because of earlier mistakes.

This was the natural law of the universe, the physics of things, and had to be played out because of God's righteousness and of Satan's claim on them. However, now they understood so much more and knew what they had to fight.... for and against. They prayed, they studied God's word, and they made the necessary changes in their lives where they could. They were determined to endure, to become overcomers, and to wait for the return of Christ. The return of Christ would happen according to plan and according to God's timing. They understood this, but their deep desire to go home with Christ inspired them, and they wanted to hurry it along. They began to wonder whether finding new souls who were longing to learn about God and about the love He so willingly gave them could speed up the process of obtaining the last soul God wanted. For they remembered that God longed for a certain number, and until that number was reached, Christ would not be sent to fetch His Bride. From these thoughts and their wonderful fellowships with other believers and seekers, they began to understand that they could help in this process by finding that last soul which God longed for. They decided that they could pray for those souls to be found. They could ask God to help them find these souls who might be alive, or had already died. Some of these souls might not know of God at all. But if the inhabitants looked for them, prayed for them, asked God to help them find them, the great plan of salvation could be completed earlier. For God had said that He would shorten the time for their sakes. In Matthew 24:22 God told them, "And except those days should be shortened, there should no flesh be saved; but for the elect's sake those days shall be shortened."

So the inhabitants began to organize a plan to pray for those whom God wanted, to pray for those who had died, those who had lost their way, and those who never had been taught about God. They began to invite others to their church and to their fellowships and into their hearts. They loved them and set an example of love for them. This aspiration to help filled their heart, and God was pleased. The angels saw the crowns of the inhabitants begin to gleam, golden in color now, because of the beauty of their aspirations. These inhabitants practiced what they were striving to achieve, truly loving others. Their attitude touched the hearts of those who did not yet believe and made them wonder who these peculiar people were who had no malice or envy, no hidden agenda, in their hearts. After all, weren't most people envious, weren't they often angry, didn't they seek friends in order to get ahead in the world and thus had a hidden agenda? But these people didn't. They seemed truly able to love and not look for anything in return. This made an impression on those who were invited into their fellowships. By their example, by the purity of their hearts, and their giving nature, they won souls to God. God was pleased, and the angels smiled. They knew that the plan was moving toward its completion. The inhabitants were changing for the better every day. But then again, wasn't this what God wanted, just what God had put into His plan, into that great engineering feat to teach the people love? Wasn't this change just part of the natural law of the universe, the physics of things, as He had created it?

Change

Without change, we are nothing, a packet of seeds.
Without change, there's no growth or love in our deeds.
Without change, we don't comfort and nurture, just spoil.
Without change, we can't be overcomers who foil.

the evil which seeks us knows what to do
to bring harm to our souls if we are not true.
So let's liken our life to the seeds of the earth
that need soil and water and sun for their birth.

And then, when we grow, the fruit we'll soon bear
will benefit all by our generous care.
For God gives the seed, and the soil, rain and sun;
but we must first see that the planting is done.
****

As the number of children of God grew, so did the number of fellowships and so did the number of teachers. Despite the growth they saw occurring, sometimes these inhabitants still had to fight their impatience, for they wanted to have Christ come quickly. Sometimes they even wondered if God had a time frame for this after all. They tried to remember that even their crops took time to grow before they could be harvested, and they compared this natural phenomena to themselves, understanding that they too needed to be fully developed before God could harvest them. But it was often a struggle, for they were impatient. They'd read God's words about reaping His harvest in Revelation 14:15: "......Thrust in thy sickle and reap; for the time is come for thee to reap, for the harvest of the earth is ripe." They wanted this to happen quickly. They longed to change the faults and failings they still had to fight, and when they didn't seem able to overcome them quickly, they were discouraged. But because they met regularly in fellowship with other believers, they had the help they needed. When one was discouraged, another lifted him up. When one felt that he was losing hope, another related an experience of faith to renew that hope. When one was sad, another told him how much he was loved. They realized that helping one another as well as teaching God's word was what God meant when He asked them to feed those in the church of God. In Acts 20:28, they read, "Take heed therefore unto yourselves, and to all the flock, over the which the Holy Ghost hath made you overseers, to feed the church of God, which he hath purchased with His own blood."

Throughout the Holy Bible, God referred to those who would someday be with Him in His kingdom as His flock or His sheep. This analogy helped the inhabitants realize that they should behave as sheep do, which is not to fight amongst one another but to have a gentle nature, to want to be near the shepherd, and to follow where the shepherd leads them. As the inhabitants shared their aspirations, they also discussed how impatient they were with many things in their lives. They helped one another understand that in time, all would work out to their benefit. Through their fellowships they learned how important it was to be with one another, to keep their faith alive, to share their hopes and joys and concerns, and to uplift one another. This not only helped them but also helped draw others to God. They were sure that this would hasten the time of the First Resurrection. Their teachers reminded them that in John 14:23 Christ said, "If a man love me, he will keep my words: and my Father will love Him, and we will come unto him, and make our abode with him." They also read in Luke 8:15: ".......having heard the word, keep it, and bring forth fruit with patience." All this was a part of the learning process which would teach them about God and what he asked of them, and help them wait in patience for the return of Christ. All this was a part of the magnificent plan, the natural law of the universe, the physics of things, which God put into place for the development his people.

Patience

Oh, Lord, I see my failings, that I want things much too fast,
that despite the many lessons, I don't learn from the past.
I know that patience shows a trust, a faith that's good and true,
that despite my need to "fix it now", I've bent my will to You.

I always want to handle the obstacles that come my way

by willfully, quickly barging through, not listening to what You say.
So help me find more patience, Lord, help me grow and learn.
Help me to listen for Your voice, and the Blessings this would earn.

I do know in my heart and soul that You truly know what's best,
and want to willingly wait in trust, as impatience is laid to rest.

****

And so they tried to be more patient and "they continued stedfastly in the apostles' doctrine and fellowship, and in breaking of bread, and in prayers" as they had been told in Acts 2:42. By being in constant fellowship with one another, they were able to uplift those who were despondent, counsel those who made mistakes, pray for those with troubles, love those who felt alone. Because of these activities, more seekers flocked to these peculiar people who were loyal and knew pure love and prayed and didn't have a hidden agenda. As the Lord saw the number he longed for being fulfilled and souls coming in not only from the ranks of the living but also from the ranks of those who had died in their sins, He was pleased. The angels rejoiced, and the heavens rang with their songs of thanksgiving. Their hope was that soon God's great plan would reach fruition. The children of God would be prepared to be the Bride of Christ and this would cause God to tell Christ to go and get them. He would take them with him to the mansions He had created for them. There they would sit at the feet of God forever.

But Satan had not been idle. All he wanted was to destroy the faith of just one of God's children, one lamb, one overcomer. Satan understood that for every new soul the inhabitants brought in to their flock, he would have to break another soul. This would allow him to remain free, to escape his fate of being bound in the lake of fire for one thousand years. So Satan and his spirit workers stepped up their efforts to cause love to diminish and fear and cruelty to grow in the hearts of the inhabitants. Satan especially wanted to be sure that those who were "lukewarm" toward God would not become the children of God. For they were the easiest to fool. Many who were lukewarm thought that they were okay with God. They thought if they just believed in God and didn't do anything particularly bad, they were okay. They didn't yet understand that it was necessary to keep the Sabbath holy by sitting under God's words or to learn God's words or to obtain the forgiveness of their sins or to prove their loyalty and obedience. Neither did they tithe to God or pray or strive to overcome. These were the inhabitants who were especially loved by Satan because he did not have to work very hard to gain their souls. So evil attacked again. Evil stalked the inhabitants as a lion stalks its prey. Evil's teeth were like fangs, bared for the feast of a kill. Evil was stealthy and silent as it sought to devour those who were just growing in faith who had not yet become children of God.

God had warned the inhabitants that this would happen in 1 Peter 5:9 where He said, "Be sober, be vigilant; because your adversary the devil, as a roaring lion, walketh about, seeking whom he may devour." The inhabitants were vigilant, carefully nurturing those newly adopted into the faith and when evil attacked, they were ready. With the help of the stronger inhabitants and the ministers and teachers who protected and strengthened them, they sustained those who were not yet fully developed in their faith, those who were evil's targets... and they resisted. They remained stedfast in faith, they were patient in their affliction, and they prayed for inner strength. They shed their desire for earthly goods so this could not claim ownership of their hearts and concentrated on the more valuable spiritual things.

Seek

Seek not your security by financial success.
But rather by your day-to-day
relationship with God and your family.
The outer financial success you cannot
take with you. But the inner successes live forever.

****

Soon the evil retreated. It was terribly angry that it had not gained access to the hearts of the inhabitants, nor even to their minds, for their minds and hearts were filled with the word of God; and their faith in that word was like a fortress. Evil was frustrated, and left these inhabitants and went where it would be welcome. It left those who hungered for and sought the word of God and went instead to those who did not know God's words and those who were complacent and who thought only of their natural life. For these would unwittingly welcome evil. Evil would entice them to remain complacent about God or to delight in envy and malice, in hatred and harm. If evil could capture and hold these inhabitants, they would become the goats who would not enter the kingdom of heaven. Satan also planned to use some of these inhabitants to harm the children of God. Evil hadn't yet given up. But evil had begun to worry. Satan could not allow God to reach the number of souls He longed for. If God did reach that number, Satan would be bound into the lake of fire. Satan had to stop God, had to find a way to draw at least some of the inhabitants away from God. So evil plotted. But many of the inhabitants had read the Bible, learned God's words, and they had put on the armour which God gave them for this attack. In Ephesians 6:11, God had said, "Put on the whole armour of God, that ye may be able to stand against the wiles of the devil." Then in Ephesians 6:14-18, God had explained what that armour was when He said, "Stand therefore, having your loins girded about with truth and having on the breastplate of righteousness; And your feet shod with the preparation of the gospel of peace; above all, taking the shield of faith, wherewith ye shall be able to quench all the fiery darts of the wicked. And take the helmet of salvation, and the sword of the Spirit, which is the word of God: praying always with all prayer and supplication in the Spirit, and watching thereunto with all perseverance and supplication for all saints." This is what the inhabitants had learned. This was the word of God. This is what they believed with all their heart. And this is how God prepared them to resist evil if they chose love instead of evil with their free will. As evil left, the inhabitants rejoiced, the angels sang, the harps of heaven played their magical songs, and the Father and the Son and the Holy Spirit smiled with love. Love radiated from them. The plan had worked perfectly. The natural law of the universe, the physics of things, had developed with perfect timing.

Precious Seeds

Despite the chaos in the world, our hearts are filled with peace
as we're gently, gently sheltered and all our stresses cease.
We gather at the end of day at home, our place of rest,

the earthly home God's given, the one His love has blessed.

We've built our little Bethany through God's amazing love,
being doers of His word, thus gaining gifts from God above.
But it wasn't at the onset, before His word we sought.
We started each day unaware that a battle must be fought.

We did not place our life and soul into His hand so kind.
We'd only known the word of God with our imperfect mind
until we realized we could do nothing on our own
and let the precious seeds of God into our hearts be sown.

****

There was still much work to do. The inhabitants were now ready to learn the warnings which God wanted to give them. God wanted them to know what would happen to them if they did not choose good or if they were not found worthy to enter the new heaven and earth where only good could live. There were requirements for entering the kingdom of God. Very specific requirements. And there were terrible consequences for not meeting these requirements. It wasn't that God wanted to be hard on these inhabitants. He loved them and wanted every one of them with Him for all eternity. He wanted them to be successful. But God was bound by His own righteousness, and He could not be found breaking the rules and boundaries of righteousness. He could not allow **anything** into His kingdom which would harm the good, the purity of love, those who had understood the requirements and made themselves ready. God had provided a way for the inhabitants to be free of the terrible evil for all eternity but only if they chose this way with their own free will. God had given the inhabitants the sacrament of Holy Baptism so they could be free of original sin and begin anew with an opportunity to enter heaven. In John 3:5, could be read, "Jesus answered, Verily, verily I say unto thee, Except a man be born of water and of the Spirit, he cannot enter into the kingdom of God." Thus, all who heard these words and desired to follow God aspired to meet this requirement and sought the sacrament of Holy Baptism. The ministers freely provided these sacraments to the inhabitants,

In addition to this sacrament, God provided the inhabitants with the sacrament of Holy Communion so their souls could be nourished and in fellowship with Christ through the forgiveness of sin.... if they took communion worthily. God told them in Matthew 26:28 that Jesus said to His disciples, "For this is my blood of the new testament, which is shed for many for the remission of sins." The ministers pointed out that in this verse God said that "many," not "all," would receive the remission of their sins. This was because Holy Communion had to be taken worthily to work. Whoever sought to be absolved of their sins had to acknowledge their sins, be truly remorseful for committing them, truly desire not to commit the same sin again, forgive those who sinned against them, and seek the forgiveness of those they harmed. Even The Lord's Prayer taught them that they would be forgiven **as** they forgave others. Holy Sealing was another gift God offered as a sacrament to those who loved Him. In Acts 8:15-17, God told the people, "Who, when they were come down, prayed for them, that they might receive the Holy Ghost. Then laid they their hands on them, and they received the Holy Ghost." The inhabitants were given further explanations of the need for them to be sealed with the Holy Spirit when they read other parts of the Holy Bible. In Ephesians 1:13 they read: "In whom also after that ye believed, ye were sealed with the holy Spirit of promise." They read in Ephesians 4:30, "And grieve not the holy Spirit of God, whereby ye are sealed unto the day of redemption." Thus, the inhabitants sought to be sealed with the Holy Spirit so that they could receive everything God offered them. The inhabitants knew that these sacraments were important for them because they found references throughout the Holy Bible which explained that these were absolute requirements to reach the kingdom of heaven. These sacraments must be followed properly and must dwell correctly in the hearts of the inhabitants. They were not to be taken lightly. They represented the three parts of God....the Father who instituted the plan of salvation, The Son who brought them forgiveness through His sacrifice for them, and the Holy Spirit which would teach them and comfort them. And so the inhabitants entered the next phase of the great and magnificent and perfect plan which God had instituted for His children. When the inhabitants had developed the proper aspirations for them to live godly lives, God would teach them even more about the power of evil and what it could bring the inhabitants and the power of love which would bring them to God. Love would bring them a heart which contained the perfection and innocence of a child. This was all a part of the natural law of the universe, the physics of things, which God had put into place so mankind could escape what his disobedience had brought upon him.

The Lord is my light and my Salvation.
Psalm 27:1

Chapter Eleven
God's Warnings

The Poems of Chapter Eleven

This know also, that in the last days perilous times shall
come. For men shall be lovers of them own selves, covetous,
boasters, proud, blasphemers, disobedient to parents,
unthankful, unholy. Without natural affection,
trucebreakers, false accusers, incontinent, fierce
despisers of those that are good.
—2 Timothy 3:1-4

And whosoever was not found written in the book of life
was cast into the lake of fire.
Revelation 20:15

The inhabitants kept their focus on the kingdom to come and the fruition of God's plan for them. With so many of their questions now answered, their hearts were filled with a greater understanding of the love God had for them even though it was difficult for mankind to fully grasp the depth of the pure love God offered them. Ther frail human minds and bodies were limited in their capacity. Only God could practice the perfect and pure love of heaven although later He would give them this perfect gift of love along with perfect celestial bodies when Christ came for them at the First Resurrection. This too was a part of the magnificent plan of salvation for all mankind. Knowing this, the inhabitants hungered for the completion of God's plan. As their understanding increased, they were also taught not to judge one another, for each of them struggled toward the same goal in a different way and with different obstacles to overcome. None could know what truly lived in another's heart, only God could know. None knew the difficult circumstances which might have caused someone to sin or the remorse they felt or the intensity of their desire to please God. God asked the inhabitants not to judge one another because only He knew what circumstances they experienced which had shaped and driven them. This is why God said that He would be gracious to whom He wanted to be gracious, not by the standards of men but by His righteousness, by His standards, knowing all things. It was difficult for the inhabitants not to judge others when they saw those who blatantly sinned or harmed another, but this too was something God required of them. So the inhabitants tried as best they could to love, forgive, and leave judgment to God alone. As they grew in their understanding of this principle, they became more tolerant and developed more empathy for one another. One inhabitant even wrote a poem to share with those who were just coming to understand God's plan in the hope that they could see what God was trying to teach them.

A Possible Philosophy

Would you trust me for a minute and accept a premise?
Suppose we were all planning to travel, and we all planned
to leave at the same time from the same place to reach the same
destination. Suppose, on the way, one of us stopped to speak with a
friend, and another stopped at a different spot to tie a shoelace.
Suppose another was hungry and stopped for a bite to eat, and
maybe one of us got sick and needed to find medicines or rest.
While each of us were striving toward the same destination from the
beginning, each of us might reach our destination
at a different time, maybe by a different path.

Therefore should we condemn any for the time or date they reached
their destination? Should we condemn the path they may have taken
if they still reached the destination?
For some simply stopped for a moment and others for a longer time.
Some stopped voluntarily, some stopped out of necessity, but all
arrived. And we too stopped for our own reasons.

Beware the conceit of thinking you are further along than someone else, for you may yet have another stop to make, perhaps one you don't expect; and the one you condemned and judged may pass you by. For we all have our stops, some more difficult than others, some more painful, some more distasteful, some divert us to another path and some are delays to help our brother or sister, but all may keep us from continuing our journey for a while.

This is the concept of our walk of faith. We all have the same goal but are on different places on the same path. Our setbacks teach us humility. They help us develop love and compassion for our fellow man and when we make mistakes ourselves, the compassion we have shown to others will be the compassion that is shown to us. From this attitude comes a noble soul. Our destination is the salvation of our soul so we may spend eternity with God. And we must remember that this is achieved only through God's infinite grace and mercy.

****

When the inhabitants discussed the content of this poem, Satan also heard both the poem and their discussion. It made him angry. He was more determined than ever to stop the inhabitants from achieving their soul salvation. He did not want them developed and ready for God. He could not allow these inhabitants to share their wisdom with others and thereby draw others to God. As the inhabitants gained godly wisdom, Satan developed false ministers, who preached false doctrines and beliefs to capture the attention of the inhabitants and sway them toward similar but distorted beliefs. Satan hoped that by using words which God might use and doctrines which were similar to what the Bible taught, he could convince some of the inhabitants to follow them. If this worked, Satan would thwart the progress of these inhabitants and delay God's plan from being completed. But God knew this and warned the inhabitants that betrayal, offense, and hate would be prevalent during the end-time, just before Christ returned. Throughout the Holy Bible, God warned the inhabitants that many false prophets would tempt them with their "new" interpretation of God's words. And many would be deceived. In Mark 13:5, the inhabitants read, "And Jesus answering them began to say, Take heed lest any man deceive you." Many hungered for God's word, but few took the time or made the effort to truly study them. If they had, they would have known that in many places in the Holy Bible, God warned them that these false doctrines would become prevalent during the end times. God wanted the inhabitants to be aware that many would come in the guise of religion and faith to draw them from true instruction and that these new doctrines could easily tempt them because of their simplicity, because they eliminated the need for men to become overcomers. Many would be tempted to follow the ways which differed from what the Bible said. If Satan could make the inhabitants believe his perversion of what was required to be a part of the First Resurrection, he would capture the hearts of many of the inhabitants. He knew that mankind looked for the easy way to do things and would rationalize away the true instruction God gave them for the right way to live. Mankind was lazy and looked for justification for his complacency. But Satan's promise was a false promise. God knew that Satan would pervert the requirements for being a part of the First Resurrection. So throughout the Holy

Bible, God warned the inhabitants over and over again of false doctrines and of those who would try to draw them to follow a person rather than God. Christ clearly warned his disciples that these perversions would come.

When the inhabitants learned this, they desired to stand firm and not succumb to these new dangers. They realized that it would be a terrible thing for them if they were led to believe that a spiritual leader was correct in what he taught them, yet he was not. In Acts 20:29-31, the Holy Bible warned, "For I know this, that after my departure savage wolves will come in among you, not sparing the flock. Also from among yourselves men will rise up, speaking perverse things, to draw away the disciples after themselves. Therefore watch." So they studied God's words and asked God for His protection and His guidance. They knew God, and God knew them. But those who had not diligently sought God's words or had been lukewarm in accepting and doing what God asked were those who Satan sought hoping to mislead them. In Revelation 3:16, God warned, "So then because thou art lukewarm.....I will spue thee out of my mouth." God also warned them in Revelation 3:3 that when Christ returned, He would do so when least expected. "Remember.......I will come on thee as a thief, and thou shalt not know what hour I will come upon thee." But through all this, the inhabitants had a promise from God, which they repeated to one another to provide courage to one another. In Revelation 3:10, God said, "Because thou has kept the word of my patience, I also will keep thee from the hour of temptation......" They wanted to learn every word God offered them. The wanted truth so that they would have the perseverance to do what

God asked of them and prevent evil from gaining a foothold on their hearts. Thus, they read another poem to one another.

There Will Be No Ostriches in Heaven on Judgment Day

There are many forms of courage and many ways of giving;
there are many forms of loving and many ways of living.
There are many forms of hiding, not doing what must be done;
there are many ways of facing things, and one is not to run.

There are living things of courage and living things of fear;
there are many things around us, which we hold too dear.
God gave us our intellect so we would assimilate and learn.
He gave us inner strength and the grace that Christ did earn.

He allowed us all our burdens so we could learn and grow.
And taught us of His wonderful love, which we could reap and sow.
God gave us Holy wisdom, so Heaven we could see;
and placed life into our souls so we'd strive for eternity.

So we must set the godly goals, let the others go;
fill our hearts with courage so that in our souls we'll know.
For God loves those who stand and fight, those who will stay.
He will not allow the ostriches in Heaven on Judgment Day.

****

The inhabitants began to realize that burying one's head in the sand they way and ostrich did was dangerous. They were asked to appreciate the effort which God and His Son and the Holy Spirit had placed into their plan to ensure the perfection of the new creation. God had done this to create the perfect home for them and the perfect future where they could help Christ reign, where they could live and love and sing and dance together in peace; where evil would be bound forever. The inhabitants were amazed as they began to grasp the enormity of God's plan and they were humbled to think that they were loved so much that God had done all that He had to help perfect them for this future. They saw that He had made this effort for everyone who was ever conceived—ever born, ever lived, and ever died— so that all of mankind would have the same opportunity for salvation. They wished that evil hadn't ever tempted mankind. They wished that man could have been stronger and never disobeyed God and never had to learn evil. They wished they could only have had to learn of good. But they realized that we don't recognize good unless we know what evil is. They also knew that all their struggles would bring an incomparable reward if they remained faithful and that every sorrow they had ever experienced would be lifted from them and forgotten. They were glad that now they recognized God's love for them, and their hearts rejoiced. Seeing this, the angels rejoiced too. The heavens rang with songs, and the harps played and the inhabitants heeded the words in Hebrews 4:11 which said: "Let us labor therefore to enter into that rest, lest any man fall after the same example of unbelief." They looked into their hearts to be sure that they were doing what was right according to the word of God. They helped one another see where changes still needed to be made. They diligently sought what God wanted to tell them. Yes, it was indeed labor, but the rewards would be beyond what any of them could imagine!

<u>What I What To Be</u>

God has taught me to look at myself, to examine the things that I
do and the thoughts that I have.
From this I have learned a valuable thing:
that if I do what God asks of me, I can like myself.

If I can truly like myself according to the standards of God,
other children of God will like me.
If I can trust myself, according to the standards of God,
other children of God will trust me.

If I desire to learn, others will respect my thinking.
If I have a happy heart, others will smile with me.
If I respect my body, it will follow my bidding.
If I offer a kind word, others will respond in like manner.

If I make a mistake and ask God to forgive me and strive not to
make the same mistake again, others will respect me.
Thus, how I treat myself and others is how I will be treated.
If I love doing God's will, others can love God's word through me.

God doesn't send difficult times for naught but to help me grow in
grace when I choose to learn and follow His word.
God rewards those who strive to love Him above everything else and
to love their neighbor as they love themselves.
This is the person I want to be.

****

God was pleased by these words. His plan—the one He had instilled in the earth as a natural part of the universe, the physics of things—to help the people, was working perfectly. But there was just a little more that the inhabitants would have to do because the dangers of the end times would be coming. To warn the inhabitants of these times, God inspired them to read the Holy Bible to learn about the time which would herald the First Resurrection. God wanted the inhabitants to know what to expect and how to prepare themselves for the evil they would witness. Even the angels prepared themselves for their part in God's plan for when Christ opened the seven seals which would begin the time of destruction from which only God's elect would be saved. The angels prepared to fight the dragon of evil and his cohorts as the children of God saw their planet enter into a time of great unrest and danger. The Holy Bible described the terrible destruction and tribulation which would occur during the end times on the cold and bleak planet earth and explained that this part of God's plan would last for seven years. God's chosen ones would be taken after three and one half years and then grace would no longer be available. The hearts of mankind would be cold toward one another, children would rise against their parents and hate testimony, evil leaders would come into power, neighbor would rise against neighbor, right would be considered wrong and wrong would be considered right, pestilence would abound, famine and turbulent weather conditions would encompass the earth, war would come to many places and Christians would be persecuted. This was the work of Satan. This was the removal of the blessing and protection of God. The Bible also warned the inhabitants that after the Bride of Christ left the earth but before the destruction ended, one third of all mankind would die by smoke and fire, one third of all the water on the earth would turn red, and the people who were still alive would be in such torment that they would plead for death. The sun would be darkened, the moon would not give its light, the stars would fall from the heavens, and earthquakes would appear in many diverse places. God also warned the inhabitants that at the First Resurrection, even from those who were believers and thought that they were worthy, only **half** would be found worthy. God explained this in Luke 17:30,35-36 where He said, ".....I tell you, in that night there shall be two men in one bed; the one shall be taken, and the other shall be left. Two women shall be grinding together; the one shall be taken, and the other left. Two men shall be in the field; the one shall be taken, and the other left." The Bible also said in Matthew 25:12: "But he answered and said, Verily I say unto you, I know you not." This was a warning that God gave them so they would know to be careful, to remain faithful, to continuously check their thoughts and actions, to watch, to pray, and to be ready at all times to go when they were called. It was a warning that only those who had been faithful and had prepared themselves and made themselves ready would be chosen to go with Christ when He returned. The Bible taught the inhabitants many of the details concerning these times and encouraged them by saying, "Let us be glad and rejoice, and give honour to him; for the marriage of the Lamb is come, and his wife hath made herself ready" (Revelation 19:7). God told the inhabitants that everyone—good and bad, dead and living—would see Christ's return and explained in Revelation 1:7, saying, "Behold, he cometh with clouds; and every eye shall see him, and they also which pierced him; and all kindreds of the earth shall wail because of him. Even so, Amen"

While the wedding feast between Christ and His Bride took place in heaven, the earth would experience wars and great devastation, and the grace which had been available on earth would no longer be available thus sin would escalate. When the First Resurrection was complete, those who remained on earth would suffer in the terrible times for another three and one half years. Some would plead for a quick death. "And the smoke of their torment ascendeth up forever and ever; and they have no rest day nor night, who worship the beast and his image, and whosoever receiveth the mark of his name" (Revelation 14:11). God explained that the terrible days of rule by the Antichrist and the beast, both of whom worshipped Satan, would continue on for three and one half more years. In Revelation 13:4-6 God said, "And they worshipped the dragon which gave power unto the beast; and they worshiped the beast, saying Who is like unto the beast? ....And there was given unto him a mouth speaking great blasphemies; and power was given unto him to continue forty and two months." One third of the remaining people would die, and the land would be devastated.   In Revelation 8:7-9 God warned, "........there followed hail and fire......... the third part of trees was burnt up, and all green grass was burnt up . . . a great mountain burning with fire was cast into the sea, and the third part of the creatures which were in the sea, and had life, died." After the final three and one half years passed and this seven-year span of devastation was finished, Satan and all evil would be bound; and Christ would return to earth with His Bride and establish the reign of His kings and priests. Peace would come for one thousand years and the inhabitants who were left and all who had died would accept the testimony which Christ and God's elect, now in their celestial bodies, would bring them. Every knee would bow to Christ; those who lived and those who had died. For God, in His infinite mercy and love for mankind, had provided a second chance in His wonderful plan of salvation for those who had never been taught of godly things, those who heard but were lukewarm, and those who heard but rejected God's offer. These people would never be able to say that they hadn't been given the opportunity to make the choice which would give them life because God would show them during this time the many times when they did receive this testimony and spurned it. God in His wisdom and righteousness had provided for this so that everyone would know that no one had been left out.

Those who were the Bride of Christ, the kings and priests, the firstfruits of God's harvest, could freely travel in their celestial bodies from heaven to earth and all over the earth. Their job for the next one thousand years would be to bring testimony to all who had not been taken at the First Resurrection. But when the thousand years were over and the testimony which they would finally believe and accept had been brought to every human being who had ever been created, God's perfect justice would require that they be tested. Thus every man, woman, and child would have been brought the testimony of Christ, would have been taught of God's statutes, would understand the prerequisites for entering the new heaven and earth and could never say that they didn't understand. Now they too would have to employ their free will and have to choose under the same conditions as God's elect who had been a part of the First Resurrection. They would have to make their choice with Satan tempting them with his evil because Satan, when the thousand years was up, would be loosed for a little while to tempt the newly converted. Just as the Bride of Christ, the kings and priests had been tested before becoming overcomers so would these newly converted inhabitants have to be tested and many would fall to Satan again, even after they had witnessed Christ's return and understood the testimony they were given. In the Apocrypha of the Holy Bible, in 2 Esdras 7:20-22, God said, "For there are many that perish . . . they did not want to be persuaded......." And in 2 Esdras 7:24, God warned, "......... the works he commanded them they perform not." In 2 Esdras 8:50 God further warned, "Therefore they shall suffer much misery and be in such state that those that dwell on earth in the last days shall have pity for them, because they have walked in great pride."

The dead would also have the same opportunities that the living had been given. God spoke of these inhabitants in Daniel 12:2, saying, "And many of them that sleep in the dust of the earth shall awake, some to everlasting life, and some to shame and everlasting contempt." After this period of testing, Satan would again be bound, this time forever. Then the remaining inhabitants would be separated into two groups. The group which did not fall to Satan, but overcame the temptation of Satan and remained faithful to God, would be those who could enter the new heaven and earth, not as firstlings but as the remaining flock, the sheep. The others, those who chose to follow Satan, who did not listen to God, would undergo a second death in which they would be bound with Satan and cast into the lake of fire for all eternity. These would be called the goats and never have another chance to be with God and suffer torment. With this understanding, the inhabitants of the cold, bleak planet prayed a special prayer to ask for help, to ask God to bring them through those days.

Let Me Learn

Let me learn Your words, let my lessons be done,
let me keep Your precepts, avoid the sorrow to come.
There will be gnashing of teeth and the horrors of hell
and the lake of fire deeper than any dark well.

The sounds of crying, and incredible sorrow,
can't now be changed, for there's no chance tomorrow.
Those who were lukewarm will also descend,
so help me change; let me make amends.

Others were blind, rebuked and chastened;
they still wouldn't listen, now their end is hastened.
Loosed are the seven seals of destruction;
help me to prevail and follow Your instruction.

The enemy wants us in the pit where he'll be,
where we'd suffer forever and never again see
the brightness of love, hearts willing to share.
Or be with those who would listen, those who would care.

Satan wants us purged from the book of life,
wants us to live and die, entangled forever in strife.
So when the end comes and the destruction begins,
while everyone heard and everyone sinned,

only those who tried, those who obtained grace,
will escape the travail and see God's holy face

****

In Matthew 25:32-34, the apostle explained the position of the sheep and the goats saying: *"And before him shall be gathered all nations: and he shall separate them one from another, as a shepherd divideth his sheep from the goats; And he shall set the sheep on his right hand, but the goats on the left. Then shall the King say unto them on his right hand, 'Come, ye blessed of my Father, inherit the kingdom prepared for you from the foundation of the world.'"* And in Matthew 25:41 and 46, the fate of the goats was further explained, *"And then shall he say also unto them on the left hand, Depart from me, ye cursed, into everlasting fire, prepared for the Devil and his angels: And these shall go away into everlasting punishment: but the righteous into life eternal."* The inhabitants had now been given everything they needed. They had been warned. They had been taught what would happen to those who did not follow God's statutes. They could no longer claim that they didn't know. Every inhabitant had been brought this testimony, some by their friends, some by their parents, some by their ministers, some by the kings and priests during the thousand years of peace, some by reading the words of the Holy Bible, some by reading books describing the prerequisites of heaven. Whatever way these truths reached the people, they would never again be able to say that they didn't know, that God hadn't found a way to tell them. And once they received this testimony, they would be held accountable to God for their actions. This would fulfill the plan which God had set into motion to create a Bride for His Son and inhabitants for His new creation from those who wanted to learn of love and live for the good of others. It was, of course, the natural law of the universe, the physics of things, just God's perfect plan, so evil would be banned from His kingdom forever. Then there would be no more sorrow and no more tears, only joy and love forever after. Now the inhabitants were to embark on their last lesson. They had been given all the tools they needed to overcome evil. But now they also needed to learn how powerful love was. They had to learn that this was the tool which would defeat evil. All the other lessons were to allow the inhabitants to develop a love-filled heart, and now they would learn how to use it.

O sing unto the Lord a new song.

Psalm 96: 1

Chapter Twelve
The Incredible Power of Love

The Poems of Chapter Twelve

And thou shalt love the Lord with all thy heart,
and with all thy soul, and with all thy mind,
and with all thy strength, this is the first commandment.
And the second is like, namely this,
thou shalt love thy neighbor as thyself.
There is none other
commandments greater than these.
Mark 12:30, 31

The inhabitants had learned about prayer, about hope, even about sadness. They had learned about being a role model, what their responsibilities were and what promises God gave them for their future. They had also learned about evil, why it stalked and harmed them and what they had to do to be protected. They knew that evil also tried to pervert God's incredible creation into an object of worship and their faith into a false doctrine. They had asked questions, and God had helped them find the answers in the Holy Bible. They developed godly aspirations for their life, and God had given them warnings about the end-time and about preparing for Christ's return. They were now well equipped for their final lesson. They now knew that many would not accept God, would not accept His invitation. They had read in Matthew 22:2-3, "The kingdom of heaven is like unto a certain king, which made a marriage for his son. And sent forth his servants to call them that were bidden to the wedding: and they would not come." As this parable in Matthew unfolded, the inhabitants realized that "his servants" meant anyone who brought the word of God to others. Those who would not come were "busy." They had other matters—earthly, material matters—to attend to and would not make the time to attend the wedding. The interesting thing about this parable was that the people who were first invited seemed to be those who knew the king and his son yet they refused to come and the servants were told to go forth and find others to attend the marriage. From this parable came the familiar saying found in Matthew 22:14: "For many are called, but few are chosen." Matthew 25:1-4 said, "Then shall the kingdom of heaven be likened unto ten virgins.....five of them were wise, and five were foolish. They that were foolish took their lamps, and took no oil with them: But the wise took oil in their vessels with their lamps."

This story warned the inhabitants that they may have been invited to the wedding in heaven, but if they were not prepared when Christ came, they could not go.....even though they had fully expected to go. Matthew 25:10-12 explained, "They that were ready went in with him to the marriage: and the door was shut. Afterward came also the other virgins, saying, Lord, Lord, open up to us. But he answered and said, Verily I say unto you, I know you not." The inhabitants had been well instructed because they had sought the word of God. But now one of their final lessons would be to learn how powerful love was and how they could use that power to prevent evil from touching their hearts. They recognized that learning and practicing love, pure love, could be likened to adding more oil to their lamps. A loving heart was part of the essence which God would look for in His children and, seeing it, would never say, "I know you not." Love was also a part of the armour of God which would help the inhabitants be protected for the end-time. The purity of the love for God and those God loved which they carried in their hearts was like the vessel or lamp of their body and would determine their place in heaven. How they demonstrated their love toward others set them apart and their conversations turned to talk of love and how they could avoid arguments. They saw how prevalent arguments were becoming and realized that they were all struggling at times with their ability to be kind and forgiving and were often angered too quickly by something someone did or said. They knew that this could indicate that they did not have enough love in their hearts toward one another and that this might allow evil to penetrate their hearts and cause anger to supersede love. This realization caused them anxiety, especially because they now knew how vulnerable they were. They laughed nervously about their struggles and teased one another about mixing up a recipe which would contain the ingredients they needed to make them more pleasing to God. Though they knew this was not quite reality, nevertheless one of the inhabitants wrote a little poem to focus their conversation on the things they needed to think about.

Recipe for Love

Take a quarter cup of warmth and a half a cup of kindness,
add love.
Combine a teaspoon of laughter with lots of common sense,
add God above.
Take a cup of understanding and a cup of real true giving,
add a kiss.
Mix in some good home cooking and a fairly tidy house,
you can't miss!
And if you'll add a special dash, doubled, of forgiveness,
you're a gem!
Then seek to learn and understand God's words,
remembering them.
And if you've sought God's blessing through your prayers,
you now can say,

you've been made a special person, one who cares,
so you're okay!

****

They laughed at the lighthearted content of this poem, but then they became serious, knowing that they needed to find a way to change how they reacted in certain circumstances. "What should we do about this?" they asked one another, and "How should we deal with the betrayal and cruelty or even just the thoughtlessness we often receive from others? What should our role be in all this?" And the angels smiled. For this too was part of the great plan. The angels knew that God termed this phenomenon "turning the other cheek" and that He told the inhabitants how to react in such circumstances. Matthew 18:21-22 explained: "Then came Peter to him and said, Lord, how oft shall my brother sin against me, and I forgive him? till seven times? Jesus saith unto him, I say not unto thee, until seven times: but, Until seventy times seven." It took a loving heart to forgive someone so many times. Yet the more a heart was filled with love and compassion and understanding, the easier it was to forgive even if they had to flee the evil they encountered. Love was the basis for everything good and the best way to win God's heart. God's heart was full of love and His heart was the kind of heart He wanted in the Bride for His Son.

So the angels waited for the final step which the inhabitants would take to bring them to the completion of the wonderful and great plan which God had established for them. But the inhabitants struggled with this achievement. Some felt that retribution and vengeance were in order for those who caused harm. They felt that punishment for a non-loving, harmful act was the only way to stop the wrongdoing. "An eye for an eye and a tooth for a tooth" was the philosophy of many. Others argued for forgiveness and to continue to be a perfect example. The inhabitants argued back and forth, unable to agree. Finally, they simply left their decision for another day. But those who truly wanted to plant into their hearts what God asked of them searched further in the Holy Bible and found God's words in Romans 12:19 which said, "Dearly beloved, avenge not yourselves..........for it is written, Vengeance is mine; I will repay, saith the Lord." With these words God clearly told them that vengeance was His, not theirs. Their job was to forgive, God's job was to deal with the sinner and woe be to those who harmed a child of God.

One evening, an argument broke out between two neighbors and cruel words were spoken. These words festered in the hearts of both. In the middle of the night, one neighbor, filled with great anger at what had occurred earlier in the evening, went to the fields of the neighbor whose words had been so hateful and burned his crop. When the neighbor saw what had been done, he went to his neighbor's wagon, set it afire, and let his horses loose. When daylight arrived, others saw what had happened. The wise among them said, "Wait, look what has come from one cruel word said in anger. This is surely a lesson for us. It should teach us that anger begets more anger." And one of the inhabitants, having been inspired by God, asked the group, "What would have happened if the neighbor that had burned the field had instead baked a fresh loaf of bread and left it at his neighbor's door with a note about the value of their friendship. Wouldn't all this destruction have been eliminated? Wouldn't the losses which both of them suffered never have occurred?" Many of the inhabitants agreed with this observation. They understood what God wanted them to do and why. But for some, they did not understand even though God reminded them in Daniel 12:10: "Many shall be purified......but the wicked shall do wickedly; and none of the wicked shall understand; but the wise shall understand."

Arguments

Whatever made me say such a mean and biting thing?
For I know very well indeed the pain such words can bring.
Where was control and patience and understanding too?
Where was the forgiveness to show my love for you?

How can I undo the wrong I did by all the things I said
and end the icy atmosphere that prevails here now instead?
I must discard the pride I feel and send a prayer above,
then go and make my peace with you and show that I do love.

For then will come the blessing for the effort I've displayed,
to make a part of our life the love Jesus wants portrayed.
For God will send the strength to me to do this thing I must,
to take another step toward a life of love and trust.

And if you don't respond to me, and if you're angry still,
I'll understand and simply wait, for I know that our Lord will
change your heart and actions and bring about the good
if I can simply do to you the things I really should.

And so I hope you will forgive me and forget the things I said
and try harder on the morrow to let our hearts be led.
For kindness and forgiveness and loving, joy-filled days
are ours if we try harder to change our hurtful ways.

****

Many of the inhabitants had reasoned on the side of love. But there were some who disagreed, some who wanted to join forces with one another and destroy anyone who they believed harmed them And because they disagreed, these inhabitants separated from the others who wanted them to forgive. They went their own way, judged, and lived by the words "An eye for an eye and a tooth for a tooth." Soon they lost sight of God. Evil smiled gleefully, raised its hands in triumph and moved to convince these wrongdoers that they were right; they were justified in what they did. The angels knew that now a great gulf was about to occur between those who would be called the goats and those who would be called the sheep. The angels knew that the sheep would be the children of God and would always choose love. This was, after all, just the natural law of the universe, the physics of things, the plan to develop the Bride for Christ, the plan to achieve pure love, and through it, forgiveness. For those who struggled to love and to forgive those who brought harm, it wasn't easy. First they had to overcome the evil spirits which wanted to plant the seeds of hate and vengeance into their hearts, to abide in their hearts and take over their lives. But little by little most of the inhabitants succeeded in overcoming and kept those evil spirits at bay until these spirits gave up and moved to more receptive hearts, the hearts of those who would be the goats. However, the struggle was not over. Evil was enlisting reinforcements because it was not content with how many inhabitants exercised their self-control not to react in hate but rather to act in love. So these spirits goaded the "goats" into helping them, and the struggle for the souls of the inhabitants resumed.

The inhabitants began to worry that they would always be battling these spirits who came against them, wanting to break them and keep them from following God's precepts. Again and again, the spirits tried to invade the hearts of these inhabitants. Even though these spirits couldn't achieve success, nevertheless they never gave up their assault, using the hardened hearts of the "goats" to bring harm. It was truly a bitter battle. It meant life or death for all eternity. This was why life on the cold, bleak planet was such a struggle for so many. But the rewards would come, rewards so great they were hard to imagine. As their heartache increased because of the anger of evil against them, the inhabitants who kept God's words in their heart used all they had learned about prayer and calling on God for help. They continued to practice love, remained an example to others, and did not seek vengeance. They learned that these things were part of the armour of God which would keep the evil spirits out of their hearts and prevent the spirits from harming them permanently. The armour was not only prayer and love but also taking Holy Communion worthily, moving the waters of Holy Baptism to break the hold of inherited sin, being sealed with the Holy Ghost, keeping the Sabbath holy, tithing, learning God's words, and keeping His statutes. These provided the armour of protection for the inhabitants.

But this didn't mean that when others sought to hurt them, the pain was less. It even seemed that the more they loved, the greater was their pain when someone hurt them. Though they knew that God would bring them through every circumstance, they wished they could find a way to lessen the pain. The pain of betrayal was the worst kind of pain. Betrayal occurred when someone they loved and trusted suddenly brought them great harm. It came as a shock because it was not expected and because it usually came from those who had been given the most love and care; from those they had trusted. The children of God lived by a code of honour which the these betrayers did not follow. When betrayal occurred, it was a disappointment which was very hard to overcome. It was one of the most difficult tests because the inhabitants still had their sinful human nature which automatically reacted to the hurt they felt. They struggled to wait, adjust their thinking, so they could deny their first reaction to the hurt and instead act with continued love, prayer and, finally, forgiveness. It was easier to remove the hurt inflicted by an enemy than the hurt inflicted by someone they once trusted. But over time, the inhabitants found that when they acted out of love and overcame their first reaction, the pain diminished. When they prayed for those who hurt them, the pain diminished even more. And when they pushed the hurtful remembrances from their minds and replaced them with God's words, the pain would finally leave. They also learned that they could pray for the peace which the Lord Jesus offered them from His own heart. Christ told them in John 14:27, "Peace I leave with you, my peace I give unto you.......Let not your heart be troubled, neither let it be afraid." They shared this information with one another. Then when they prayed, they asked God to give them the peace which the Lord Jesus had promised them. And He did.

Betrayal

I loved so much and tried to be a true and loyal friend
but was so very hurt, and thought my heart would never mend.
I don't know why some do the cruel things that they do.
They lose their love, know no remorse, and never ever rue.
One day they hurt then hurt some more and even tell a lie;
I can't believe such vehemence and for a long time wondered why.
But now I see that jealousy and, sadly, envy too
can cause hatred in a hardened heart; and this makes me feel so blue.

For what a waste of energy and what a loss is had
when we could have been so loving and could have been so glad.
And so I hope with all my heart that the light will shine one day,
and the Lord's forgiveness will be sought. For this I'll daily pray.

For God will make us answer for all the things we've done,
though I hope our soul salvation is the reward we will have won.
Help me pray, Dear Father, and forgive and even love.
For I strive to be worthy for Your kingdom up above.

For without love as You've taught us, none will be the bride.
Christ deserves an equal yoke, not one all bent with pride.
So I thank You for the sacrifice, the forgiveness that I see.
For even when I try, I fail and need the grace You've granted me.

****

The angels smiled when they heard these words. God smiled too. God gave His children all they would need when the evil spirits struck so they would not succumb. He fortified the armour they had taken as a shield. The plan—the great and magnificent plan to overthrow evil, to sow the seeds of pure love into the hearts of God's peculiar people—was working. After all, this was just the natural law of the universe, the physics of things, which God's righteousness had put into play. But there was one more lesson to be learned about love. The inhabitants needed to tell one another of their love. Sometimes their pride held them back from saying these words. The fear that they would be rejected or laughed at, that they were too expressive, that they wore their hearts on their sleeve often held them back from saying these words. But God wanted them to say these words. He wanted them to understand that He often told them that He loved them. Christ did this too. Even the Holy Spirit comforted them with His love. If God could so openly express His love, why should the inhabitants not express their love for one another....and for Him?

The inhabitants thought that they only needed to tell their spouse and their children that they loved them. But they were wrong. They needed to tell others that they were loved. To hear that someone loved you was a comfort, a reassurance. It bonded and cemented relationships. It was pure love, perfect love and demonstrated that pride did not live in their hearts. They did not always know when a friend was carrying a burden, but by expressing words of love, they provided a balm for the burdened soul. The words "I love you" reminded that friend that God loved them and had provided them with someone to comfort them. Since the inhabitants needed to learn this,

God allowed a certain type of sorrow to occur in their lives. Sadly, with the heart of man, pain was often the best teacher and taught the quickest lesson. These children of God were ready for a quick lesson rather than one that could take years to accomplish. Their hearts were open and receptive.

One day a group of people gathered in fellowship and began to talk together. They expressed their concern over the deep sadness in their hearts which remained with them under certain circumstances and wondered how they could relieve this terrible anguish. They were speaking about the sudden death of someone they had loved very much, someone who had been a great support in their life. They spoke of the regrets they had. One inhabitant told of an argument he had with his brother just before his brother died and how this made him wish he could speak to his brother one more time to assure him that he loved him and was sorry for their silly argument. It ate at him because he'd said things to his brother that he hadn't had time to retract, hadn't had time to apologize for. This left him with a heavy heart. Another inhabitant had a grandmother whom she loved very much. Her grandmother had been her role model and had always taken time for her. She had taught her of God and never failed to give her a hug whenever they were together. While this inhabitant loved her grandmother very much, she'd never taken the time, never sat her down to tell her how much she meant to her and how much she appreciated all she had done for her. When her grandmother died, suddenly it was too late. She could never tell her grandmother how much she'd loved her. Her anguish over this was terrible. This made the inhabitants think about how important it was to tell those close to them that they were loved.....and say so every day!

Grandmother

How I loved you

How I loved the way you always made me feel so loved

How I trusted you, How good you were to me

How I watched you carry your burdens with such dignity

How you smiled and helped

And hugged....And loved

What a wonderful example you always were to me

How perfectly you taught me about God

I wish I had told you what this meant to me.

I wish I had told you every day while I still had you with me

I wish I had told you this before it was too late.

"Grandma, I love you"

****

The very act of discussing the pain they were feeling by having missed their last opportunity to tell someone they loved them, or to tell them they were sorry for an argument they had, opened the eyes of the inhabitants to the importance not only of loving one another but of telling one another that they were loved. They knew that they themselves were comforted when they heard these words, but now they knew that they should speak them freely to others whom they loved. From these losses the inhabitants learned an important lesson: they should not only love one another but should speak of their love for one another in case it would be the last opportunity to do so. The inhabitants were learning the comforting nature of love. They remembered the commandment which Christ gave to His apostles and read it again in the Holy Bible in 1 John 4:21: "And this commandment have we from him, That he who loveth God love his brother also." They knew that to love someone also meant to care about their heartache, to uplift when they were down, and to comfort when they hurt. They learned to speak words of love and remembered the words from Hebrews 6:10 where God said, "For God is not unrighteous to forget your work and labour of love, which ye have shewed toward his name, in that ye have ministered to the saints and do minister." Loving and speaking of love was a form of ministering. As they practiced this, they began to see that both hearing and speaking of being loved was uplifting and that when something was said which seemed less than kind, it was easier to let it go, believing more the other conversations which had been loving.

This made them less sensitive to the misspoken word. Hebrews 10:24 told them, "And let us consider one another to provoke unto love and to good works." They began to see what God meant when He told them that love was powerful. God had told them in 1 John 4:7: "Beloved, let us love one another; for love is of God; and every one that loveth is born of God, and knoweth God". And in 1 John 4:11 said, "Beloved, if God so loved us, we ought also to love one another." And 1 John 4:17-19 adds, "Herein is our love made perfect.....There is no fear in love; but perfect love casteth out fear; because fear hath torment. He that feareth is not made perfect in love." The inhabitants also noted that the deeds of love which they performed when expressing their love for one another brought them joy. The inhabitants now recognized that their loving words had to be backed up by loving deeds as well. They were ready to learn of the power that this love had against evil.

Jesus loved His disciples and told them that if they fed His sheep, it would show Him that they loved Him. He even exacted a promise from Simon Peter to feed His sheep. This meant to care for, teach, and be an example to those Jesus loved, those whom He hoped would become His Bride. The Holy Bible recorded His words to Peter in John 15-17 where He said in the sixteenth verse, "He saith to him the second time, Simon, son of Jonas, lovest thou me? He saith unto Him. Yea Lord, thou knowest that I love thee. He saith unto him, Feed my lambs." This verse connects the verbal expression of love in the words "I love you" with the deed of love performed by doing something out of that love. The inhabitants were amazed and saw that this was very important. This was surely an example for them.

This ended the lessons. The inhabitants had all they needed for that terrible yet great day when Christ would come to take them home and tribulation would erupt on their planet. They were finally equipped to win the crown of glory and be ordained as sons of God. There were many names for those God longed for: the Bride, the kings and priests, the martyrs, the overcomers, the saints, the firstlings, the lambs, the sheep, the firstfruits, the elect, a peculiar people, the chosen, and the children of God. They were those who readied themselves for God, those who loved Christ. They would enter heaven either at the First Resurrection or the Last Judgment. The inhabitants who were taken at the First Resurrection had given their love, their direction, their help, and their prayers to others. They had learned God's words and had remained faithful to Him. They had resisted Satan. When the days of tribulation ended, they would write of the days of peace, of freedom from sin, and prophecies of what would come when Satan was again loosed for a little while. Others would learn from what they had endured. Others would see, by the glorified bodies of those taken at the First Resurrection, the rewards of heaven. They rejoiced at the magnificence of God's plan where every soul God had created would have the same opportunity to attain what they had and enter heaven. They would live forever in perfect peace, in perfect celestial bodies, and sit at the feet of their Heavenly Father and His son, the Lord Jesus. For all eternity there would be no sorrow, no tears. The new earth would shine brighter and be more beautiful than anything they could ever imagine. The inhabitants began to sing a new song which told the story of how they had learned to dance in a terrible storm waiting until it passed, and as the storm tried them like gold is tried in a fire, they learned of perfect love. It told the story of their struggle to rise above temptation, to put aside the imperfections of the human condition, and put on the white garment of the overcomer. It was the story of how they learned to dance in the midst of a terrible storm.

Dancing in the Terrible Storm

There once was a terrible storm that came
and crashed on the shores of life.
It was filled with a fury they'd never seen
and brought horrible pain and strife.

They tried to ignore it, escape from it, run;

but it unrelentingly followed and thrust
its sharp-edged dagger into their hearts
diminishing hope and strength and trust.

Without concern or compunction, it harmed and destroyed,
and they didn't understand why.
Then they learned that it came from the devil,
who through sin wanted them to die.

Finally, it passed; they looked at themselves; they were different,
stronger, more loving, and good.
They had empathy, kindness, could even forgive.
Tried in the fire, they'd learned as they should.

Then they understood the fury of the storms, their rage
and their cruelty, and pain.
They saw that from each they can learn and grow,
that from each their souls can make gain.

They also had learned that there were those in life
who would be used by evil and sin
to hurt the children of God by their acts,
but if they trusted and prayed, they'd win.

They thanked their Father for allowing the storms
and for everything that taught them of love.
They thanked Him for letting them see it was Him
who gave them hope and strength from above.

They now danced in the storms and threw their heads high,
sang and never sighed with despair.
They danced in the midst of the painful winds,
rejoiced in their God, and His wonderful care.

They let the winds flow and listened to their fury,
smiled in their hearts, and decided to stay.
For evil could try them but do no harm
because God had taught them to pray.

Yes, they danced in the midst of each terrible storm,
and sang with incredible joy.
They twirled and swirled to the music they heard
as God thwarted the evil one's ploy.

They allowed their souls through strife to prepare
to bring God's perfect love to all.
For this was the plan, the magnificent plan,
the reason the Bride was called.

****

Preserve me, O God:
for in thee do I put my trust.

Psalm 16:1

Epilogue
Sarah's Decision

Sarah sighed as she finished reading. Her heart was filled with love for Grandma and what Grandma had taught them. She remembered how she and Caleb and Josh had responded to the story of God's plan of salvation and how it had filled their hearts with wonder and with understanding and wanted that same wonder to fill the hearts of the children she and Matt hoped to have one day. She wanted to share the gift of Grandma's story with others. She remembered that every time Grandma read them her story, they learned something new and opened their understanding. Children understood far more than adults ever gave them credit for. They hungered for and understood principles which adults struggled to understand. *Why don't we teach the principles of kindness and forgiveness which Christ taught since they help us deal with the unfairness of life?* Sarah wondered. *When God's word is planted into hearts we are better equipped for life. Perhaps if everyone could develop the heart of a child, we could please God more easily. Perhaps God calls us His children because He is looking for purity in us, a heart willing to follow, to trust, to love, to forgive by understanding another's situation. When godly lessons are provided at a very young age, we remember them. We grow into what we are taught. Even if we leave the congregation of believers as teenagers or adults, we have a greater opportunity to come back to God because the seeds of love and righteousness had been properly planted. The seed might lie dormant for a while, but it takes very little for it to bloom once again.* Suddenly Sarah knew that this beautiful story of the angels and the inhabitants of the cold, bleak planet was one of the catalysts which had cemented her faith. God likens the purity of a child's heart to the heart of a lamb which willingly follows the shepherd. If we view a child's heart as something precious to God, all adults should try to emulate the same trust and innocence . . . especially when we are trying to be role models for these children. One should never take lightly what they plant into the heart of a child, nor take lightly what they neglect to plant either. Not only are we held responsible for what we do but also for what we don't do. And parents are the first role models a child encounters, therefore the most important. When the parents fail in their responsibilities to teach their child about God or even about a simple thing such as diligently doing their homework, the child suffers because of it. School teachers and Sunday school teachers often become the role models who have to make up for what the parents hadn't done properly. Luckily for children, there are also grandparents, youth leaders, ministers, and many others who give of themselves and serve God by helping children learn about God. These role models recognize that children are our future spiritual leaders and that they learn best by example. Suddenly it was very clear to Sarah why Grandma had written this story. *Grandma knew that whoever read her story would understand that children not only understood so much more than one realizes but would carry the story in their heart all their life....and God would open their understanding of it as they developed! This is why Grandma had told this story to them!* Quickly Sarah reread some areas of the story, with some she smiled and with other she wept. Now she understood that knowledge about their Heavenly Father and His plan of salvation was what would provide what everyone really needed. She marveled at Grandma's decision to place the manuscript in her desk knowing that one day Sarah would find it....and use it. She wanted Sarah to use the manuscript to open the eyes of many to the great need in this world to love and teach all children and to understand that they had their struggles too even if different than adults.

Each one of us can help, Sarah thought. *Whether it is to teach our own children, teach those around us, or join a church or organization where we can help. There is something for everyone to do, and these activities move the heart of God and bring us His blessing. That blessing not only rests upon us but also on our families and on future generations. But before we can teach, before we can speak to the children about God, we need to know of Him ourselves. We need to know how to answer the insightful questions others may ask. Reading Grandma's story would be such a great start because it outlines God's plan for us and shows us why our struggles can seem so difficult. It helps us understand what we are working toward and how inconsequential and brief our difficulties are when compared to an eternity with God. It would help children learn that they have an enemy who wants them to fail . . . spiritually and naturally.* Sarah knew that the story in Grandma's manuscript was Bible based and that scripture supported its statements. *I will ask Matt if we can publish this story, for our children, for all the children in the family, and for all the children we meet,* Sarah thought. *Adults too! What lives in the heart of a child is striking: the depth of their understanding, their innocence and willing acceptance, the simplicity of their faith, and sometimes, the forgiveness of the evil that goes on around them even when they should not be subjected to such an experience. They continue to love, despite what is done to them . . . or not done for them. We adults have often lost these qualities and can gain so much when we immerse ourselves in the faith and trust of these little ones.* All of us need to remember that *the return of Christ is real. It is imminent. It is important. Every one of us can help someone by bringing them testimony. We all should help, but we cannot teach what we don't know. In fact we not only place those we teach in jeopardy when we do not teach the word of God properly, but we place ourselves in even greater jeopardy.* Sarah recalled the warning in the Holy Bible in Revelation 22:18, 19: *"For I testify unto every man that heareth the words of the prophecy of this book, if any man shall add unto these things, God shall add unto him the plagues that are written in this book. And if any man shall take away from the words of the book of this prophecy, God shall take away his part out of the holy city, and from the things which are written in this book." These were the final words written in the Bible. These words were the culmination of what God wanted us to know. This is to remind us that it is important for us to learn God's words . . . **all** of them . . . and teach them correctly.* Sarah wished Matt would get home so she could talk to him about Grandma's story of God's magnificent plan. She wanted him to read the manuscript so he too could see that it might move hearts and inspire people to learn more about God's word, about the love He has for them and about His promises for the future. She couldn't wait to share her idea about publishing the story. Sarah thought it would be wonderful to share Grandma's story with her family and friends. Sarah's heart filled with thankfulness to think that perhaps this story would become the tale of choice as a bedtime story for children, just as it had been for her and her brothers. If it was explained along the way by their parents, a wonderful bonding would occur and unity would develop as their hearts and God's heart melded. From this story, they would learn of God and of the times to come. Sarah also knew that it could be a tale for both older and younger adults, so they too can prepare themselves for the end times which was already beginning. Sarah knew that Matt would feel the same way she did. She knew beyond a shadow of a doubt that she and Matt would have Grandma's story published so all could share in the beauty of God's magnificent plan of salvation and learn of the incredible love and patience He has for His children. And just at that moment Matt walked into the house. Sarah jumped from her chair, ran to Matt, threw her arms around him, and said, "Matt, just wait until you read this manuscript . . . It's wonderful . . . It's what Grandma always read to us as children, to Caleb and Josh and me . . . It's what we will read to our children . . . we will share it with everyone . . . Ohhh, Matt, it's wonderful!" Matt smiled at her, loving her with all his heart, happy with how happy she was. He could see that reading Grandma's manuscript had truly moved her heart. "Okay, okay, honey, I will read it. I promise!" Matt laughed. And they sat together and talked about Sarah's great plan.

Before lunch on the following Saturday, Matt had finished reading Grandma's manuscript and when he turned the last page and rested the manuscript on the lamp table, he began to think of Sarah's desire to publish the manuscript. Even though she didn't say it, in his head he could hear her asking, "Are you done yet, did you finish reading yet, what do you think?" It was that enthusiasm, that goal oriented joy and the accompanying courage to dive right into things which had first attracted him to Sarah. He'd felt that his own nature—which was to be cautious, careful, slower to act—was somehow enhanced by her different characteristics. But it was a two-way street; they each contributed to one another. She gave him enthusiasm, and he gave her practicality. She bounded into the heavens, and he kept her grounded! They both agreed it was a perfect combination for them. But Matt was worried. He knew that to publish Grandma's manuscript would be a good thing, but he also knew that it would awaken their enemy, Satan, and that he and Sarah would have to be ready for an attack. Satan was a formidable enemy. Matt knew that Satan didn't have time to bother with those who were already in his pocket or those who were complacent about God or even those who were strong in faith but didn't try to influence others. Surely, this project *would* influence others. This *would* alert Satan. Satan would be angry and try to stop the project because Satan did not want any new people in God's circle. His life depended on it. Satan had to prevent God from reaching the number of souls He wanted for the First Resurrection. Satan wanted to delay that day and remain free. Suddenly, just as Matt had predicted, Sarah bounded into the study after peeking into the room and seeing that Matt had finished reading.

"Well, what did you think? Isn't it wonderful? Can you picture Caleb and Josh and me listening to that story over and over again over the years when we were growing up? See how we gained so much understanding at such a young age? Don't you think it could help others? Isn't it wonderful? What do you think? Do you—"

"Sarah, hold on a minute, how can I answer so many questions at one time, or even remember them?" Matt asked, laughing at the jumbled words spilling so quickly from her in such great enthusiasm. As he pulled her into his lap and gave her a sound kiss on the cheek, Sarah smiled and put her arms around his neck, feeling so much joy in sharing this moment with him. She was so happy to have found the manuscript and to think of sharing these precious childhood memories with Matt. *How lucky I am to have found Matt; how blessed I am that God gave him to me. How many other men in this world would understand me so well, would put up with me, would listen to my impulsive ideas, would share my faith, would anchor me?* Sarah wondered.

"Well, what did you think? Did you like it?"

"Sarah, whoa, slow down, honey. Yes, I liked it. And, yes, I can picture you sitting with Grandma listening to the story. And, yes, I do think it helped shape your faith as a child . . . helped you understand what life was all about . . . And, yes, I do think it would benefit others to read the story. But Sarah there are a lot of things we need to discuss . . . so we can go into this with our eyes wide open."

"What do you mean, Matt? Do you mean the work we'd have to do to publish it?

"No, not at all. We'd both enjoy the work. What I mean is that this project will surely alert Satan. He would know of it and hate the thought of it. He'll attack and he'll send his cohorts to attack too. He'll want to stop us. He'll want to discourage us and break our faith or our relationships, maybe even our health, our jobs, or our hope. Remember how Grandma warned that he not only attacks personally, but also sends his fallen angels to attack, and uses other people to bring harm. Are we up to this? Are we willing to take this on?"

"Gosh, Matt, I hadn't thought of that. You're right. We should discuss this with Caleb, in fact with the whole family, even our minister, and pray about it . . . but I do think we should do it . . . I think that we need to discuss it, ask for everyone's prayers, explain to God how we feel and how we want to lay everything into His care . . . we can ask God to direct and protect us . . . and if we feel that God wants us to do it, I think we shouldn't back down."

"I agree, Sarah, but I just wanted you to know what might happen and that we will have to 'put on the armour of God' like we never did before. As soon as a child of God begins something which might draw others to God, a red light goes on in the world of evil and war is declared. In fact we'd better pray right now about it." And they did. They prayed in the same manner that they had taught Mary and Kevin to pray and covered the same things that Grandma had taught them to cover when they prayed so that God would know what lived in their heart,

Dear Heavenly Father
How can we thank You for all You have done for us?
For the love You have bestowed upon us?
How can we find the words to praise Your perfection and Your glory, Your honor and Your righteousness,and for loving us and providing for our freedom from evil?
Dear Father, You know that publishing Grandma's story
is something that we feel is right to do. But we need your guidance Lord, we need to know that You want us to embark on this project, so please Father,

give us a word that lets us know what direction we should take that will be in accordance with Your will.

Help us Father to be strong in our faith and in learning Your words and ways, that we may always help others and become what You wish us to be. Let our hearts be filled with love Father, so we can give, forgive, and understand others.

Help us to develop the kind of love that You have toward us; unselfish, pure, good, unconditional. Please help all who come to you with heartache, those who seek your counsel and love.

Move the hearts of those who do not yet believe, that they too might believe. We know we too falter from time to time, Father, in many ways but we yearn to be all You would have us be and need Your help to do so.

Thank you for giving us Your love. Thank you for the gift of Christ and for the sacrifice He made for us so we could have the forgiveness of our sins. Let us always recognize what You have done for us and help us protect that gift with every ounce of our being and with the strength of faith.

Father, let us be an example that through us others will know You. And Father, let those who entered into eternity without knowing You come now to Your altar of grace.

Bind the forces of Satan, the powers and principalities that he sends against us and let our homes and our families and our hearts always be our Bethany. We love You Father and we ask all these things in the name of Your Son, the Bridegroom of our soul, Jesus Christ, Amen

****

When they finished praying, Sarah said, "God will help us, Matt. He will see us through this project. Remember that old saying, 'If He leads you to it, He will lead you through it'? And we might even hear something from the altar tomorrow that will inspire us."

Let's run over to Office Depot right now and make copies of the manuscript, and see if they can put a plastic spiral binding on them. If they can do it right away, we can give one to each family tomorrow." Kissing one another again, Sarah climbed from Matt's lap. Then hand in hand they walked from the study. They were about to embark on a project which would indeed raise the ire of their enemy and bring about incredible consequences.

****

Bibliography

The Holy Bible, King James Version, published by The New Apostolic Church, Canada, Thomas Nelson, Inc., Camden, NJ, 1972

James Strong, LLD, STD, *Strong's Exhaustive Concordance of the Bible*, Abington, Nashville, thirty fourth printing 1996, copyright 1890

Ray C. Stedman, *Spiritual Warfare*, Word Books, Publisher, Waco, Texas, 1976

Sophy Burnham, *A Book of Angels*, Ballantine Books, New York 1990

Henry H. Halley, *Halley's Bible Handbook,* Zondervan Publishing House, Grand Rapids, Michigan, 24th edition, Copyright 1965

Henry M. Morris, *Many Infallible Proofs*, Moody Press, Chicago, 3rd printing 1977

Henry M. Morris, *The Bible and Modern Science*, Moody Press, Chicago, 1951, 1968

Donald Grey Barnhouse, *The Invisible War,* Zondervan Publishing House, Grand Rapids, Michigan, 12th printing 1976 copyright 1965

Robert Boyd, *Boyd's Bible Handbook*, Eugene, Oregon: Harvest House, 1983

Note:

One of the poems appearing in this novel is titled "Where Were You" and was written by Helen Glowacki, the author of this book. The premise of the poem was taken from the story generally known as "Footprints in the Sand". At the time of this writing, no legally recognized author for this work has been attributed although many claim authorship. There is a pending lawsuit, initiated on May 12, 2008 by Basil Zangare, son of Mary Stevenson, to have his mother acclaimed the original author. Burrell Webb also issued a legal document claiming to be the original author. Following are the authors listed in Wikipedia as claiming authorship of "Footprints in the Sand" and those who wrote hymns, songs, and sermons about this subject.

Ella H. Scharring-Hausen, 1894-1985, "Footprints in the Sand", June 6, 1922
Mary Stevenson, 1922-1999, copyrighted "And You Carried Me", 1976
Floyd Keeton, born 1921, copyrighted "Poetry Anthology #1" in 1944
Carolyn Joyce Carty, born 1957, copyrighted "Footprints" in 1963
Margaret Fisback Powers, born 1939, copyrighted "I Had a Dream" in 1964
Burrell Webb, born 1958, wrote "Footprints"
Mary B.C. Slades wrote the hymn "Footsteps of Jesus" in 1871
Charles Haddon Spurgeon wrote the sermon "The Education of the Sons of God" in 1880
P. Magnusen, D. Krueger, R. Page, S. Cowell wrote the song "Footprints in the Sand"

Many of the novels in The Grandma series contain the poem titled "Where Were You" written by Helen Glowacki.

Scriptural References

The material used in this book was taken from the following verses which are grouped together under the following twelve alphabetically arranged headings which reflect the content of this story:

- ASPIRATIONS
- BRIDE, KINGS, PRIESTS
- CREATION
- EVIL, SATAN, THE DEVIL
- HOPE
- LOVE
- PRAYER
- PROMISES
- RESPONSIBILITIES
- ROLE MODELS
- SADNESS
- WARNINGS

A

Aspirations
2 Esdras 4:22 (I beseech thee, O Lord let me have understanding)
Acts 2:42 (continue in the apostles' doctrine, fellowship, breaking of bread, prayers)
Ephesians 1: 18 (your understanding being enlightened)
Ephesians 1:13 (after . . . ye believed, ye were sealed with the holy Spirit)
Ephesians 1:9 (Having made known unto us the mystery)
Ephesians 4:14-15 (That we henceforth be no more children)
Ephesians 4:30 (and grieve not the holy Spirit of God whereby ye are sealed)
Ephesians 4:30 (Ye are sealed unto the day of redemption)
Ephesians 6:11 (armour of God that ye may be able to stand against the devil)
Ephesians 6:14-18 (Stand with righteousness, peace, faith, quench darts of the wicked)
Galatians 5:22 (the fruit of the Spirit is love, joy, peace, longsuffering)
John 3:5 (Except a man be born of water and Spirit, he cannot enter the kingdom
Lamentations 3:40, 41 (Let us . . . turn again to the Lord)
Luke 24:45 (that they might understand the scriptures)
Mark 10:14 (little children to come unto me)
Philippians 2:3 (let each esteem other better than themselves)
Psalm 25:4 (You are the God of my salvation)
Psalm 62:8 (Trust in him at all times, you people; pour out your heart)
Psalm 79:7 (Turn us again, Oh God . . . cause thy face to shine; and we shall be saved)
Psalm 119:18 (Open thou mine eyes)
Psalm 146:5 (Happy is he . . . whose hope is in the Lord)
Romans 10:14 (how shall they believe in him whom they have not heard)
Romans 12:1 (I beseech you therefore ,present your bodies acceptable unto God)

B

Bride, kings, and priests, lambs
Revelation 7:16,17 (the Lamb shall lead them unto living fountains, wipe away tears) 8

Revelation 7:9 (a great multitude of all people, clothed with white robes)
Revelation 20:12 (the dead were judged . . . according to their works)
Revelation 20:6 (he that hath part in the first Resurrection, be priests of God and Christ)
Revelation 20:8 (shall go out to deceive the nations, to gather them together to battle)
Revelation 21:7,8 (He that overcometh shall be my son; unbelieving, in the lake of fire)

C

Creation, the
Isaiah 37:19, 20 (they were no gods, but the work of men's hands)
Isaiah 47:13 (Let astrologers, stargazers, prognosticators, save thee)
Job 36:27 (he maketh drops of water, rain according to vapour, do drop upon man)
Job 37:14 (consider the wondrous works of God)
Job 37:3 (He directeth . . . the lightning unto the ends of the earth)
Job 38:4 (Where wast thou when I laid the foundations of the earth?)
Matthew 6:26 (Look at birds, your heavenly Father feeds them. Are you not more value)
Psalm 33:6 (By the Lord, heavens were made, fear, stand in awe, He spoke, it was done)
Psalm 148:4 (the number of the stars; He calleth them)

E

Evil
2 Thessalonians 2:9 (can produce signs)
Ezekiel 13:22 (with lies ye have made the heart of the righteous sad)
Genesis 3:1 (the serpent was more cunning)
Isaiah 14:12-15 (How art thou fallen from heaven, O Lucifer)
James 4:7 (Submit yourselves to God. Resist the devil, and he will flee from you)
John 8:44 (he is a liar and the father of it)
Mark 4:15 (take God's word from men's hearts)
Matthew 4:10 (saith Jesus, Get thee hence Satan: thou shalt worship the Lord thy God)
Matthew 4:3 (Then was Jesus led up of the spirit into the wilderness to be tempted)
Matthew 12:44,45 (seven other spirits more wicked than himself . . . enter and dwell)
Revelation 12:7-9 (there was war in heaven , dragon was cast out, angels were cast out)
Revelation 13:4 (they worshipped the dragon . . . they worshipped the beast)
Revelation 14:9,10 (if any man worship the beast, he shall be tormented)
Revelation 16:13-14 (they are the spirits of devils, which go forth to kings, to battle)
Revelation 19:20 (the beast , the false prophet, both were cast alive into a lake of fire)

H

Hope
1 Corinthians 13:7 (Hopeth all Things)
1 John 4:18 (perfect love casteth out fear)
2 Peter 3:8 (one day with the Lord as a thousand years, and a thousand years as one day)
Acts 24:15 (have hope toward God)
Colossians 1:5 (hope which is laid up for you in heaven)
Hebrews 3:6 (rejoicing of the hope firm unto the end)
Hebrews 6:18 (hope we have as an anchor of the soul)
John 14:16 (he shall give you another Comforter)
Psalm 16:1 (in thee do I put my trust)
Psalm 90:4 (For a thousand years in thy sight are but as yesterday when it is past)
Psalm 119:105 (Your word is a lamp to my feet)

Psalm 146: 5 (Happy is he whose hope is in the Lord)
Romans 5:2 (rejoice in hope of the glory of God)
Romans 8:24 (For we are saved by hope)
Romans 8:25 (we hope for that we see not)
Romans 12:12 (Rejoicing in hope; patient in tribulation; continuing in prayer)
Titus 3:7 (heirs according to the hope of eternal life)

L

Love
1 John 3:10 (the children of the devil . . . loveth not his brother)
1 John 3:18 (let us not love in word, neither in tongue, but in deed and in truth)
1 John 4:11 (God . . . loved us, we ought . . . to love one another)
1 John 4:17-19 (There is no fear in love . . . perfect love casteth out fear)
1 John 4:21 (he who loveth God love his brother also)
1 John 4:7 (love one another; for love is of God, one that loveth, knoweth God)
Hebrews 6:10 (God is not unrighteous, ye have ministered to saints and minister)
Hebrews 10:24 (let us consider one another to provoke unto love and to good works)
John 15-17 (He saith to him . . . lovest thou me? . . . Feed my lambs)
Mark 12:30, 31 (love the Lord with all thy heart . . . love thy neighbor as thyself)
Matthew 18:21,22 (how oft shall , I forgive him? Jesus saith, seventy times seven)
Romans 12:19 (avenge not yourselves . . . Vengeance is mine)

P

Prayer
Colossians 4:2 (Continue in prayer . . . with thanksgiving)
James 5:13, 14 (any among you afflicted? Let him pray)
James 5:16 (fervent prayer of a righteous man)
Luke 18:11,14 (everyone who exalted himself in prayer as the Pharisee)
Luke 18:13,14 (this man went down to his house justified)
Mark 11:24 (when ye pray, believe that ye will receive them)
Matthew 6:5 (When thou prayest, thou shalt not be as the hypocrites are)
Psalm 30:4 (give thanks, His anger endureth but a moment , joy cometh in the morning)
Psalm 96:1 (Sing unto the Lord a new song)
Psalm 102:1 (Hear my prayer, O Lord)
Psalm 136:1, 23, 24 (the Lord, remembered our low estate , and redeemed us)
Romans 12: 12 (patient in tribulation, continuing instant in prayer)

Promises
1 Corinthians 3:9 (we are labourers together with God, ye are God's building)
1 John 1:7 (if we walk in the light, the blood of Christ cleanses us from all sin)
1 Peter 5:6 (Humble yourselves . . . that he may exalt you in due time)
1 Thessalonians 4:17, 18 (we which are alive, shall be caught up, be with the Lord)
2 Chronicles 6:36 (For there is no one who doesn't sin)
2 Corinthians 11:1 (I have espoused you to one husband)
2 Corinthians 3:14 (their minds were blinded, until the vail is done away, with in Christ)
2 Esdras 2:14 (I have broken the evil in pieces, and created the good: as surely as I live)
2 Esdras 4:26 (The more thou searchest the more thou shalt be astonished)
2 Esdras 9:25 (if thou will implore the Most High . . . I will come and talk with thee)
Acts 8:15,17 (that they receive the Holy Ghost, hands on, received the Holy Ghost)
Acts 11:21 (the hand of the Lord was with them)

Deuteronomy 11:26, 27, 28 (The blessing, if you obey the commandments)
Deuteronomy 12:28 (obey these words, that it may go well with you and your children)
Deuteronomy 31:6 (do not fear nor be afraid of them)
Ecclesiastes 3:1 (To everything there is . . . purpose under the heaven)
Ecclesiastes 3:6 (A time to get . . . to lose . . . to keep . . . to cast away)
Galatians 6:9 (in due season we shall reap)
Genesis 3:14,15 (Because thou hast done this thou art cursed)
Hebrews 3:5 (I will never leave you nor forsake you)
Hebrews 12:11 (no chastening seems to be joyful , afterward it yields, righteousness)
Isaiah 43:2 (I will be with you)
Isaiah 49:12 (these shall come from far)
Isaiah 49:26 (all flesh shall know that I the Lord am thy savior and thy redeemer)
James 1:12 (Blessed is the man that endureth temptation, he shall receive crown of life)
James 2:22 (by works was faith made perfect)
Jeremiah 24:6 (I will plant them and not pluck them up)
Jeremiah 33:3 (Call to Me, and I will answer you)
Job 23:10 (when He has tested me, I shall come forth as gold)
John 6:53 (except ye eat the flesh, drink his blood, ye shall have no life in you)
John 14:23 (If a man love me, he will keep my words)
John 14:27 (my peace I give unto you . . . Let not your heart be troubled)
Leviticus 26:6 (none shall make you afraid)
Luke 8:15 (an honest, good heart, having heard the word, keep it, bring forth fruit)
Luke 12:32 (Fear not, flock; it is your Father's good pleasure, give you the kingdom)
Luke 18:7, 8 (he will avenge them speedily)
Matthew 24:22 (except those days . . . be shortened, there should no flesh be saved)
Matthew 25:13 (Watch . . . for ye know neither the day nor the hour . . .the Son cometh)
Matthew 25:21 (faithful over a few things, I will make thee ruler over many things)
Matthew 26:28 (my blood . . . is shed for many for the remission of sins)
Proverbs 3:25,26 (Be not afraid , For the Lord, shall keep thy foot from being caught)
Proverbs 4:20-27 (attend to my words, they are life, health, remove thy foot from evil)
Proverbs 30:5 (God is . . . a shield unto them that put their trust in him)
Psalm 16:3 (the saints that are in the earth . . . is all my delight)
Psalm 34:7 (angel of the Lord encamps around)
Psalm 118:5 (I called on the Lord in distress; the Lord answered me)
Revelation 2:26 (he that, keepeth my works, to him will I give power over the nations)
Revelation 3:12 (Him that overcometh . . . I will write upon him the name of my God)
Revelation 3:21 (him that overcometh will I grant to sit with me)
Revelation 3:5 (He that overcometh, I will confess his name before my Father)
Revelation 5:10 (hast made us, kings and priests: and we shall reign on the earth)
Revelation 7:13,14 (These, great tribulation, washed robes white in blood of the Lamb)
Revelation 7:16,17 (shall hunger no more, neither thirst, God shall wipe away tears)
Revelation 7:9 (great multitude, all nations, kindreds, tongues, stood, white robes)
Revelation 14:15 (Thrust in thy sickle and reap . . . the harvest of the earth is ripe)
Revelation 14:4 (they which follow the Lamb . . . were redeemed)
Revelation 19:7 (the marriage of the lamb is come and his wife hath made herself ready)
Revelation 21:4 (there shall be no more death, neither sorrow)
Revelation 22:17 (whosoever will, let him take the water of life freely)
Romans 2:7 (To them who by patient continuance in well doing seek . . . eternal life)
Romans 8:28 (all things work together for good to them that love God)
Romans 8:38,39 (neither death, nor life, shall separate us from the love of God)
Romans 10:2 (I bear them record)
Romans 14:9 (Christ died, and rose, that he might be Lord of the dead and the living)
Timothy 2:3,4 (God our Savior, would have all men, saved, come into the knowledge)

Zechariah 9:14 (And the Lord shall be seen over them)
Zechariah 13:9 (I will bring one-third through the fire , test, say, "This is My people")

R

Responsibilities
1 Esdras 2:15 (Embrace thy children . . . make their feet firm . . . for I have chosen thee)
1 Peter 1:22 (have unfeigned love of the brethren . . . love one another with a pure heart)
1 Peter 2:9 (ye are a chosen generation . . . a peculiar people)
1 Peter 3:8,9 (be of one mind, having compassion, not rendering evil for evil)
Ephesians 5:1,11 (have no fellowship with the unfruitful works of darkness)
Exodus 18:20 (teach them the statutes and the laws)
Galatians 5:22,23 (love, joy peace, longsuffering, gentleness, goodness, faith, meekness)
Philippians 2:1-5 (be like-minded, love, accord, nothing through strife, esteem the other)
Proverbs 4:11 (I have taught thee . . . led thee in right paths)
Proverbs 4:20,21,22 (incline your ear to my sayings, Do not let them depart)
Proverbs 8:13 (hate evil: pride and arrogancy, and the evil way)
Proverbs 22:6 (Train up a child in the way he should go)
Psalm 119:100 (I keep thy precepts)
Romans 12:9,10 (Abhor evil; cleave to good. Be affectioned one to another)
Romans chapter 12 (show mercy, hate evil, cleave to good, be constant in prayer)

Role models
Acts 2:42 (they continued in apostle's doctrine, fellowship, breaking of bread, prayers)
Acts 5:29 (the . . . apostles . . . said, we ought to obey God rather than men)
Acts 6:4 (But we will give ourselves continually to prayer, and to the ministry)
Acts 20:28 (Take heed, feed the church which he hath purchased with his own blood)
Acts 28:31 (Preaching the kingdom of God, those which concern the Lord Jesus Christ)
Ephesians 4:11-13 (he gave apostles, prophets, evangelists, pastors, perfecting ministry)
Galatians 6:2 (Bear ye one another's burdens)
Romans 5:18,19 (offense of one, came upon all men, righteousness of one upon all men)

S

Sadness
1 Peter 3:14 (be not afraid of their terror, neither be troubled)
Ecclesiastes 7:3 (by the sadness of the countenance the heart is made better)
John 14:27 (Let not your heart be troubled, neither let it be afraid)
Luke 24:17 (ye walk, and are sad?)
Matthew 14:27 (Be of good cheer: It is I: be not afraid)
Psalm 5:11 (Let them ever shout for joy)
Psalm 73:1-3 (But as for me, my feet had almost stumbled)
Psalm 118: 5 (I called on The Lord in distress)
Revelation 3:18, 19 (as many as I love, I rebuke . . .)

W

Warnings
1 Corinthians 10:12 (him that thinketh he standeth take heed lest he fall)
1 Peter 4:17 (What will be the end of those who do not obey)
1 Peter 4:18 (if righteous scarcely saved, where shall ungodly and sinner appear?)
1 Peter 5:9 (Be vigilant; the devil walketh about, seeking whom he may devour)

1 Timothy 6:11 (flee these things; and follow after righteousness)
2 Esdras 7:20-22 (there are many that perish . . . they did not want to be persuaded)
2 Esdras 7:24, (have not acknowledged his ways, works commanded perform not)
2 Esdras 8:50 (they shall suffer . . . misery . . . because they . . . walked in . . . pride)
2 Timothy 3:1-4 (last days perilous times, men shall be despisers of those that are good)
Acts 20:28 (Take heed to feed the church of God)
Acts 20:29-31 (savage wolves will come, speaking perverse things, draw disciples)
Daniel 12:10 (none of the wicked shall understand; but the wise shall understand)
Daniel 12:2 (many that sleep in the dust shall awake, some to life, some to shame)
Deuteronomy 32:27 (I know thy rebellion, and thy stiff neck)
Ephesians 4:30 (Grieve not the Holy Spirit of God, ye are sealed, the day of redemption)
Ephesians 6:11 (put on the armor of God . . . to stand against the wiles of the devil)
Ephesians 6:13 (take up the . . . armour of God . . . to withstand in the evil day)
Exodus 20:3 (have no other gods, graven image, nor serve them; I am a jealous God)
Hebrews 4:1 (Let us therefore fear . . . to come short of it)
Hebrews 4:11 (Let us labor to enter, rest, lest any man fall after example of unbelief)
Isaiah 14:12-15 (thou shalt be brought down to Hell, to the sides)
Isaiah 25:11 (he shall bring down their pride together with the spoils of the hands)
James 2:14 (though a man . . . hath faith, and . . . not works? Can faith save him?)
James 2:20 (faith without works is dead)
John 5:29 (good, unto the resurrection of life . . . evil, unto the resurrection of damnation)
Leviticus 26:19 (I will break the pride of your power)
Luke 12:48 (or unto whom much is given, of him shall be much required)
Luke 17:30,35-36 (one shall be taken, and the other shall be left)
Mark 13:5 (Take heed lest any man deceive you)
Matthew 10:21 (the children shall rise up against their parents)
Matthew 22:14 (many are called, but few are chosen)
Matthew 22:2,3 (a king, marriage for his son, them that were bidden would not come)
Matthew 24:12 (because iniquity shall abound, the love of many shall wax cold)
Matthew 25:1-4 (foolish . . . took no oil . . . the wise took oil . . . with their lamps)
Matthew 25:10-12 (They that were ready went in . . . and the door was shut)
Matthew 25:12 (I know you not)
Matthew 25:31-32 (he shall separate them as a shepherd his sheep from the goats)
Matthew 25:41,46 (them on the left hand, Depart . . . into . . . everlasting punishment)
Numbers 14:18 (iniquity of the fathers on the children to the third and fourth generation)
Psalm 78:58,59 (they provoked him to anger with graven images, God was wroth)
Revelation 1:7 (every eye shall see him, also which pierced him, all kindreds of earth)
Revelation 3:15, 16 (I will vomit you out of my mouth)
Revelation 3:16 (because thou art lukewarm, I will spue thee out of my mouth)
Revelation 3:3 (Hold fast, repent, I will come, thou shalt not know what hour)
Revelation 8:7-9 (f ire, on earth, trees, grass, mountain into sea, creatures die)
Revelation 9:11 (a king over them . . . is the angel of the bottomless pit)
Revelation 9:15 (an hour . . . a day . . .a month, and a year, to slay the third part of men)
Revelation 11:2,3 (forty and two months , a thousand two hundred and threescore days)
Revelation 11:8 (bodies in the street . . . three days and an half . . . nations shall see)
Revelation 12:12 (For the devil is come down unto you, having great wrath)
Revelation 13:4-6 (they worshipped dragon, beast, power given forty and two months)
Revelation 20:15 (whosoever was not found in book of life was cast into lake of fire)
Revelation 21:8 (Sorcerers, idolaters, liars, shall....lake, fire and brimstone)
Revelation 22:18, 19 (if add, take away, words of this book, God take away his part)
Romans 6:16 (whom ye yield, ye obey, sin to death, obedience to righteousness)
Romans 14:12 (every one shall give account of himself to God)
Zephaniah 2:11 (he will famish all the gods of the earth)

About The Author

Helen Glowacki is an interior designer, writer, teacher, and motivational speaker. She was the host, writer, and producer of the television series "The Contemporary Woman", broadcast by UA Columbia Cablevision. Her writing credentials include an extensive background as a freelance feature and staff writer for four newspapers and for various newsletters and magazines. A graduate of William Paterson University, Helen received a Bachelor of Arts degree, magna cum laude, in Communications. She also received an Associate of Science degree with honors and is a registered nurse.

Desiring to use her gift for writing to help others find the love and comforting presence of God, Helen donates her books to cancer centers, drug rehabilitation centers, prisons, youth centers, hospitals, to New Apostolic Sunday schools in Pakistan and to mission schools of *The Henwood Foundation* in Zambia. She also emails books to those who are willing to receive testimony or will help in the quest to bring testimony to others. She also writes amazing articles based in scripture which are filled with insight about how God wants us to conduct our lives and she posts many of these on her Face book pages and on her website.

Those who have provided reviews of Helen's books tout the beauty and spiritual inspiration of the stories in her novels and many have noted that her non-fiction books are "spiritually uplifting and biblically correct". Her greatest joys are her husband, two children, four grandchildren, and time spent in her New Apostolic faith and in fellowship.

To order additional books, to become a distributor of these books, or for more information, visit Amazon.com, the author's website at: www.helenglowacki.com or email the author at: helen@helenglowacki.com.

You can also visit her Face book page for her books at: http://www.facebook.com/pages/The-Grandmother-Series/155300907853909?ref=ts and also her personal page at: http://www.facebook.com/pages/Helenglowacki/

Description of the novel:

Abiding Faith, Hidden Treasure

Jim lost his faith in God when he saw how devastating the terrorist attacks in Iraq were to its people. How could a loving God allow such heartache to occur? Why didn't He use His power to stop these acts of violence? Could God really be that complacent in the face of human suffering and if so, why?

When Jim first met Barbara and recognized the depth of her faith, he knew that they could never have a future together. Angered by everything he witnessed; how his mother's minister's had mistreated his mother when his father died; how her neighbor, who professed to be a Christian treated her.....how could religion of any kind make a difference?

Thus Jim fell into responding to kindness and religious philosophy with pithy comments inspired by his television hero, Bill O'Reilly. Anyone who tried to get close to Jim had to first break through the cynicism of his cutting remarks. Barbara did however. In fact, she fell in love with him and saw through his remarks and into his incredibly loving and sensitive nature.

When she brings to a Thanksgiving Day dinner with her family, and Jim meets Grandma for the first time, Grandma challenged him asking him to form a question...any question....and see if the Bible could answer to his satisfaction. So Jim asked how creation and evolution could coexist and to his surprise Grandma answered with quotes from the Bible which made him reassess his position.

Despite the reply which gave him so much food for thought, Jim's hardened heart remained imprisoned until letters from the grave bring him a miraculous experience of faith and he realizes that God's plan of salvation actually allows for heartache. Even he began to understand why and how evil could bring about the conversion God wanted in His people.

Grandma told Jim to read 2 Peter 3:9 where Peter reminded the congregations: *"The Lord is not slack concerning his promise, as some men count slackness; but is longsuffering to us-ward, not willing that any should perish, but that all should come into repentance."* And 2 Peter 17-18: *"Ye therefore, beloved, seeing ye know these things before, beware lest ye also, being led away with the error of the wicked, fall from your own stedfastness. But grow in grace, and in the knowledge of our Lord and Savior, Jesus Christ. To him be glory both now and forever."*

This poignant story of a gentle hearted young man's journey to learn why evil prospers, why God allows what He does, and to find a God in whom he can place his trust, is fast paced, uplifting and heartwarming. Abiding Faith, Hidden Treasure is Helen Glowacki's sixth novel, all a part of the Grandma saga and is another story her readers will love.

****

Novels

by Helen Glowacki   (Book Size 6 x 9)

When God Broke Grandma's Heart: (208 pages) Rising from sorrow to become a beacon of faith Grandma struggles in an abusive marriage until God moves her from unequally yoked and broken to the healing of His love and forgiveness. Her granddaughter Sarah learns where to find answers to her problems and carries that legacy to those she loves. **Paperback: ISBN 978-0-9847-2110-8**

When God Took Grandma Home: (260 pages) About the heartache of drug addiction, of the enemy who destroys children through drugs, why God allows righteous anger, why we should pray for those in eternity and a description an incredible experience of faith for Matt and Sarah about why God allowed such heartache to occur. **Paperback: ISBN 978-0-49847-2111-5**

When Grandma Chased the Spirits: (208 Pages) The magnetism of idolatry, it's invisible power, and the heartache of bearing a child out of wedlock brings debilitating panic attacks to Mary and affects her husband Kevin. When Matt and Sarah tell them about their faith, God engineers a miracle to solve what that they thought impossible to resolve. **Paperback: ISBN 978-0-9847-2112-2**

The Granddaughter and the Monkey Swing: (284 pages) A wedding, a broken engagement, renovating and decorating a home through Divine Proportion, the truth about Halloween, and the gift of role models create a tender story of friendship. Helping through the planning and problems of a wedding culminates in the unveiling of a secret. **Paperback: ISBN 978-0- 9847-2113-9**

The Story of God's Plan of Salvation: (299 pages) This incredibly beautiful, touching and whimsical story for all ages, begins when Sarah finds a manuscript in Grandma's desk and recognizes the story Grandma read to her and Josh and Caleb when they were children. Angels narrate as they watch and encourage the inhabitants on the planet below them struggle to learn of God's magnificent and all encompassing plan for them. **Paperback: ISBN 978-0-9847-2114-6**

Abiding Faith, Hidden Treasure: (262 pages) Serving in Iraq, Jim loses his faith to see a loving God allow so much heartache. Barbara invites him to dinner where Grandma shows him why creation and evolution co-exist and God's enemy creates the injustices Jim blames on God. Letters from the grave bring an incredible experience of faith. **Paperback: ISBN 978-0-9847-2115-3**

And Then They Asked God: (295 Pages) When Rebecca and Jayden arrive at their college campus they are overwhelmed by betrayal. Losing the values Rebecca once cherished fills her with guilt so monumental that she cannot forgive herself. Chaldeth the evil angel is defeated when God's grace frees Jayden and brings Rebecca's recovery. **Paperback: ISBN 978-0-9847-2116-7**

Caleb's Testimony: (262 pages) Caleb would have taken bets on his ability to trust God explicitly....until his accident.. Now, he and Ann must face the wrath of Satan aimed at causing them to blame God for their misfortune. Can they give up everything they worked for if God asks this of them? **Paperback: ISBN 978-0-9847-2119-1**

Caleb's Zeugnis: This is the same book as listed above but has been translated into the German language. **Paperback: ISBN 978-0-9890-2140-1**

All books by Helen Glowacki are also available as eBooks

Non-Fiction Books
by Helen Glowacki   (Book Size 5 ½ x 8 ½)

Politically Incorrect: The Get Some Gumption Handbook When Enough is Enough: (406 pages) Fifty timely and controversial issues are examined under the politically correct approach and compared to what scripture tells us is what God wants His children to do. **Paperback: ISBN 978-1-4507-9074-1**

Overcoming Depression: How To Be Happy: (258 pages) We all face heartache, and all feel sad from time to time. But depression can linger and come from many different causes. It can rob our hope and destroy our relationship with God. Thus our Heavenly Father tells us through scripture how we can tap into His blessing and direction and brings joy out of tribulation. **Paperback: ISBN 978-1-4507-9077-2**

What No One Tells You About Addictions: (216 pages) Discussing the merits of tough love, the selfish co-dependency of the enabler, what scripture tells us about spiritual warfare and invasion, and generational sin, make this book a must read. **Paperback: ISBN 978-1- 4507--9075-8**

"Why God Why" mini-series
by Helen Glowacki   (Book size: 5½ x 8½)

To What Purpose?: (126 pages) This first book in the *Why God Why* series answers questions about why we are here, what we must learn, and what God plans for us. It is an excellent book for testimony and to share with others. **Paperback: ISBN 978-1-4507-7580-9**

Why God, Why?: (126 pages) This second book in the *Why God Why* Series describes why we experience heartache, its purpose, and how to face it. It answers questions about God's plan for us and what we need to do to be found worthy. **Paperback: ISBN 978-1-4507-7581-6**

Why Trust Scripture?: (126 pages) This third book in the *Why God, Why* Series addresses the challenges against scripture, who wrote the Bible, the importance of the sacraments, what role Satan plays, and how health and the Bible are related. **Paperback: ISBN 978-1-4507-7582-3**

What Should I Know about Life after Death and the Coming Tribulation?: (126 pages) What occurs following death, what will happen during the tribulation, and what the seven seals could mean to us are explained in this fourth book of the series. **Paperback: ISBN 978-1-4507-7583-0**

What Does God Want Me to do Right Now?: (126 pages) A concise explanation of what God asks of us, how we can live up to His expectations what is required to become a part of the Bride of Christ, and what God plans for the future with or without us. **Paperback: ISBN 978-1 4507-9076-5**

Do My Little Sins Really Count? (126 pages) Most of us believe that the little sins don't really matter but scripture explains why they do and teaches is about the seven deadly sins, sin by proxy, and sin by commission and omission which can affect whether or not we take Holy Communion worthily. **Paperback: ISBN: 978-0-9847-2117-7**

What Do Angels Do? (126 pages) Few of us know that there are three levels of heaven in which nine different ranks of angels exist. Nor do they know that these angels have been assigned three very different tasks. This little book takes the mystery out of what angel's do, who rules them, and how they affect our lives. **Paperback: ISBN: 978-0-9847-2118-4**

Book Reviews

Reverend (District Apostle Ret.) Richard C. Freund, President of The New Apostolic Church, USA, Sea Cliff, New York: Magnificent writer, a story which makes the reader become emotionally involved, a joy to read, strong Christian values. *"When God Broke Grandma's Heart",* best seller quality.

Reverend (District Apostle Ret.) Richard C. Freund, President of The New Apostolic Church, USA. Helen's new novel, *"When God Took Grandma Home"* "Delights, brings comfort to those who grieve. Inspires, gives insight into the after-life, masterful portrayal.

Reverend Andrew Muliokela: New Apostolic Church in Alexandria, Virginia, formerly from Zambia Africa: *The Granddaughter and the Monkey Swing* and this series of books are awesome! A journey unlike another, I was reading a great novel, learning about confidence, love and support but also learning Bible verses at the same time! Helen Glowacki teaches through her books and I recommend them 100%. You'll enjoy the journey!

Reverend Frederick Rothe, (Ret. New Apostolic Church, New York) Palm Beach Gardens Congregation, Florida: Spent 48 years serving God and another 30 in the congregation. These books contain an accurate account of what God wants of us and why we suffer. The application of scripture and the people in the stories stand for the principles God wants in all of us.

Reverend Kevin Speranza, New Apostolic Church, Palm Beach Gardens, Florida: *And Then They Asked God* so happy I read this, weaves, documents biblical precepts, addresses political correctness, moral & political corruption, biased teaching, insidious growth of socialism renamed progressivism, self-importance, guilt and its debilitating power. WELL DONE! Identifies danger, artfully and Biblically!

Reverend Luke Jansen, Sr. V. P., Medical Connections, Boca Raton, Florida: "To Ms. Glowacki, author of **The Grandma Series**: grateful for your books, refreshing to find a Christian author who sees the *difference* between religion and spirituality AND that the two can and should be used in the same sentence.

Reverend Derryck Beukes, Montana-De Aar Congregation, Northern Cape, South Africa: Dear Helen, I personally often use your articles in my soul care visits, especially where youth are involved. I can assure you that your articles made a difference to my way of thinking, and I am busy encouraging fellow priests to read your works, as they are so factual and insightful! Thank you for your hard work. I thank God for you, and the wisdom He gave you! Please continue with the excellent work.

Deacon Shadreck Wilima, Overspill Congregation, Ndola, Zambia: Your articles prompt realistic examples which New Apostolic Christians need for their everyday living.

Youth Chairperson, Sunday School Teacher, Mulenga Ernest, Lusaka Central Congregation, Lusaka, Zambia: Through your writing I am constantly reminded of what to be aware of. I pray that God keeps you in the hollow of His hand, guards you and guides you to reach your brethren as you do me. Thanks for caring for the souls of many.

Reverend Aurelio Cerullo, Atripalda Congregation in Campania, Southern Italy: Dear Helen, your books and articles, and social networking bring brothers and sisters the words of our faith and touch the hearts of those who do not know our faith. Our goal is found through the grace of the apostolate and in this sense, the word's from 1 Corinthians 15:58 assumes an important meaning: "*Therefore, my beloved brethren, be steadfast, immovable, always abounding in the work of the Lord, Knowing That your labor is not in vain in the Lord*". Now that I am a minister of God for about a year I too am grateful to our beloved Father in Heaven for having opened the eyes of my soul, for having removed the plugs from my ears of my heart to hear and listen to His will in connection and communion with those who precede us, guided by the light of the Holy Spirit. God's work always evolves and adapts to the times and even via computers, cell phones and smart phones. I Thank God for having been able to know you, you're a very valuable pearl. God bless you richly.

Rev. Fred Krueger, (Ret.) Lutheran Minister 12 yrs and Clinical Social Worker 26 years, Dallas, Texas: "Inspiring, grabs the heart, author headed to the bestseller list, a pleasure to read, masterful. *"When God Took Grandma Home"* filled with insight into God's plan!

NOTE: The articles which are referred to in these reviews are excerpts from Helen Glowacki's non-fiction books. Not shown are reviews by the ministers who oversee *The Henwood Foundation*'s New Apostolic Mission Schools in Zambia and review all reading materials prior to distribution.

Edith Stier, wife of a Ret. District Evangelist, Clifton, New Jersey: *The Grandma Series* helps those in need, inspirational, heartwarming, ends with a beautiful example of how God explains our pain, renews hope, shows us the way, creates miracles. I love this series.

Patricia Robinson, wife of a Ret. Rector, Indiana: 5 star rating: *When God Broke Grandma's Heart*: WONDERFUL INSPIRATIONAL NOVEL, enjoyed this book, well written, Bible references, how to achieve peace of mind and soul.

Rosemarie Schaal, wife of an Ret. Reverend, New York: *Abiding Faith, Hidden Treasure:* Reader develops empathy, feels emotion, hears a battle between scientific and spiritual knowledge. Skillful, detailed, brilliant, vivid, teaches that nothing happens that is not planned by Him.

Colette van Loggerenberg, wife of a Minister, Scottsville Congregation of Pietermaritzberg, South Africa: *Grandma's Little Book of Poetry: The Story of God's Plan of Salvation:* This has to be one of the BEST EVER books that I have read....If you ever get the chance to get one of Helen's novels...READ IT. It's like a fairytale but a TRUE fairytale.....Close your eyes and picture this: Grandma with her hair in a bun, glasses perched delicately on her nose, sitting in a rocking chair and her grandchildren sitting on the floor with BIG eyes hanging onto her every word.....but with a twist!!!!! If you have doubts about PRAYER...read this book. I LOVED IT...thank you!

Debbie Espeland, wife of a Rector, Palm Beach Gardens Congregation, Florida: 5 star rating: *When God Took Grandma Home:* HEARTWARMING! Touched my heart. Heartwarming and spiritual.

Aletta Venter, wife of a Deacon, Scottsville Congregation, Pietermaritzburg, South Africa: *"Grandma's Little Book of Poetry: The Story of God's Plan of Salvation".* What a learning process for me. Oooh I just **love** the way the angels are telling the story, **very original!** When is mankind going to learn? The inhabitant's lesson was to learn of good and evil. And they failed miserably each time. The devil has his agenda, and the inhabitants are the target. They call on God for help, the angels rejoiced. Great....!!!

Aletta Venter, wife of a Deacon, Pietermaritzburg, South Africa: *"Abiding Faith, Hidden Treasure"* is the deepest and most rewarding novel I have ever read, touched my soul, made me cry, author's understanding of God's work is astounding, opens the mysteries

Lisa Mayo, wife of Minister, Palm Beach Gardens Congregation, Florida: Helen's *Why God Why* series of books gave me a new understanding of my faith. They are informative, so enlightening and in-depth, but in a way that is easily understood!!

Tammera Shelton, M.S. Psychology, Odenton, Maryland: I find *"When God Broke Grandma's Heart"* inspirational, beautifully portrays letting go of the negative and despite injustice, no pain is for naught.

Robert W. Rothe, USMC 1970-1976, Nevada: 5 star rating: *When God Broke Grandma's Heart:* Outstanding writer, kept me riveted, an angel sent to help through trying days. Thank you for helping.

Katharina Leipp, Schopfheim, Germany: This is the first time I have ever heard of a female New Apostolic author and I am very impressed by your articles. I have sent your link to my Shepherd and German friends and would like you to consider advertising in our German *Our Family Magazine*.

Claudine Visagie, South Africa: I'm trying to think of a way to introduce Helen's books and articles to others... especially to our youth. They are life changing!

Rabecca Mukuta Mukato, Lusaka, Zambia, Africa: Speaking on behalf of my Dad, District Elder Mukato, your articles are brilliant; they have changed me! Because of your articles my Dad has less headaches!

Robert Henry Parkes, Pietermaritzburg, South Africa: You are gifted with the verses and writings you do and are so inspiring to others. God is really using you as His special servant. You are really a wonderful person and we thank the Lord for you our sister in faith.

Frank Geores, from Port St. Lucie, Florida: *"When Grandma Chased The Spirits:* beautiful spiritual experience, can see caring nature and loving heart of author, eloquently reveals her love for God and search for truth. Worthy of the Star of Bethlehem rating. Thank you for sharing your magnificent gift.

Ben Lodwick, Avid Reader., from Brookfield, Wisconsin: Wow! An eye opener about God's plan of salvation, and why bad things happen to good people. Reminds me of Jim LaHaye and Jerry B. Jenkins "Left Behind Series". MUST READ!"

Dr. Walter Forman From North Palm Beach, Florida: *Grandma's Little Book of Poetry: The Story of God's Plan of Salvation:* a "wonderful book about success and failure in life. All Helen's novels are wonderful, a balm for the soul and an education to the seeker."

Susan Day, From Jupiter, Florida: *Abiding Faith, Hidden Treasure* : I hated to put it down, couldn't wait to pick it up, read all Helen's books, proves every point, shows what to do through God's words. I am 90 and Helen's books have helped me call on God.

Georgette Rothe, From Fort Piece, Florida: *Abiding Faith, Hidden Treasure* was more than I expected; a Biblical course making you re-evaluate your beliefs, enjoyed the journey very much.

Fred D'Alauro, from Palm Beach Shores, Florida: Internet 5 star rating: *When God Took Grandma Home:* Remarkable! Inspirational, moving. Fascinating storyteller with a real message.

Debra Forman, Chester, New York. Internet 5 star rating: *When God Broke Grandma's Heart:* Written from the heart, shares strong beliefs that shelters us in times of need, courage captivates the reader.

Anonymous: Internet 5 star rating: *When God Broke Grandma's Heart:* WHEN LIFE GETS YOU DOWN, PICK THIS BOOK UP, it wrapped its arms around me. A wonderful read. Congratulations. Inspiring work.

A reviewer, a reader in Kentucky: Internet 5 star rating: *When God Broke Grandma's Heart:* Well written, heartwarming, overcoming heartbreak through God, touches your heart. A worthwhile read.

A reader: Internet 5 star rating: *When God Broke Grandma's Heart:* a must read! FANTASTIC!

A reviewer Internet 5 star rating: *When God Took Grandma Home:* Moves you, captivating.

A reviewer, a Kentucky reader: Internet 5 star rating: *When God Took Grandma Home:* MUST READ!

www.ingramcontent.com/pod-product-compliance
Lightning Source LLC
Chambersburg PA
CBHW031103260626
47172CB00001B/197